SCREAM CANYON

A Dalton James Investigation

G. L. BOLDREY

outskirts
press

Outskirts Press, Inc.
http://www.outskirtspress.com

Paperback ISBN: 978-1-9772-4100-9
Hardback ISBN: 978-1-9772-4138-2

DEDICATION

I would like to thank everyone who helped me along the way with the production of the book.

I dedicate this book to my late parents; My father Garry L. Boldrey Sr.; inspired me a to take whatever path I choose and to be proud of your accomplishments. My mother Kay; handed me her artistic talents and creativity.

Thank You to all Firefighters present, past and future.

PROLOGUE

The morning was cold and windy a slight snowfall had powdered the open areas during the night. The night had been uneventful, other than the dream of everlasting damnation. That she had been told would become of her soul, for sins against the father. Today would be the day to leave, to escape, and to see if the Great Spirit would watch over her or would the father of the white people burn her in hell.

The village appeared to be asleep. This would be her chance to escape, she slid quietly from the family hut if she could get a mile or two from the village, she would still have enough time to do a ceremony to the Great Spirit before passing over into his hands. The feel of a cold wind blowing on her face as tears were swept back along her temples the moccasins made of moose hide and buckskin falling quickly on the half-frozen path. The fringe of her buckskin dress, and long raven hair waving, every breath showing as her lungs, and arms pumped, as she ran to the sacred place.

The voice of the black robes inside her head telling her she had sinned against god, unable to hear the search party who were just minutes behind her. The sun a mere sliver peeking above the horizon. The cold air gusting up from the face of the cliff, to the top of the outcropping where she stood. Singing her death chant and praying asking for forgiveness from the Great Spirit. Pleading to be let into his village.

The time was too short for a long prayer. The search party was closing in, this would be a leap of faith. To end this life and to begin a new one.

The floor was cold and damp when she awoke to an agonizing pain in her leg and arm. It was dark and voices could be heard yelling her name. She screamed for help holding onto her faith and praying but, no one came, and the Great Spirit did not come. No one for a very long time. Then someone did come, not to release her, but to join her in this purgatory...

CHAPTER ONE

The morning was starting out as usual, a small fire in an apartment complex. I had been dispatched via my cell phone, from central dispatch to respond to a fire scene.

The commanding officer on scene was a young Captain who I had seen on other fires and he recognized me when I drove up and parked behind the fire engine that was hooked to a fire hydrant.

"Hi Dalton I wasn't going to call, but I'm a little rusty on my investigation techniques".

"That's all-right Captain I had to get going this morning anyway. What do you have?"

"Well, it's nothing major, I'm not sure how to classify it as accidental or negligence or both.

"Let me get my coveralls on and we can take a look." I went to the back end of my Yukon and pulled out a green tote. Where I kept a set of coveralls, boots and a helmet grabbed a flashlight and a clipboard from the back seat. Well, Captain let's see what you got.

We headed toward the apartment complex and into the front door. The Captain began ordering the firefighters to start mop up procedures. This didn't mean they were actually going to use a mop it meant to pick up and finish putting anything they were using back on the truck, and to make sure the scene was under control and the fire was out.

The Captain led me into the laundry room that was shared by the tenants.

"Dalton the fire appears to have started in here somewhere in the wall or next to the wall back here." He was pointing behind a commercial size clothes dryer.

"I think your right Captain I would say it was the lint in the vent stack it's pretty common. The supervisor of the building been in here yet?"

No not yet but I talked to him before you came and he said." "He had been having trouble with this particular dryer. That's why I thought I better call you just in case he torched it for insurance reasons."

"It doesn't look like it so far, did your guys pull it out from the wall?"

"Yes, they had to get into the wall a little bit to get at the fire."

"That's what I figured, it looks like it just overheated and caught the lint inside the stack that's what I'm going to put down as the cause. The reason is lack of maintenance, even though you empty the lint trap there is still going to be some get by the filter and into the stack. That's why he was having trouble with it."

"So, there isn't anything suspicious?"

"No Captain just put it down as accidental. I looked at my watch realizing it was already 8:00. Captain I have to get going I have a class to teach in one hour, are you okay with my conclusion?"

"Yes, all set Dalton thanks for coming."

He released me from the scene. I put my dirty gear back into the tote, and headed for my class that was about a twenty-minute drive away. I called the dispatch center and told them I was cleared of the scene at 0800 hours and that I was going to be giving a class until 1500 hours. The fire service uses military time so it's less confusing when logging times on documents there isn't any reason to ask A.M. or P.M.

The drive to the fire station where my class was being held was slow, rush hour traffic in Detroit can be brutal, everyone is always late they drive like the speed limit is just, a suggestion. I was going with the flow at about 80mph in a 65mph zone and it was bumper to bumper the guys that run the NASCAR races at Michigan International Speedway had nothing on this bunch. The term bump drafting and door rubbing or trading paint was evident on a few commuters' cars. I hoped there wouldn't be any caution flags come out before I got to my class. These usually came in the form of a police car directing traffic and a rescue squad and EMS vehicles. No cautions today, which was a good thing that meant nobody got hurt. I arrived at the fire station on time and a little tense from the drive, you would think after twenty odd years I would be used to it.

The old station was red brick probably built in the forties or maybe earlier, it held two rigs an engine which is the water pumping truck and a ladder truck that were fairly new and in well-kept condition. When I visit other stations, I can usually tell if the fire company is dedicated just by looking at their equipment, if it's all shiny and new looking then they take pride in their work.

I parked in the visitor's spot marked by a sign that said the same, grabbed my box of training materials and briefcase from the back seat and headed for the front door of the station.

The weather was a bit chilly for the middle of April temps in the mid 50's but a heavy overcast was hanging low, just one of those dreary days. I liked teaching on this sort of a day it meant I wouldn't be missing any of the sunny days of spring, which I enjoyed so much after being locked down all winter. With the snow and ice and freezing temperatures of Michigan not that I didn't enjoy winter but after seven or eight months I had enough it was time for spring with baseball, green grass and sunshine.

The receptionist at the front desk was smiling and she recognized me from a previous visit.

"Hello, Mr. James can I help you with that box?"

"Hi Jane, no I can get. The same room as last time?"

"Yes, sir same room, I'll get the door."

"Okay, thanks"

Jane was in her mid-thirties, with a wonderful smile and a want to please attitude, her hair was done in a corn row braid and she had been to the nail salon to get the multicolored art work done. The last time I saw her she was sporting a small Detroit Piston's logo on her nails and I complimented her on them, this time when she reached for the door grabbing it about eye level, I noticed they had been done in red and gold and had little fire helmets and axes on them.

"Nice nails Jane, did you just have them done?"

"Yes, sir yesterday I'm glad you like them I was a little worried they wouldn't turn out"

She was talking as she walked ahead to get the classroom door. "If you need anything just give me a shout and I'll see what I can do Mr. James."

"Okay Jane, and please from now on call me Dalton." She smiled and went back toward her desk. She was attractive and had an air of confidence. The classroom layout, was a podium in the front and a chalkboard behind it, and along the one wall was a table that had various snacks and beverages on it. I went to the front and set the box on the podium and my briefcase alongside of it

The group of firefighters were setting in old school desks and some were mingling around the snack table getting their morning coffee and doughnuts. I walked over and grabbed a bottled water and a bagel.

"How are you guys this morning?" I asked walking past a group guarding the doughnut box.

"Pretty good Captain, how are you?" A young African American firefighter from the Warren area responded, his shoulder patch was stretched tight against his bicep, and easy to read.

"I'm doing good, looks like you been working out a bit."

"Yeah, you could say that keeps me ready for action and Jane likes the muscles to.

"Oh, the Jane at that front desk?"

"Yeah, that's right."

"Good for you, she seems pretty nice, treat her good, or I might have to kick your butt."

"Ha ha I'll be good to her Captain."

He knew I was joking and doubt if he thought I could kick his butt; I know I did.

After finishing my bagel, I started to sort out some training materials from the box, and asked the group. To find their seats.

"Okay let's get started I have some materials to hand out, while I do this please sign in on the sheet being passed around so you can get your certificate. Does everybody have a booklet and folder?" Nods and yes answer came back

I took my place behind the podium. "All right let's get started with a brief introduction of myself, some of you already know me but for those who don't, my name is Dalton James

I am currently a Captain in the Detroit Fire department I am an arson investigator and sit on the arson task force where I am the lead investigator and training officer, my background is in fire science, arson detection, crime scene investigation and teaching classes to the various departments in the metro area, I have a Master's in this area and have twenty-five years' experience all of them with the city of Detroit, with that said let's begin."

The training was an overview of basic fire investigation not so much to make them into investigators but to make them aware of things to look for at a fire scene. How not to destroy evidence and how to preserve a scene until investigators arrive. The training lasted most of the day, with a half hour lunch break on the premises of pizza. The trainees all passed their written test and were told they would receive their certificates in the mail.

I packed up my stuff said my good byes and was out and in my Yukon by 3:00 pm.

Not bad timing, it still gave me time to go home and get cleaned up and maybe head down to the local watering hole and get some supper and a few drinks. I was driving back enjoying the fact that I was going to just miss rush hour, when my phone started to beep, damn it so much for a night out. Checking the number on the small screen it was a URGENT from central dispatch.

My cell phone mounted on the dash had speed dial programmed for the dispatch number and speakerphone, I punched the number and got an answer immediately.

"Hello central dispatch who is calling please."

"Hello central this is Captain James what do you have?"

"Hi captain you are requested to respond to a scene on the corner of Gratiot and eight mile there is a fire company on scene and the Battalion Chief is standing by for you on the command frequency channel 232."

"Okay central I'm almost there right now, thank you." I hung up and got off the expressway onto Eight mile. I could see some smoke coming from the general direction the dispatcher had given me, the overcast day was holding the smoke down toward the ground. The closer I got the more you could smell and see it. The intersection was blocked off and a few city police were rerouting traffic. I got out my portable light and stuck it on the dash and turned it on, the officer waved my through. The fire apparatus was in position on two sides of the burning structure, and it just so happened I was able to park right behind the Chief's rig.

The Chief was standing between the curb and his car as I pulled up, he came towards me, I recognized him from a fire I had been at a week ago. It was a department store one where the upper floor is living quarters or a rental, they use to call them tax payer's apartment, let's see, I thought what the hell was his name? Jackson, I think.

He came around to the driver's door as I got out.

"Hi Captain James, Battalion Chief Jackson he stated sticking out his hand.

"Hi Chief what do you have for me?"

"Well Dalton we have a three-story warehouse converted into offices, ground floor major burn second floor seventy percent, and third floor minor smoked and water damage."

"The fire didn't make it to the third floor or did you guys get a good stop on it?"

"Both, we did get a pretty good stop but we had help from the sprinkler system."

"From the sprinkler what do you mean did you hook up to the standpipe?"

The standpipe is the pipe you see on the outside of most commercial buildings it allows the fire department to hook their hose to it and pressurize the sprinkler system.

"No, we didn't right away because the sprinkler was working, but it was only on the third floor, that is partly why I called you."

How's that?

"The place was torched but the arsonist didn't figure on the third-floor system to be on a separate valve the dumb shit left all this evidence unburned on the top floor."

I got into my bunker pants, coat, and helmet. I usually wore coveralls but I had used my pair I had this morning and it probably was going to be wet work anyway.

"Okay Chief let's go take a look." I had brought along my grab bag is what I called it. It was an old waterproof duffle bag that contained some tools of the trade so to speak, a small shovel like the army hands out, some zip lock bags in different sizes, rubber gloves, leather gloves, dental picks and forceps and a clipboard with some drawing paper, also in my pocket I carried a flashlight and a digital camera so I could photograph the scene and then down load it on my computer, and to top it all off a 35mm camera just in case the digital was not clear enough.

The Chief and I walked up to the building and then around the outside as I took some pictures from different angles to analyze when I got back to the office, you could tell a lot from outside photos like how the fire spread how the elements of wind, rain, and fire suppression had affected the personality of the fire as it burned. The building was a three-story brick structure that was about thirty years old it had at one time multiple windows but now they had been remodeled to where there was only three per side and they supported an arched top to give it a country style, the exterior doors were steel with a full window also sporting an arch top. The landscaping around the outside was low maintenance washed stone for mulch and a few shrubs the sidewalk was a flagstone of sort's kind of a blue tint it looked quite nice I assume before the fire.

The Chief was inside now giving orders to direct a large fan to get the rest of the smoke out and to get some fresh air inside so the firefighters could work without their breathing apparatus.

I began taking pictures with both cameras as soon as I entered the front door, the bottom floor was a total burn everything inside was destroyed the desks and chairs and office equipment had been turned into steaming piles of black charcoal. The fire had gutted the first floor, all the walls and ceiling were covered in a heavy black soot and water was running and dripping through in spots, a slight haze of steam was still rising off the scorched and burnt office furniture. The water was about 5 to 6 inches deep on the floor, not much sense in looking for a fire track on the floor. I turned my light on the stairway and noticed a burn line going up that appeared deeper in charring than the rest of the area I took my flashlight out and propped it up so it lit up the area for my cameras to get a clearer image the first floor was going to be difficult to determine the actual cause until some of the water disappeared. The first floor was a wash a lot of interior damage, but the structure itself appeared to be sound and safe from collapse.

The Chief came over and asked if I had enough light for my cameras. I told him I thought so and he went about giving other tasks to the firefighters inside. The room appeared to have burned from the ceiling down the charring on the walls had a pattern, which was consistent with this.

When the Chief came over, I asked him if any of the attack firefighters were in the building yet.

"Yes, they are Dalton they are upstairs on the top floor looking for hot spots and checking for fire spread."

"What did you say about this being a treasure trove of evidence? All I see are some irregular burn patterns on the walls sort of like it burned from the top down."

"The treasure isn't on this floor it's on the top floor, my guys are securing it for you, and I told them not to touch a thing just watch for fire spread."

"Okay Chief thanks I'll get up there and see what we have."

I went up the stairs there wasn't an elevator so I figured the fire probably spread up the stairway, but upon checking the stairway there seemed to be minimal burn, except for the deeper char line I was looking at now. The second floor was in better condition than the first not as much damage to the office furnishings and the burn pattern looked like it was from the top down this was starting to look like an arson job. When fire burns it burns in an up and out fashion if it can't go up then it tries to get out. If you think of a mushroom that is kind of how it works, when the super-heated gases rise, they are carried in a column of hot air like a chimney would work, if the chimney becomes plugged or you have a stop over it, then the fire tries to spread sideways. If you have a fire inside a room and it starts on the floor then it will try to go up it will spread across the floor or up a wall as it burns up the wall it will create a V pattern because the fire is increasing in size therefore it needs more fuel, when it reaches the ceiling it gets stuck so it spreads out in a V pattern across the ceiling from the point of ignition or from where the fire came up the wall. However, in this particular room the fire didn't even burn to the floor the bottom of the desk and chairs were not even touched. This got my attention if the fire had started on the ground floor then spread to the second floor there would be more burn on the floor. The carpet was only burned in a few spots and the desks tops and chair seats were burned but nothing lower to the floor. The ceiling showed a more extensive burn, meaning the fire burned there longer.

I began to look along the area just above the stairwell when I noticed that same faint line of charring in the plaster wall. What could have caused this? I took some more photos and decided to go upstairs and see if I could get an answer from the evidence left in the unburned room.

When I got to the top of the stairs, I noticed along

the wall there was some toilet paper lying there. Just then one of the firefighters noticed me and came to the top of the stairs. He was holding a short-handled pike pole used for interior work. The handle is shorter so the person handling it can maneuver.

"Hi Captain you need a hand with anything?"

"No not yet but I will, were you on the attack team?"

"Yes sir, I and Ron were the first ones in."

He said pointing toward another firefighter.

"Good get Ron over here I want to ask you two some questions." He hollered for Ron.

"Were you guys the first ones up here and into the structure?"

"Yes, that's right came in hoses spraying knocked the first floor down without much trouble and started going to the second. When our air ran out."

"So then did you come back in and were you two the only ones in here?"

"No there were two other attack crews but Ronnie and I went out for new bottles and then came back up to the second floor, we kind of rotate crews so there are at least two crews inside at all times kind of cover each other's ass so to speak, we rotate back to the area that we left so the crew inside can be relieved."

"So, you and Ronnie end up on this floor up here?"

"Yes, sir that's right, then we noticed all the balloons and shit hanging everywhere when, we came up kind of odd how the water was running down the steps when we hadn't even been up here to spray any."

"So, the water was running down the steps and did you notice if it was running through the ceiling on the second floor, was there any toilet paper on the steps, like that right there along the wall?"

"We did notice some on the top of the landing right where it washes up by the wall but nothing on the steps itself probably got washed down with the water, course we weren't really looking for it either, until we came up to the top floor."

"Good job guys knocking it down I think we better get some of that paper collected for evidence and take some pictures, would one of you run out to my rig it's parked behind the Chief's car and grab two of those empty paint cans out of the back?"

Ronnie volunteered and the other firemen started to help me gather some of the paper in the landing area.

"Hey Capt. There is a lot more inside balloons and all kinds of shit looks like the asshole was loading it up for a fast burn but the sprinklers shut that idea down."

"Okay let's put some of this stuff in a zip lock and then we can work the inside of the room, anybody else in there beside you two?"

"Yes, sir two more Jimmy and Sarah, they got orders not to touch anything until you tell them."

"Good idea, did I hear you say Sarah?"

"Yep, one of the best hose handlers on the department. HA, HA, HA!"

"That will be enough of that Benny, I heard that, if I ever get a hold of that little hose of yours, you'll be squatting to piss like me."

I could see that Sarah had a way with the boys and she wasn't afraid to mix it up, that was good, in their profession there had to be a way to release some of the stress from the tragedy that they faced day in and day out and most I've found, do this by using humor or ribbing each other.

"Sarah I'm Captain Dalton James," I said sticking

out my gloved hand. "Did you come in with the attack crews?"

"Yes, sir me and Bobby were second crew in right behind Benny and Ronnie."

Sarah had a certain swagger in her talk and actions, just treat me like one of the guys but don't fuck with me, she had blonde hair cut short not butch length but short enough to not stick out around her collar her smile was mischievous and she looked to be in really good shape like she did a bit of weight training not bulky but fit she had her coat undone and her small hard breast sat just above the belt line of her bunker pants she was maybe 5'6" 130# but she must be good to handle the rigors of firefighting.

"You must be Bobby." I said to the tall fireman that was leaning against the wall inside.

"Yes, sir that's me what can I do for you?"

"Well, when Ronnie gets back with the paint cans, I'm going to need some help collecting samples of everything in here anything from carpet to copy paper on the desks including a couple of these balloons that are hanging from the ceiling." Just then Ronnie returned.

"Here you go Capt. This what you wanted?" Ronnie asked handing me paint can.

"Yes, Ronnie thank you, were you able to find any signs of fire spread up here?"

"No nothing yet, but we want to check the ceiling," Benny answered making a motion with his pike pole.

"Okay let me have a quick look first, the four of you stay put and does anybody have flashlight?"

"Yes sir, right here." Bobby offered his to me.

"I don't need it just yet Bobby, but I will for some

pictures."

The room was set up with desks and chairs with small dividers in between them forming small cubicles. The walls were a stucco finish and the ceiling had been dropped down with a suspended grid of tiles and florescent lighting.

"You guys call Haz. Mat. Yet?"

Sarah was quick to answer. "Yes, they're on standby as soon as you are done, they will come in, the Chief said you would want to take some pictures."

"Yes, that's right. Was this toilet paper on the floor like this when you entered the room?"

"Yes, and there was some on the stairway on the landing but the water washed most of it down you seen what was at the top." Ronnie answered.

"Okay Bobby follow me and shine your light on the ceiling so I can get some pictures and try not to step on any of the paper on the floor if you can help it, I have some pictures of it already. I directed to him where I wanted the light for the best images of the room.

Now step back toward the entrance and shine the light toward the wall where the paper runs up it so I can get a shot, see where that paper is hanging off the balloon in the corner that is where he wanted it to start the chain reaction. Ronnie and Bobby, I want you to take down one of those balloons really careful like and put in one of the paint cans, Benny and Sarah bring the other one and we can get some more of this paper that isn't too wet off the wall in the corner."

"The balloon is in the can Captain." Exclaimed Ronnie. Anything else?"

"No, that should do it I'm going to work a little more on this paper trail and see if I can figure out how the chain reaction was planned to work, it might help with some other cases I'm working on, you guys do what you need to for fire spread checking, just be careful not to knock down any balloons."

The arsonist had strung about thirty balloons across the ceiling, which was filled with gasoline I assumed and trailed the paper up the walls and across the floor leading back to the stairway. The paper worked like a fuse it would burn across the floor, up the wall, igniting a balloon full of gas this would intern explode creating a fire ball, causing other balloons to rupture, the larger the fire the more balloons broke. The chain reaction of balloons would burn very hot and fast igniting everything in the room because the ambient temperature would increase to somewhere around 1200 deg. F.

The contents would flashover because they had reached their flashpoint, a quick hot burn, that's why the second-floor furniture had burned on the top. The water from the sprinklers had created steam thus dropping the temperature from the flashpoint. That is where the arsonist screwed up, he didn't shut the sprinkler system down for the top floor; the heat sensors for the bottom floors tripped the system for the whole structure. I had been working on two other fires with the same patterns but I was unable to figure out how he was getting such a fast burn before any fire departments arrived on scene. This would work for showing the way the structures were set and possibly convict him for three fires instead of one.

The firefighters had donned there S.C.B.A. [self-contained breathing apparatus], even though the air was clear it wasn't a bad idea, one of them was pushing up the tile with the pike pole and one would look above it while standing on a short stool that Ronnie was steadying and Sarah being the shortest had the hose line ready to hand to Bobby if he needed it, good team effort, they were moving down the room in a zig zag kind of way.

I was looking at the small burn pattern on the floor left from the burnt paper and making a hand drawing of it on the note pad from my duffle bag, when I noticed something shiny back under the corner of one of the desks. What the hell is that, I thought as I crawled under, shining my small light on it? BOOOOMMM!

An explosion threw me under the desk my face pressed into the wet carpet my first instinct was to cover my face with my gloved hands. The fire coat I was wearing was not closed I had just undone it because it is difficult to bend down, the bunker pants I had on offered some protection to my legs and lower torso, the coat had been blown over my head which helped to keep my head protected the helmet had been blown off probably right over the desk before I was forced under it. When the coat flipped up it left my middle and upper back exposed to the fire, I could feel the fire burning my flesh and smell it I was trying to dislodge myself and to roll over but I couldn't move there was something on my legs the room was an inferno, the heat and pain the smell of burnt flesh and the cries of agony from the other firefighters could be heard then I blacked out the world became dark. I thought I was dreaming I felt coolness and heard sirens and people voices and a bright light and more voices but, where was I? In some macabre nightmare.

CHAPTER TWO

I woke up unfamiliar with my surroundings face down on my belly looking through a hole in the bed.

"What the hell?" I tried to roll over but I had been restrained, my back hurt like hell and the smell of burnt flesh and antiseptic filled my nose, hospital the light came on in my brain but how did I get here? The sound of someone entering the room became apparent, some white shoes and a pair of legs covered in white tights came into view in front and slightly to my right.

"Hello! Hello! Could somebody tell me what's going on?" My patience had run out.

A soft feminine voice answered. "Oh, Mr. James please don't move, I'm going to stand you up, so you can see me better, don't worry you won't fall out just relax." The bed started to rotate upwards and a lovely face came into view.

"Hi is that better? I'm Kathy and I'll be your nurse today if you need anything just press this button that I'm placing in your hand."

"Hi Kathy could you tell me what I'm doing in a hospital strapped to bad?"

"Well Mr. James you have been in here going on two days and your back has been severely burned, second and third degree you have skin grafts that's why the back of your legs may hurt. Are you in much pain?"

"I'm just sore in the back area, not my legs too much, but I do feel kind of fuzzy in the head."

"That's normal you're on morphine and some other medicine. The doctor will be in shortly to see you, we were not expecting you to wake up already, and I'll leave you upright until the doctor comes in. would you like me to bring you some reading materials?"

The nurse left and a short moment later the voice of a man came from outside the door even though I couldn't see him I figured it was the doctor.

"Hello Dalton; how are you feeling I'm Dr. Brice I did the surgery on you when you came in."

"I'm sore and tired, but I feel okay. What happened, how did I get here, and how long do I have to stay strapped in this bed?"

"You were brought in by EMS and you have been here for two days going on three its 2:00 pm right now."

"So, tell me doctor what is my condition?"

"You have multiple burns to your back area, starting from your waistline and extending up to the top of your shoulders, mostly third degree and some second, I expect a full recover, but you are going to have some scarring and a long regiment of physical therapy to get the skin stretched and the muscle working in and on your back."

"Is my face scarred, and how long in this custom straight jacket?

"No, your face is fine and most shirts will cover any scarring on your back, as far as the bed restraints, just until tomorrow, the nurse will change your dressing and give you a scrubbing, I'm not going to lie to you it's going to hurt like hell."

"Okay doc thanks."

"Quite alright Dalton just holler if you need me or have any more questions. The nurse will be in to check on you again shortly."

He patted my arm as he left the room and gave me one more, "get well."

The nurse came back in and checked my vitals and left a small T.V. that she placed on the floor so when my bed was in the down position, I could watch it, the remote was tied to the bed so I could reach it.

"Your vitals look good Mr. James and I brought you a T.V. to watch here is the remote in your left hand just two buttons one for channels and one for volume. You are in a room by yourself so don't worry about disturbing anybody, is there anything else Mr. James?"

"No: just one thing please call me Dalton if you are going to see me naked please use my first name."

"I see you have a sense of humor, that's good you may need it before were done,

Okay back down you go and if you need anything just press the call button, I'll be back in an hour, take care Dalton."

"Thank you, Kathy." I was still a little having trouble trying to remember what had happened to me, my head was still swimming from the drugs and my concentration was fading in and out, man was I tired, well let's see what's on the T.V. the afternoon variety of soap operas was on and very uninteresting, I didn't really care if John was sleeping with Karen who had memory loss and thought she was his lover and not his ex-wife sister. How the hell could anybody watch this shit all day? My sleep mode started to kick in and I must have dosed off. The next thing that came to me was someone playing with my finger on my right hand and pressure being applied to my bicep. I awoke slightly startled.

"What are you doing to me?"

"Not to worry Dalton it's Kathy and I'm just taking your vitals again."

"Oh, I thought you just did that a little while ago, and aren't you going to stand me up so I can see you?"

"Yep, just as soon as I'm done you have to have your collection bag dumped."

"Collection bag?"

"Yes, you have a catheter in for your bladder, it will only take a minute sleepy head."

"Sleepy head I just fell asleep. Didn't I?"

"No, you have been out for about two hours, you didn't even know I was here the first two times, there your catheter is all set. Do you feel up to a visitor? There is a Chief Jackson outside and he has been here every afternoon since you came in."

"Oh yes of course send him in, but could you stand me upright and shut the T.V. off?"

"Sure Dalton, T.V. is off and is that high enough for you? All set?"

"One more thing could you scratch my nose?"

"Better yet, how about you do it yourself. The doctor said, to remove your arm restraints as long as you didn't move them around too much and try and scratch your back. Now when I take these off remember your arms are going to feel heavy and there is going to be some pulling sensations on your back so move gentle. There is the right one and now the left. How does that fell any pain?"

"Oh, thank you I thought my nose was going to split as much as I was wiggling it. Ouch dam you weren't kidding when you said pull, is my skin even hooked on back there?”

“Yes, it’s hooked just not stretched, I’ll send the Chief in, see you in an hour, just have the Chief stop by the station when he leaves so, I can put your bed back down.”

“Okay Kathy and by the way nice smile, thank you.”

It never hurts to compliment the nurse especially when she is, I charge of the catheter tube. The Chief entered as soon as Kathy left.

“Hi Dalton how you feeling are they taking good care of you?”

“Yes, pretty good; I’m glad you came now maybe you can tell me how I ended up here because it’s kind of fuzzy to me.”

“Oh, they didn’t tell you?”

“No, they didn’t tell me, all the doctor said was that EMS brought me in and I woke up after two days with severe burns on my back and skin grafts that require me to lay strapped in this bed for another day.”

“Well, if you think you are up to it, I can tell you, let me pull over a chair.”

The Chief went to some unseen corner and slid a stuffed chair over the kind for visitors to lay in or take a nap while they waited for their loved ones to get better.

“Okay Dalton where do you want me to begin?”

“I faintly remember going to a fire scene and you were there, the structure had been torched, some odd thing about balloons and firefighters putting one in a can and that’s it.”

“It sounds like I better start at the beginning or close to it, I called you on Saturday afternoon, for an arson fire that are company had been dispatched to.

When we arrived, the structure was fifty percent engulfed and it appeared to have water being put on it from somewhere, we later confirmed that the third-floor sprinklers were working, the asshole didn't shut them off, we thought he forgot or didn't know there was two valves. Now after what happened to you and my four fire fighters, I think he did it intentional."

"Why, do think that?"

"Well, I believe he was trying to kill you, you were getting too close and by setting off a bomb and killing you he might have figured that because the lead investigator is gone so is the investigation or at least the detective work, someone else would have to start over."

"What do you mean lead investigator, was I working something similar?"

"As near as we can figure it's the same guy that torched the two apartment complexes last month."

"How do you know that?"

"The lab boys say that the balloon fragments from the apartment fires are the same composite material as the one that you canned from the office complex, and the burn patterns are consistent with the ones you took pictures of on your digital camera that was in your coat pocket, I had it taken to the lab after the paramedics found it in the pocket."

"Now it's starting to come back, the first two floors were burned and the top floor was loaded and ready but the sprinklers doused it, did they get any ideas from the other evidence they compared, as to who it might be?"

"No not yet but we'll get the cocksucker, you can count on it."

The Chief's disposition changed from cordial to pissed off and sad, his eyes started to water a little.

"Damn Chief settle down I'm going to be alright; I just have some bad burns but it's okay I didn't figure one being a back model for swimsuit calendars.

"I'm sorry Dalton. I shouldn't unload this on you, but I have some other bad news and I'm glad you are going to be okay, really."

"Other bad news, what are you talking about?"

"Do you remember the other firefighters that were in the building with you?"

"Yes, I do somewhat Chief, there was a blonde girl Sherry or something, a tall guy name was Bobby, ah let's see Ronnie and Benny. Yah, that's it what about them?"

"I shouldn't tell you but here goes and please bear with me, damn I have a hard time at this. The girl was Sarah Johnston and when you get out you might want to buy here a steak or something, because if it weren't for her you and Ronnie wouldn't be here. That little shit saves both of you guys by hanging on to the hose line even after she was blown off her feet. Ronnie had been thrown backwards and over a desk, while you had been thrown under a desk but your coat had been flipped up somehow and your back was on fire, she had the presents of mind to put some water on it even though she herself was on fire from the gasoline flying everywhere. Ronnie was a bit luckier than you he only had second degree burns on his ears and around his mask because his helmet came off."

"What about Sarah did she get burned, and the other two, Benny and Bobby what happened to them?"

The Chief's face started to contort and his eyes began to flood big tears that started streaming down his ebony cheeks his lower lip was quivering and his voice was cracking. He buried the heel of his hands in his eyes, placing his elbows on his knees.

"Ah shit Dalton they didn't make it. The explosion took Benny in the face and melted his mask, just disintegrated, it he was dead from smoke inhalation Bobby was worse he took the full blast and it pretty well decapitated him, he didn't know what hit him. The arsonist had booby trapped the ceiling tiles knowing that we would eventually look to see if the fire had spread."

"I'm very sorry Chief Jackson when is the funeral, I would like to give my condolences to the families."

"I could do that for you Dalton the service is tomorrow at eleven o'clock"

"Thank you Chief, is there any way I can thank Ronnie and Sarah, or maybe call them on a phone if you have the number?"

"I'll do one better they are coming to see you tomorrow afternoon, the nurse said you would be able to sit in a different bed and she thought the company would be good after you get a scrub, so with that said Dalton, I'm going to be going I have a lot to do before the funeral tomorrow, it's going to be full dress trucks and all off duty fire personal we want to give them and the families the respect they deserve, it's sure good to see you awake and on your way to recover."

"Thanks again Chief I'll see you later." The Chief slid the chair back and was left alone with my thoughts of regret and anger toward the lost firemen and the asshole who burned them and me, myself no longer taking priority. I wondered if they had a family or if they had a wife and kids, man that's tough knowing that your dad was never going to come home

The rest of the day and into the night I was poked

and drained checked and rechecked how they ever thought you could sleep in a hospital was beyond me, every hour they came in. I finally had enough painkillers to put me out until morning. Kathy had left and another nurse took over my care the doctor stopped by before he went home for the day at around seven o'clock, man those guys worked long days. My new nurse's name was Polly and she had the disposition of an angry pit bull, I was glad I could sleep through her shift.

The morning shift started at 7:00 am and the first face I seen was Kathy. The first thing on her agenda was to see if I was up to a little bit of food, so she stood me up and fed me a bit of breakfast, mostly juices and soft stuff. My stomach had been without food in it for four days and it didn't take long to get full. Once the feeding was done, she took my vitals and gave me some pain medicine along with a check of my morphine drip on the I V tube.

"How are you feeling Mr. James, was the food okay on your stomach?"

"Yes, I almost forgot what it felt like to eat, I didn't miss it, what do they put something in that I V to curb the appetite?"

"Yes, it is something like a diet drug but we don't like to have you on it for long.

I'm glad the food went done okay, you are going to need it more then you know it helps the pain killers to take effect and to last longer. The scrub room is going to be unpleasant to say the least."

"When do we have to do that?"

"As soon as I check your IV, we can have two orderlies wheel you into the tank room."

"Tank room, what's that?"

"It's the room where we scrub the dead skin off the burn area and put new dressings on."

"Oh, I see and why do you have to scrub it?"

"The problem with a burn is that a lot of the recovery is trying to keep it from getting infected. The skin tissue from the graphs is new and some of the damage tissue is dead so you could actually get gangrene on your back and infect the surrounding area, we have to scrub it with a brush to kill the bacteria."

"Sound pretty unpleasant."

"I'm not going to lie it's going to hurt so if you want to yell or cry do whatever, we have seen it all and don't be embarrassed. The orderlies will be right in I'm going to change and I'll see you in a bit."

The orderlies arrived and transferred me to a small gurney and wheeled me down the hall to the scrub room. They were big guys probably 250 to 270 pounds and muscled heavy through the arms and chest. One had a constant grin and the other said nothing just kind of hummed a song that he only knew. They wore a rubber apron, which they cover with green scrub suits. They took me from the bed and placed me in a warm whirlpool type tub big enough for six to eight people. Nurse Kathy and one other nurse I didn't know came in wearing a set of scrubs also and got right into the tub with me. The two gentlemen stood outside the tub alongside the edge. Kathy and the other nurse gently rolled me onto my stomach and undid my wet gown and left I kind of float there with my head hanging over the edge as the two orderlies held my arms to keep my head up.

What came next was the most painful thing I ever

experienced in my entire life, the bandages were removed after they had been thoroughly soaked exposing my raw back to the water that wasn't too bad but when to nurses started scrubbing the area it was worse than having your fingernails pulled out or a dentist drilling on a nerve, the two big fellows were there to keep me under control so the nurses could work as quickly as possible. With the scrub done I was patted dry and new bandages put in place new gown and just barely conscious, I was wheeled back to my room and transfer to my bed just before passing out.

The weeks of scrubbing and dressing changes went by slowly and painfully. The firefighters that stopped by for a visit or to play cards and tell war stories were greatly appreciated and to numeral to remember all of their names. Sarah and Ronnie stopped by about every other day sometimes to say hello and other times to play cards or just pass the time we did have a common bound I guess and I did owe Sarah my life and she was trying to come up with all kinds of ways I could repay the debt, anew truck a million dollars etc. I knew she was only joking and would not take a thing other than a thank you.

The days turn into weeks and then into months. Chief Jackson stopped by every so often and kept me filled in on any news about the arson case.

I had been through almost all of my rehabilitation and was looking forward to getting out the skin and muscles were healing good and I had to where a sock type of a thing to help the skin have more support and to maybe lesson the scarring.

The Chief came by one day and informed me of some good news regarding the arson cases that I had been on and the one that put me in the hospital.

"Hi Dalton I got some good news about the case.

I had just returned to my room from rehab and the Chief was setting in the reclining chair watching soap operas.

"Okay Chief let's hear it and by the way I have been wondering who actually watched that stuff on the tube."

"Oh, I don't usually watch it, but some of the gals on these things are knockouts, well enough have a seat you are going to like this news." He shut off the T.V and pulled out some pictures from his shirt pocket and tossed them up on the bed. "Here Dalton takes a look at these. The first one is from your camera and the rest are from a recent fire, recent as in last night, I couldn't get here fast enough once I found out."

"I see yes very similar in the way the balloons are hung and the toilet paper, but what's the good news, did you catch him in the act?"

"No not really he caught himself the photos are from the first floor of a four-story office similar to the one you worked the top story was where he was found, we pulled up and noticed a lot off steam and not much smoke and it was confined to the top floor, here are some more pictures." The Chief was sitting on the edge of his seat and enjoying telling me his story.

"It looks just like the room where they drug me out did a bomb go off in there?"

"Yes, it did and it fucking fried the cocksucker right where he stood, the trigger must have tripped somehow when he was placing it and he didn't have the sprinklers shut off yet, probably figured on doing it on the way out. We got the bastard that fried you and killed my guys no trial no wasted tax dollars spent on jail time a perfect ending I would say."

"Yes, a perfect ending, but do think it is really him, do the crime scene guys have a match on any of the bomb materials or balloons?"

"No not yet too early but I'm guessing it will come back a match, oh I'm so happy I could just piss. The families of Leroy and Bobby will be glad to hear they finally got their justice."

"Yep, that's great now all I have to do is get out of this hospital and I can be a very happy man, one more week, they tell me and then some outpatient rehab and I'm all set to move."

The Chief's face went from a lock of joy to a look of confusion his move hung open trying to decide on what to say.

"All set to move, what do you mean, can't you stay on the task force when you get healed up?"

"Oh, I can stay but I don't want to I'm moving and as soon as I can drive, I'm going to look at some property I found in the Upper Peninsula."

"What do you mean Upper Peninsula, of Michigan, across the bridge, why there isn't anything up there but black flies and snow, has this hospital stay made you crazy?"

The Chief was acting like he was losing his best friend, but my mind was made up and nothing he said was going to change it.

"Yes, the upper peninsula of Michigan across the bridge god's country I've heard and no more assholes like the one in the picture to chase after all the time and no more worry if some sonofabitch is going to blow you up while you're doing a job, I have had it with this shit hole city and all it's killing and fires and gangs and traffic and dirty air, fuck it I'm out of here and you won't change my mind so don't even try. The care and friendship you have shown me I can never repay but when I get settled, I'll call you and you and the wife can come see me, maybe do some fishing or go deer hunting."

"Well okay Dalton, but I think you are making a mistake." We can worry about that latter, but I'm telling you it's time for me to go. I found a piece of ground and I'm going to call on it as soon as I'm out."

"Please remember Dalton you always have a friend in Detroit, let me know when you go and give me a call when you get there."

The Chief gave me a hand shake and bid me a good future as he left the room. The rest of my stay went well the scrubs had long ceased and the rehab was pretty routine. The day had arrived that I was able to drive and when I returned to my home, I called the real estate office that was listing the property and set up an appointment for the following Saturday. This was going to be my new beginning.

CHAPTER THREE

The realtor was located in the town of L'Anse in Baraga County. The area was known for fishing, hunting, snowmobiling and just about every other outdoor activity. I was hoping to get into town on the Friday before my appointment and take a look around at the local sites and see if this was really what I wanted.

The drive up to L'Anse is about twelve hours from Detroit, so I decided to leave on Thursday and take my time not really knowing what to expect from my injuries and to give me enough time in case I had to stop and stretch every so often. I stopped in Marquette and spent the night the drive had been somewhat painful but the scenery was great I had never been to the western Upper Peninsula before and was enjoying the leisurely pace I had set. Tomorrow I could make it to L'Anse in about an hour so there was no need in getting up to early, maybe sleep in a little I did need the sleep after being in the hospital my schedule was all messed up.

I called the realtor in the morning and told her I would be there Saturday for sure and that I was in Marquette and wondered if there were any attractions in the area that I could take in until our meeting. She recommended that the iron-mining museum was good and that there were several roadside parks and lakes to take in on the way to L'Anse. Thanking her I set out toward L'Anse and stop along the way at some over-look areas and a campground at Michigamme Lake, this might be a place to visit and go fishing I thought. The road to L'Anse is very scenic it has mountains and streams crossing that look promising for hiking and fishing, the sturgeon river has a waterfall that can be seen by pulling off just after the bridge crossing. The town of Alberta is not far from it. I didn't know that there was a town I Michigan named this evidently it was a company town owned by the ford family there is a large sawmill on the property that manufacture wood parts for the automotive industry and a Michigan tech-nological university school of forestry school also, the ford's donated the surrounding property and buildings to the university. I made a quick tour of the grounds, and thought it must have been a busy place when the mill was running.

I drove into the town of Baraga which is located roughly across the Keweenaw bay from L'Anse the lo-cal Indian tribe has a casino there and it felt like a good place to spend the night and try my luck at the card table.

The night at the casino was not so lucky having lost a hundred dollars I decided to call it a day and turned in.

The next day I went to L'Anse for my appointment, the day was sunny and bright but the breeze from Lake Superior had a slight crispness to it.

The green ford explorer parked in front of the real estate office I assumed belonged to the agent I was go-ing to see. I parked on the other side of the street and crossed over to the small building, which now had an open sign in the window.

There was a sound coming from the copy machine in the corner, but no one was in the room.

"Hello is anybody in here?"

From one of the side offices a woman appeared, she had a small folder in one hand as she came towards me extending her other for me to shake.

"Hi Cheryl Johnson Baraga County Realty, how can I help you?

She was a smaller woman about 5'2" to 5'4" blonde hair cut short, blue eyes maybe 120 pounds, thirty to thirty-five, a pleasant joyfulness was apparent in her voice, added with a genuine smile across her face.

"Hi Ms. Johnson, I'm Dalton James; we have an appointment this morning."

"Hi Mr. James, and please call me Cheryl."

"Only if you call me Dalton, please."

"Okay, I have a few more descriptions to run off and we can be on our way."

She went to the copy machine and was explaining that she had some similar parcels that I might want to see if the one I called on wasn't quite right.

"Okay Cheryl sounds good."

"All finished Dalton, shall we be on our way?"

She asked turning the open sign to closed and locking the door as she held it for me

"Would you care if I drove?" I asked

"No not at all just let me grab my jacket, from the car."

I was glad she didn't object. The explorer was a bit too small for my 6'2" frame and my back were still tight not a good combination for a small car.

Cheryl got in and started giving me directions as

we drove, pointing out certain aspects of the town of L'Anse, we had traveled out of town in a northerly direction towards the old settlement of Skanee and then turning toward the Huron river onto a gravel road. There were a few old farms and hunting cabins along the way.

"Stop right up here Dalton this is one of the parcels I pulled up this morning, right here on the left-hand side its thirty acres and has electric and phone available."

"Is it the one I called on?"

"No but it is on the way if you want to take a look at it."

"Why don't we go see the one I called about and if I don't like it, we can see the others."

"Okay you are the boss, so what do you do in Detroit Dalton?"

"I'm a retired arson investigator."

"Oh, that sounds interesting, but you don't look old enough to be retired."

"Well maybe I should have said just tired, I'm in the process of making a major life change in priorities. How about you Cheryl have you been a realtor long?"

"No not long about five years."

"It sure is a nice day," I said trying to change the subject. The sun was shining through the trees along the road giving way to shaded areas that flashed bright and dim light onto the roadway, my thermometer on the rearview said sixty-two degrees. I was looking forward to a walk in the woods just to see how peaceful a place like this could be.

"Do you plan on moving up here, or is this going to be a vacation place?"

"I'm planning on moving here, build a house before

winter and start over so to speak."

"Does your wife share the same ideas?"

I knew the question of marital status would come up sooner or later.

"No, I'm not married, never have been, and spent too much time on the job. But that could change once I get settled." Answering her question before she could ask it. A slight smile started to appear on her face.

"Well let's hope you like this parcel so we can see more of you around here, I still can't believe you are single, please forgive my forwardness but you are nice looking, dress properly, seem to be intelligent and are easy to talk to."

"Cheryl Johnson are you hitting on me? I don't think Mr. Johnson would appreciate it very much."

"Oh no, I'm sorry sometimes my mouth has a mind of its own, I was merely making an observation that all. How did you know I was married?"

"Um let's see, there was hand prints on the back windows of your explorer, too small for an adult, family pictures in the office where you work, and on your left hand is a ring,"

"You are the observant one, aren't you? And again, I am sorry about my questions into your personal life."

"Don't worry about its okay Cheryl, now where is this piece of property at?"

"Just a bit farther, there should be a real estate sign nailed to a tree out by the road and just past it there is an old driveway that I think you can park in."

"Is that it?" I said pointing to a sign on her side of the road.

"Yes, that's it just be careful backing into the drive it's kind of brushy."

I pulled past and backed in so I was just off the road. Cheryl got the land description and plat out of her folder and stepped out of Yukon and took out a small compass she had in her pocket.

"Well let's see Dalton," she said walking to the back of the Yukon where I was retrieving my jacket. "The main road runs east and west and according to the survey map there is an old trail that bisects the property in a diagonal manner, see here." She offered the map to me for a look.

"Yes, I think you are right, but haven't you been here before?"

"No, the surveyor just came out here on Monday and he dropped this map off Thursday, he marked the front corners and strung some orange tape along the borders."

"So, you aren't familiar with it then, let's have a look at the map again. I think if we just push through this thick brush we will be in the clear, stay by the truck Cheryl and I will have a look" I pushed through the brush which had seemed to be the thickest out by the road, where it could get more sunlight, about twenty feet in the woods opened up, the canopy of the larger trees had voided the area of sunlight and the underbrush had not been able to grow.

"It isn't too bad in here Cheryl, just push through and you will be in the clear in about twenty feet, I'm standing on the trail right now." She pushed through and look kind of ruffled and nervous, looking herself over for any critters that may have gotten on here from the thick brush. Taking out her compass she confirmed that this was probably the diagonal trail.

"This trail should give us a fairly good look of the

parcel it runs corner to corner."

I could she Cheryl wasn't really content on tromping through the woods and wanted to stay close to the trail.

"Sounds good Cheryl let's walk the trail and if I see anything that interests me, I can go look, and you can stay on the trail, okay?"

The forest consisted mostly of hardwoods, hard maple, beech, red oak, white and yellow birch, with some different species of pines. The terrain was hilly and dry, some large boulders were sticking up through the leaf litter here and there. We had gone about two hundred yards down the winding trail that bisected the parcel when a high bluff came into view.

"Cheryl, I want to walk up that hill and look around it may be a nice spot for a house, do you want to follow or stay on the trail?"

"I'm coming with you that hill looks like it would be a nice setting for a house."

The incline wasn't too steep and when we reached the top, the view was spectacular, on the backside a large deep gorge or canyon traversed the entire length of the hillside, and you could look out over the tops of the trees that grew up from the bottom.

"This is great Cheryl it's like a canyon or a gorge look you can see over the trees, is this part of the property?"

"Yes, I think so Dalton according to the surveyor's map it has a small stream running through the bottom, it starts in the canyon and runs out towards the southeast corner so the stream is on the property too."

"I wonder if you can see it from the edge." I walked out to the edge and looked down the small creek was visible in spots through the treetops and the wall of the gorge was probably hundred feet straight down.

"This is awesome come take a look Cheryl."

"No that's okay Dalton, I'm a bit afraid of heights, and I'll take your word for it."

Cheryl was standing about fifty feet behind me and wasn't coming any closer to the edge.

"Okay, Cheryl I've seen enough let's go back and draw up the papers I'll take it."

"You will? But you haven't even seen the whole parcel yet."

"That's okay I'll look at all of it later, I'm satisfied with it so far."

We walked back to the Yukon, Cheryl was talking a mile a minute, excited that she had made a sale I assumed. We drove back to her office all the while she was talking about the area and how everybody is so friendly and that once a few people got to know me, I would fit in, and her kids were almost out of school for the year and she was planning a trip and she was glad that I liked the first parcel because she wasn't real keen on walking through the woods.

"I'm sure glad you liked it; the other ones don't have road through them."

We arrived back at the office in shorter time than it took to get out to the parcel. I guess I was excited too.

"What do you need from me Cheryl, a down payment or some sort of holding fee?"

"If you want to put something down, that's fine or I can just hold it, if you need more time to decide."

"No, I already decided, and I want it, what did you say was the price?

"It's a forty-acre parcel and it is wooded with a stream and road frontage with power and phone, the asking price is fifty-five thousand, is that fair enough for you?"

"That sounds more than fair, here is a check for fifty-five hundred, consider it a down payment or a holding fee."

"Okay, I'll just get you a receipt and have you fill out some forms and you can be on your way."

Cheryl was getting the paper work together and jabbering excitedly about anything and everything, explaining where to sign and what I was signing.

"How long do you think the lawyers will take to draw up the papers and do a title search on it?"

"Do you want, a lawyer of yours to do it or one from the area/"

"Why don't we use one from up here, and that way I can just move here right away?"

"You can move that fast?"

"I told you I was ready for a change and the quicker the better"

Cheryl grouped the paperwork together into a folder after making me copies, noting her business card numbers and where I could reach her if need be, she also put the lawyer's card in the folder.

I pulled it out reading the name out loud, "Jessica Whitehorse?" That's a name you don't hear every day.

"Yes, she is a Native American, her office is in Baraga, and the address is on the back with directions."

"Oh no kidding I'm looking forward to meeting her, when do you think that will be?"

"Let's find out, I'll give her a call right now." Cheryl dialed the phone, showing a happy face that the lawyer was still at work on a Saturday.

"Hi Jessica this is Cheryl Johnson over at Baraga

County reality, I'm fine how are you, good I have a buyer setting in my office and he would like to know how long before you could do a transaction on a piece of property. Yes, he is pretty eager to get it done, ah uh okay I'll tell him thank you bye. She said next Saturday would be good for her and to just give her a call if that was okay with you."

"Saturday would be fine; do you know if there are any cabins for rent around here and perhaps a good contractor that may want to build a log home?"

Cheryl went into the back office and came out handing me two more business cards.

"Thank you, Cheryl you have been more than helpful, and I'll see you next week"

"You are welcome Dalton and thank you very much, give me a call next Thursday and I can be sure to have everything ready for Saturday."

Would you like me to buy you lunch? I'm starving.

"No Dalton I have to get back the babysitter is expecting me by 12:30 and it's already noon, but thanks for the invite." That's quite all right, can you maybe suggest a place a guy can get a beer and a burger? She gave me directions for a bar downtown, I thanked her again and said I would call on Thursday.

I left her office and went into the downtown area looking for the bar which was located on the main street. I had read somewhere that at one time there was thirteen bars in L'Anse, now there were only a few. I parked out front at the curb, the place had been there a while the brickwork was old and the facings around the windows and doorways looked hand carved. Once inside you noticed the worn wood floors and the dark stained varnish on the wood trim and bar top, yes,

I'm sure there had been many a beer tossed back in here. I took a seat at the end of the bar; the place was pretty empty for a Saturday. There were two different couples setting at separate tables and one old grizzled looking guy at the other end of the bar. He was talking to the bartender and from his reaction it appeared he was telling a joke. The barkeep noticed me and came over chuckling.

"What can I get you sir?"

"I'll have a beer and maybe something to eat, do you have a menu?"

"Okay, I'll bring it back with the beer." He said retreating back into the kitchen to grab a menu and returning with a beer from the cooler behind the bar.

"Thanks.

"Ya sure just let me know when you want to order." He went back into the kitchen and came out with a food order for one of the tables. The old guy was checking me out probably wondering who the stranger was. I have found the best way to make friends in a bar is to buy them a drink when the bartender came back, I motioned him over.

"What will you have?"

"I'll have a burger and another beer and give the old guy at the other end whatever he's drinking on me."

The bartender placed a fresh beer in front of me and one in front of the old gent, who gave him a puzzled look, which the bartender answered by pointing towards me. The old timer got up and sat down on the stool next to me with his beer in hand.

"Thanks for the beer young fellow."

"No problem I can't stand to drink alone, the name

is Dalton James, how are you," I said offering my hand to shake.

"Gus Jorgenson, glad to meet you." He said offering his hand, it was huge looked like a baseball mitt when it grabbed mine.

"What brings you to a place like this/"

"I'm buying some property up here and the realtor said this place had good food."

"They do come here all the time." Gus took a long pull from his beer, he was about seventy I would guess in good shape not to heavy just thick as they say around 6'4" maybe taller when he was young, his pants were wore through at the knees and had what looked like a couple of days dirt on them, the yellowed tee shirt was sticking above his flannel shirt, and a greasy ball cap with the word CAT in yellow letters, a three days growth of white whiskers covered his round face and his pale gray eyes gave away his Scandinavian ancestry.

"Would you like some lunch Gus?"

"No thanks just finished, where did you say the property was that you were buying?"

The bar tender brought my food and I ordered two more beers. I told Gus where the forty acres was and he started to fill me in on some of the local history after about an hour of bullshitting, I told him I would look him up and maybe do some fishing next week when I moved up here for good. I think that we became friends right then and there.

The sun started heating up the afternoon and it may just get to 75 degress, the local radio station stated, as I drove south back to Detroit. Hopefully for my last visit to the motor city.

CHAPTER FOUR

I drove around L'Anse on Thursday, checking out all the stores and trying to get more familiar with the area, passed the bar I was in the week before and thought I should go in and see if old Gus was in his stool at the end of the bar. I had called Cheryl the day before and told her I couldn't wait in Detroit any longer so if she had any question, she could reach me on my cell phone.

The day was fairly nice with some cloud cover to break up the glare of the sun as it glimmered on the lake surface a soft northwest wind was rippling the water giving it a gemstone look. It was great to be up here and I was looking forward to seeing old Gus. I entered the bar, standing in the doorway letting my eyes adjust to the dimmer light and trying to see if Gus was in there through the cigarette smoke. He was seated in the same spot as the week before and I took the stool next to him, he didn't even notice me. The argument he was having with some young kid was keeping him focused, the kid had a pierced ear and a gold loop through his left nostril and Gus was explaining why it wasn't right for a man to have that kind of shit hanging off himself, and why didn't the kid have a job and for being in a bar giving some old guy like himself a hard time.

I just sat there grinning overhearing the

conversation, ordered two beers using the universal hand signal that every bartender knows, two fingers and point to who gets them.

The bartender slid one in front of Gus, who still hadn't noticed me sitting beside him.

"I didn't order any goddamn beer."

"I know that, he did." The bartender countered and hooked his thumb in my direction.

Gus turned on his stool to face me placing his elbow on the bar, and holding his beer with his left hand clanked the neck of the bottle with mine, like a toast.

With that movement by Gus the earring kid headed for the back door.

"Well, hello, glad to see you found your way back, and thanks for the beer."

"Hello Gus surprised to see me? What was that all about with the kid? Did you eat lunch yet?"

"I'm a little surprised that you came to see me, and no I haven't eaten yet and that fucking kid was getting on my nerves. I don't understand why the hell some guy has to put an earring in his nose, he looked like some kind of a queer."

"That's the way the younger ones dress now and there are worse things than wearing an earring in your nose."

"FUCK! I think the little fucker had perfume on too, smelled like some French whore or something."

"That wasn't perfume, it was cologne, and you shouldn't get all worked up about it, he'll probably grow out of it in a few years." I was thinking the perfume smell might not be too bad considering the aroma coming off of Gus when he placed his other elbow on the bar. I think those were the same clothes he had on last week and I kind of slid over a bit to give my sinuses a break. I ordered some burgers and fries and another beer for us and started grilling old Gus on some fishing spots we might hit later in the day.

"Hey, Gus how long did you say you have lived here seventy years or so?"

The food arrived and Gus tore into it before answering me.

"Yah that's right give or take a few, why you asking?"

"Well, I thought after we eat you might want to take me fishing, I'll drive and supply the beer you just have to show me where to go."

"That sound like a hell of an idea, it's time to get out and get the stink blown off anyway."

He didn't know how right he was. Man, that old guy was getting ripe. We finished lunch and stepped out into the fresh air, thank god, he smelled like B.O, mixed with wet dog, cigarette smoke and a sprinkle of frying grease. I was definitely driving with the windows down. It was nice to have the air blowing the smell out as we drove out of town, Gus was giving directions and I was trying to follow as he reached back and grabbed us each a beer from the cooler in the back seat.

"You see that two tracks up there take a left and here is a beer so you can see well."

I was enjoying the company and I think he was too. "So, what kind of fish are we going after Gus?"

"What kind do you want, we got'em all around here, rainbows, browns, speckled trout, walleye and pike just to name a few."

"Speckled trout, what kind is that?"

"Well, you trolls call them brook trout I think."

"Trolls? What do you mean trolls?"

"That's what we call down state people up here, because you live below the Mackinaw Bridge." Ha ha.

I was beginning to like this old coot; we drove down several more two track-changing directions more than I would remember. The last one was an old railroad grade, after our third beer from the cooler Gus decided that there was a little pond just up ahead that might hold a speck or two.

"Just ahead Dalton there is a place where the beaver has the old bridge washed out and a nice little pond made, it's usually good for a couple of nice trout, so stop right here and walk up there and try your luck."

I parked the Yukon and opened the back, getting out my fly rod and a small box of flies, which imitate grasshoppers. "Aren't you going to fish Gus I brought an extra rod for you?"

"No, you go ahead, I got to piss like a gut shot panther and beside someone has to guard the beer, and I'll catch up with you."

"Okay, bring the net when you come, I think we may need it."

Gus stayed back and pissed, while I went ahead, I had tied on a small hopper imitation and was kneeling by the edge of the pond trying not to spook the fish when Gus came up behind me.

"What the hell you fishing with a bullwhip?"

"No, it's a fly rod."

"A fly rod, what you got on for bait?"

"It's called a grasshopper see here." I pulled the line in so Gus could take a look.

"That don't look like no grasshopper I ever seen, looks like a bunch of feathers and hair, and are you praying or fishing down there on your knees?"

"The fish think it's a grasshopper and there isn't any praying just skill here watch and learn old-timer." I was getting a bit cocky with him and laid the next cast perfectly on the surface of the beaver pond. The area surrounding the pond was low and the cedar trees crowded the edge and gave way to maples as the terrain increased in elevation.

Gus was still giggling about his praying comment when the pond surface exploded where my hopper was.

"I got'em! Gus get the net over here it feels like a nice one." The fish made a couple of runs and finished off with a tail walk before giving up, Gus bent down and netted it.

"What do you say now Gus? I told you the fish couldn't tell the difference, and it looks like my first speckled trout is about sixteen inches long."

"That is a nice one Dalton, I've caught bigger ones in here with a worm, good job, now get three more and we will have enough for supper."

I continued to fish for about an hour catching six more and keeping three but none were as big as the first. Gus gathered the fish and put them in the cooler with the beer and ice and I packed the rod in the back-end of the Yukon.

"Hey Dalton good job on the fish, but could you not tell anybody where you caught them."

"I'll do one better I won't come out here unless you come with me, how does that sound?"

"Sounds good, here have another beer it's the last one, no sense in letting it spoil."

We left the fishing hole and Gus directed me through the back trails and out onto a gravel road, that looked familiar.

"Gus this is where my property is right over there is the old driveway."

"I know that, I told you I worked up this way in the woods cutting pulpwood and I knew where your place was, all them trails we just came off of, I used to drive every day for work.

"Gus you mind if we stop, I kind of want to look around some more."

"Hell no, I'm starting to get sore riding around in this metal buggy and I think I could piss again."

I pulled into the old drive where I had parked the Saturday before and got out Gus stood by the fender relieving himself on my front tire.

"You pissing on my tire? Well, when you get done go through this brush back here, I'll be waiting for you."

"Okay Dalton."

He joined me on the trail, and stood their kind of in thought, and started walking toward two big pine trees about a hundred yards ahead.

"What are you doing Gus?"

"I'm looking for old man Ford's fishing camp, if I remember right it used to set right by these two big Hemlock trees."

"Who's old fishing camp?"

The old man was turning in circles trying to remember his bearings. The trees all looked the same to me but he seemed to know where he was going.

"Henry Ford the guy who built the model T, ever hear of him?"

"Yah, I heard of him, but I never knew he used to come up here."

"Well, he used to own a bunch of this around here, you see them Hemlocks?"

"Hemlocks, what are they, the ones that look like a pine?"

"Yep, I believe Ford's cabin used to set right on the other side of them."

"No shit! Gus you're a hell of a tour guide, you know anything else about this property?"

The old tour guide started thinking and talking as he walked.

"I think if we walk right that way, through those maples on the ridge, we will come to the gorge with the creek in it."

I was following Gus and he was pointing out different trees and the way the loggers cut and cared for the forest.

"Dalton, I don't think this forty was ever cut off. You see those big Hemlocks scattered here and there on this place and the two big ones I pointed out earlier?"

"Yes, what about them?"

"If this was cut off once the Hemlocks on here would have went too, they wouldn't be that big, the loggers would have knocked them down and stripped the bark off."

"Stripped the bark off? What would they need that for?" I was starting to take an interest in what Gus was explaining, maybe he wasn't just an old codger, who sat in the bar and smelled bad.

"The big-time companies, would come through an area first and take all the premium timber, the money timber, but the Hemlock wasn't worth much as far as lumber quality, so after the big outfits went through and took the good stuff, they sold the lower quality to someone else or let it go back to the state who sold it again. The smaller companies would come through and take the less desirable timber for pulpwood, and posts etc., the Hemlock was cut and the bark stripped off for use in the tanning industries."

"The tanning industry, what did they do with it?"

"The tannery would boil it down somehow and extract the chemicals from it for tanning leather, you have to remember that leather was a big necessity, everything from shoe to coats and just think of all the horse harnesses. They would haul it out on carts and sleds and load it on train cars for shipment to the big tanneries in Chicago and other places."

This is all very interesting Gus, but what about the big maples on this ridge?

"They should have been cut too but no one knows why old man Ford said no. We should be coming up on the edge of that canyon soon, just over this hill."

We walked up to the edge and the view took my breath away again.

"Scream Canyon." Gus said to no one in particular.

"Scream Canyon, where is that Gus?"

"Right here, you are looking at it."

"Why is it called that?"

The old man kind of turned his face from me. "I'm really not sure Dalton."

We started back for the truck and I had the feeling that Gus wasn't telling me everything he knew about how Scream Canyon got its name. We both got in the Yukon and Gus wasn't really talkative anymore so I spoke up.

"Hey Gus you want to come over to my cabin I rented? I'll cook up those trout for supper."

"Sounds like a hell of a plan just take me to my truck at the bar and I'll meet you there."

"Okay, but I'll need to get a few groceries so give me a few minutes after I drop you off or just go in, I didn't lock up its cabin number six right down by the water."

I dropped Gus at his truck and went to the store and picked up some coleslaw and potatoes and some cooking oil and flour for the fish, and another twelve beers the old man had cleaned out the cooler and was probably working on my refrigerator by now. The old boy could drink beer.

Gus was parked out front when I returned and was drinking a beer in his truck.

Gus why didn't you go inside and drink that?

"I just slid in and grabbed one out of the fridge, ain't right sitting in a man's house when he ain't home. So, did you get some groceries, you get started and I'll clean the fish how does that sound?

I went in and started cooking the potatoes and mixing the coleslaw Gus came in with the fish ready for the fry pan. We ate like starving wolves and by the end of supper we both had a few beers down and were looking tired.

"Thanks a lot Dalton that was a good day, but my ass is dragging and I'm going home see you later."

"Yah mine's dragging too, what do you say we go fishing again tomorrow, meet me here for breakfast at 7:30?"

"Okay Dalton, see you in the morning."

I turned in for the night and was up at 6:00, cooking breakfast and all the while thinking about what Gus had told me about me property. I cooked pancakes, sausage, scrambled eggs, and some left-over potatoes. That ought to hold the old fart, he could eat just as much as he drank.

Gus arrived at 7:00 knocked once and came right in.

"Morning, Gus you are looking well today."

He was all cleaned up, fresh pair of pants and shirt, clean-shaven, but he still had on his CAT hat.

"Yah, Thursday night is bath night and I decided to go for it."

"Hope you are hungry, have a seat, coffee?" I sat the food down as his sipped his coffee and we dug in.

"You're damn good cook Dalton, but I have to tell you I'm still a bit confused about what you used to do in Detroit, you were a fire cop or something?"

"Well not exactly I started out as a volunteer fire-fighter and then I got interested in arson investigation so I went to school and got some training and a degree in fire science and investigation. I worked for the Detroit fire department on their arson task force. I solved crimes and fire causes using science and forensics. Understand?"

"Yah I guess so Dalton."

"Well, enough talk, where we going fishing today Gus, more brook trout?"

"No, today is a good day for herring off the pier, I was checking the wind this morning before I got here and it's blowing the right way for the herring to be in close, you might even pick up a steelhead or two."

"It's sounds good to me, what do I need for tackle?"

Gus explained what I needed and what I didn't have he did. We arrived down at the pier and I could see there were some other fishermen already there. The pier was located at the mouth of the Falls River that emptied into Lake Superior at the bottom of the Keweenaw Bay. There was a Celotex plant on both sides of the river and they piped steam or something across overhead in large insulated pipes.

We each took a folding chair, a five-gallon pail, and our fishing gear and walked out onto the pier. The several fishermen already there greeted Gus and me as we went down the line past them, setting up on the far end of them. Gus was rigging his poles and mine and explaining how to catch herring, because I was a greenhorn at it, he must have thought I needed a lesson. Once everything was tied on and the lesson over Gus reached into a small cooler and threw a handful of salmon spawn into the water that he had collected the previous fall, and in went our lines, we propped the poles on the handrail and sat back and waited.

Gus started the introductions with the two gentlemen sitting next to us, one was a State trooper from the Baraga post and the other one was the Fire Chief of Baraga. It didn't take me long to figure out this was more of a social gathering then a fishing trip, as the conversations went back and forth down the line of fishermen.

The state trooper was the first to ask me a question. "Did you say you were Dalton James?"

"Yes, that's right, from Detroit."

"I've heard of you, you were with the arson task force, wrote some books and stuff on fire scene investigation techniques."

"Yep, my books were the called The Smoke Sniffers."

"Yes, that's it, I read both of them good reading."

"Oh yah, now I know you." The Chief piped up. "There was an instructor up here from Lansing last year teaching an arson investigation course at the college in Houghton, he said you wrote the book that he was using, everyone in the class got a copy."

"The name Dalton James didn't register at first, but the Smoke Sniffer title did, he said you had a nose like a bloodhound when it came to arson."

"So, I have been told, and thanks for reading my book."

The Chief wasn't done yet and I could tell he was thinking up something.

"You know Dalton we don't have a full-time arson investigator around here; we have to use the State Police detective when we need one sometimes, we have to wait half a day or night because he is out on another scene, do you think you might be interested in helping me out on some fires if I need it, just voluntary of course."

"I don't see why not I'll give you my cell phone number. I'm going to be staying at those cabins across the bay over there until my house gets built."

We fished and talked a while longer and around noon, Gus and I decided to call it quits. On the drive back to my cabin I realized old Gus had set the whole thing up with the Chief, he just couldn't stand seeing a young guy like me sitting around retired.

I went into the cabin and grabbed a couple of beers and Gus and I went out to sit on a bench by the water in front of the cabin. Gus and I sat watching the shore birds dart around and skimming the water with their bills.

"Hey Dalton I have something to show you about your property." He reached into his shirt pocket and pulled out a folded pack of papers yellowed from age.

"What do you have their Gus?"

"It's a cruiser's map of your forty."

"What does that mean a cruiser's map?"

"It is a map or survey of the timber in a given area done by a timber cruiser. Before anything is cut a cruiser working for the timber company or an independent firm, goes to the woodlot and does an estimate of the board footage or cordage of each tree species and makes a map or drawing for the cutters to follow, he usually marks the boundary in paint or in the old days he axes blazed the trees. The only problem is your forty never got cut, but everything around it did."

"How do you know this Gus?"

"Because the cruisers' map that we are looking at was done by my father."

"Why are you bringing this up about the timber on my property, does it make a difference if it wasn't cut?"

"No not really Dalton, but when I got home last night I got to thinking about those big trees on the ridge, and wondering why they were never harvested, they're close to a good road, easy picking so to speak. The ones in the canyon are a different story you would need a lot of special equipment for them. But the hard maple on the ridge could be cut easily."

"I'm still not following you Gus, why are the trees such a mystery to you?"

"Listen up Dalton and I'll tell you. Do you have any idea what hard maple veneer sells for or is worth or what it is?"

"No, not really I know it is used in the furniture business, and for doors and trim, but I never really thought about it".

"The thing about hard maple is the Japanese love it and so do some of the other countries where it has been harvested off. The area around here and the Keweenaw

Peninsula grow some of the highest grades of hard maple in the world. When we were out there yesterday, I did a little cruising of my own."

"Is that what all the circling was about and the blank looks on your face when you looked at the wood on the ridge?"

"Yep, and don't hold me to it because I'm not a timber cruiser, but I figure on the ridge alone you have somewhere in the neighborhood of fifty to sixty thousand dollars' worth of veneer hard maple and that's not counting the birch and oak. So now do you see why I was questioning it?"

"The trees are worth more than double of what I paid for the property; well, it isn't mine yet, not until tomorrow. I never would have guessed those trees are worth that much."

"No? I didn't figure you did that's, why last night I got to digging through my dad's old stuff, and found this map. You have made quite a find for yourself. Who is doing the transactions for you?"

"I have a meeting at the lawyer's office with the realtor Cheryl Johnson and the lawyer is Jessica Whitehorse".

"The Johnson lady is alright, but watch yourself around that Indian, and whatever you do don't mention the value of them trees."

"I won't, but what's the matter with Jessica?"

"Do you remember the name of that canyon out there?"

"Yah scream canyon, what of it?"

Gus took a long drink of his beer and leaned back on the bench, his demeanor turning more serious.

"The other day when you asked me how Scream

Canyon got its name, I wasn't quite honest with you. There is a legend about it and it goes like this.

"The Indians in these parts a long time ago used to hold ceremonies up on that bluff that overlooks the canyon, sacrifices and shit like that. They held it in high regard religiously. But that isn't where the screaming part comes in. the Jesuits snow shoed into these parts one winter and tried to bring Christianity to the tribes. Father Baraga came later. There is a statue over there of him. These were the first black robes, they came with the French fur traders, they weren't, as tidy as him. They sometimes stepped out of the black cloth if you get my drift. When they showed up, they told the tribes it was forbidden to hold ceremonies on the bluff it was "pagan and devil worship" they said. The story doesn't stop there, it seems somewhere along the way the Chiefs daughter fell in love with one of the Black Robes, which was not a good thing a Frenchman yes but not a Jesuit. The Chiefs didn't trust them like the fur traders. The Catholic Church kind of frowns on this shit too. There was no talking the Indian princess out of it. The Chief found out and he fixed here up in a forced marriage with one of his most trusted braves. The night of the wedding the bride's mother stayed in the wigwam to make sure the marriage was consummated. The next day the princess was in a hell of a state of mind so she went to the Jesuit priest and confessed because she wasn't sure if she was really married and didn't know how this would stand with the him and the Christian beliefs. Well, the story goes that the priest told her that it really wasn't a real marriage because it wasn't held before God and that she had committed a sin of having sex before marriage. They say she went kind of nuts after that and went around saying the ro- sary to herself and praying out loud trying to be for- given. Then nine months passed and the princess gave birth, the Chief and his wife thought the baby she had carried for nine months was the product of the wed- ding night with the brave. The day after giving birth the princess disappeared. The tribe formed a search party and tracked her to the bluff overlooking the can- yon. When the search party arrived at the canyon, she was standing at the edge praying. Then she jumped, screaming all the way down."

"That's a great story Gus, so that's why it's called Scream Canyon?"

"No, not quite. The search party went around to the bottom to retrieve the body so they could perform a burial ceremony on it but they couldn't find her. They stayed and search for two days and all the while they could her screaming, it freaked them out thought it was her spirit haunting them so they packed up and left never to go back"

"Oh, this just keeps getting better all the time, first Indians and then priest and now a ghost."

"Hold on, I am not finished. When the search party returned to the village the princess' mother had given the baby to the Black Robe that the girl was in love with."

"The grandmother didn't want the baby, why not?"

"Well, it looked like a little Indian except for one thing."

"Gus, what was the one thing?" I was beginning to get impatient with him and his yarn. He was chuckling as he held me in suspense.

"It is said the little bundle of joy had blue eyes; you

ever see an Indian with blue eyes? The tribe figured the girl thought it was a devil child bad medicine as they say. I kind of got a different idea on where the blue eyes came from. I think the old Black Robe was dipping the holy pole in the unholy hole, if yah get my meaning. That is why the girl jumped, to save her Jesuit lover from being thrown out of the church."

But didn't the other Jesuits know or figure it out?

"No, it's not that they didn't figure it out, without the confession of the girl, they didn't have a leg to stand on and the holy daddy wasn't going to tell them anything different, let them think it was a devil child, give them all the more reason to covert."

"Why did you tell me this story Gus?"

"There is a little more to the story and it is closer to the present day. The Chief of the suicidal princess has the last name of Whitehorse, Chief Whitehorse to be exact."

"So, what you are telling me is that Jessica's ancestor was the girl that jumped?"

"That's just what I'm telling you Dalton so be careful around her."

Gus got up and stretched his legs and back and headed for the truck with a look of satisfaction after telling the story. "Give me a call tomorrow Dalton after your meeting, I'm going home see yah later."

"Okay Gus sees yah."

The bench was hard on the ass and I thought a good long shower and maybe some T.V. with a big sandwich would finish off a good day of fishing and storytelling.

CHAPTER FIVE

I woke up unrested and tired from all the dreaming and nightmares of screaming Indian maidens and burnt corpse and firefighters being blown up. I showered and shaved, made some strong coffee to see if I could get kick started, gathered all of my paperwork and cashier's check.

I was going to meet the great, great, great whatever granddaughter of the Indian princess, Ms. Jessica Whitehorse at her office in Baraga.

I arrived at her office at 9:00 am sharp and parked out front right behind Cheryl's Explorer. My briefcase in hand I entered the office where a receptionist asked if I was Dalton James?

"Please go right in Mr. James, Jessica is expecting you."

She held the large wooden door open as I entered and stood just inside after it closed behind me, taking in the office décor around me. The room was finished in oak trim and the ceilings and floors were hard maple flooring done in a diamond pattern, toward the back was a large oak desk in a half moon shape with all the modern technology apparent, fax, pc, copier, etc. on one wall was a massive oak book shelf containing a fullest of law books and encyclopedias. The decorations were a Native American motif, bows and arrows hung on walls with snowshoes, furs and paintings depicting scenes of Indian hunting parties and dances. There was a large one just below the crossed snow shoes of a Jesuit priest blessing the small band of natives kneeling before him, he had a pair of snow shoes strapped on his back and his face and hand were turned toward the heavens, I figured this must be Baraga the one the statue is of.

The next thing I set my eyes on was the woman standing behind the desk, Ms. Jessica Whitehorse. She invited me to sit down in a large overstuffed chair by the corner of her desk it was covered in buckskin and adorned in beadwork. She was wearing a pair of designer jeans, a white cotton blouse that accented her full breasts and a tweed-hunting jacket with leather patches on the elbows and on shoulder. The clothes didn't give justice to the beautiful woman that stood before me smiling. The long raven black hair was braided into a ponytail that nearly reached her narrow waist, a thin face with a jaw that kind of squared toward the back, her nose was petite with a slight hook on the end, a small full lipped mouth with a pouting look to it, her skin tone was a reddish brown, like a someone with a good suntan. The white blouse accenting her skin color, making it appear darker than it actually was. She was tall and slim 5'9" to5'10" maybe 130 pounds, with a slight curve to her hips more athletic than a super models thin build. What I noticed next and I'm sure everyone else did when they met her, was her eyes. They were large ovals of the deepest brightest glacier blue I had ever seen and you couldn't help but stare into them, they held your attention, she spoke with a feminine huskiness in her voice not butch but seductive. I could just imagine that everywhere she went her presence was noticed. She started to speak, and I was brought out of my daydream. She was sitting behind her desk, now the tone was all business.

"Mr. James, thank you for coming in today, Mrs. Johnson has prepared the proper paper work and I would ask you to read it over and if there are any questions please feel free to ask." Jessica handed me the packet and I checked the title search and taxes and was satisfied that everything looked on the up and up, so I handed it back to her.

"When you looked at its Ms. Whitehorse did you notice anything unusual?"

"No, Mr. James everything seemed okay to me, so if you are satisfied, we can get started."

The transaction went smoothly, with her and Cheryl passing papers back and forth from each other than to me for signatures. I noticed Jessica had a slight gap in her front teeth not a Dave Letterman, but enough to make herself conscious about it so she covers her face with her hand when she smiled. The documents were explained to me before signing by her in all the while talking in that bedroom whisper of a voice she had. I was not really paying to close attention to the paperwork. Her voice was distracting me, I don't think I said three words the whole time just nodded and signed, and she had cast a spell on me. With the paperwork done I popped open my briefcase and handed her the cashier's check and placed my copies inside. Jessica stood and thanked us for coming, shook each of our hands. When she grasped mine across the desk, I felt an odd warmness inside, yes, this woman had cast a spell on me.

Cheryl and I walked out of the office and exchanged goodbyes at the curb where her car was parked, I crossed the street, got into mine and headed back to L'Anse, I was in town and not really knowing how I had gotten there, I had been daydreaming about Jessica, when I nearly missed the turn I wanted to take into town.

Snap out of its Dalton, my god it's just a woman a very beautiful woman, I was acting like a freshman in high school who just seen the senior cheerleader bend over and noticed she had a thong on, my heart was racing, I had sweaty palms.

The bar was just around the corner and I had agreed to meet Gus when I was done in Baraga. I did need a drink; Gus was sitting in his usual spot at the bar and when he seen me, he motioned me over to a table along the back wall away from the bar.

"What's up with the privacy thing Gus, why are we sitting at a table I just want a drink?"

Gus tilted his head toward the bar, and hooked his big thumb in that direction. "Old long ears have a way of flopping his pie hole about things he shouldn't know about."

The bartender came over and took our drink orders and left before Gus would speak again.

"So, Dalton how did you make out at the attorney's office are you the proud owner or not?"

"Yes, sir it's all mine bought and paid for; the deed should come through in about a week."

"Good for you. What did you think of Ms. Whitehorse?"

The bartender brought our drinks and Gus clanked his against mine.

"Congratulations Dalton, so spit it out what did you think?"

He kind of caught me off guard with the question and could see I was going to lie.

"I thought she was very professional Gus."

"Bullshit, you fell hook line and sinker for her, didn't you? I told you to be careful of her, but you wouldn't listen to old Gus."

He went on preaching and to me in a scolding fashion.

"I knew you was going to come back all starry eyed and pumped up like a two pecker Billy goat in a sheep herd."

"Now hold on Gus, it's not like that at all, she is very attractive, but I'm not interested."

"Fuck it isn't, she is just like that ancestor of hers all pretty and shit, fella can't hardly stand to be around her without getting all stiff legged, if you know what I mean. She isn't anything but trouble."

"Wow, wow hold on Gus, what is the problem you have with Jessica?"

"There is a lot more too little Ms. Indian attorney then you think."

"Yah like what? He was starting to piss me off."

"It's a long story Dalton."

"Well why don't you fill me in, I got all day."

"All right you hard head, I will. Jessica Whitehorse has the same curse as her great ancestor; she is just too damn good looking. Men used to follow her around like dogs and get into all kinds of trouble fighting each other over her."

"How old is she Gus?"

"I would say maybe forty or so, I'm not real sure,

but she ain't always been a Miss, she was a Mrs. now she is a widow."

"A widow, I didn't think she looked old enough to be a widow."

"Well, she is, want to know how and why?"

"Yes, I would Gus please continue."

"Her daddy is on the tribal council, seems like the old blood line still means something. He wanted her to get a good education, so he sent her down state to some college and she got herself a law degree, while she was away at school, she fell in love with one of the professors, he was about five or six years older than her at the time. When she came back from college, she brought the good professor with her they had gotten married. This didn't set to well with big Chief daddy. He wasn't real welcome, about like a fart in church. The mother smoothed things over with dad and Jessica and the professor went into law practice together representing the tribe's affairs, she handled the small stuff and the husband handled the big money deals. She would represent the drunks and the petty shit in court."

"I'm with you so far, but what does that have to do with her being a widow?"

"Hold on to your horses I'm getting to it. The professor was getting a bit impatient with his capital gains so he started handling all the land transactions for the tribe, they were making good money off of the casino and wanted to invest. He was skimming off the top, he would tell the tribe an inflated price, knowing damn well they could pay it, and when they did, he would pay the seller the asking price with a slight stipend to keep his mouth shut."

"How did the tribe find out Gus?"

"It was working good for him than he got greedier so he hooked up with some slippery fuck of an insurance investigator and they would put insurance on the piece of property and make the professor the beneficiary, then somehow they would burn the place collect the money and split it. He got away with it for a while."

"How did he do that don't they investigate fires up here?"

"Yah they do, you know that fire Chief you met yesterday, he would do the investigations and could not come up with the cause, then when the insurance investigator showed up, he would agree with the fire Chief and recommend they cut a check to the professor."

"That still don't seem right, didn't they call any other investigators?"

"You are right, but when you were investigating in Detroit did you get called to every fire?"

"No, not all of them just suspicious ones or if there was a fatality, you know if someone was killed."

"Exactly, that's the part I'm getting to now. The two of them had worked the scam three times I think and had split around two and a half million, then the tribe bought this old warehouse and were going to convert it into a recreation center for the kids to use. The professor handled the transaction and tried the scam again for a big pay off, but the arson job got botched somehow and somebody got killed."

I was listening intently now. Who got killed Gus?

"The professor, that's who, Jessica's husband."

"Then they had to call in a State Police investigator because it was a fatal fire, right? So, what happened during the investigation, did they figure out how they were doing it?"

"They did just that and he determined the professor was killed before the fire, somebody killed him then torched it. Whoever it was didn't get a full burn, the old sprinklers still worked all there was, was some water and smoke damage. The insurance company didn't want to cut a check for the full amount of total building replacement. The tribe got involved and found out the professor had been scamming them and the insurance company. When the insurance company checked their records, the check had already been cut for the building in the amount of one million dollars two days prior to the fire and then it was cashed one day later, before they could cancel it."

"I still don't see how the insurance company, could insure something that the professor didn't own."

"It doesn't matter who owns it, I could take out a life policy on whoever and be the benefactor as long as I paid the premium it doesn't matter."

"Now Gus, you are saying that Jessica is involved somehow?"

"No, that's not quite true. The investigators turned up the scam and when the check came back to the insurance company it was signed and cashed by the professor or someone forged it, anyway the money came up missing and the finger was pointed at Jessica, she was cleared later when they realized the insurance investigator was missing too."

"So, they never found him either?"

"No, not yet anyway. They found his car at the airport in Marquette, the police figured he killed the professor, pocketed the money and fled; she's off the hook. The tribe didn't question the other fires because they were going to tear the buildings down anyway, less cleanup cost and believe me don't you think the cops didn't rake them over the coals, thinking they burned the buildings and collected the money. The insurance company cleared them of any wrong doing once they looked at the canceled checks."

"That's a lot off story old man and not much proof, why do you still think Jessica was involved?"

"Because she was paid a million dollars from the professor's life insurance policy, that's why."

"Oh, I see, interesting. Does the fire Chief still have the records from the fires?"

"Hell, I don't know. Why don't you go ask him, you said that you would help him if he needed you?"

"Maybe I'll go see him tomorrow. Well Gus once again you have piqued my interest, but now I have to go see my contractor about getting me a house built."

CHAPTER SIX

From a vantage point a half a mile away, an arsonist was watching and waiting for the show he had directed to begin.

It was 2:00 a.m. a stiff wind was blowing in land from the Keweenaw Bay towards the town of Baraga. The arsonist had been working in the department store since 10:00 p.m. the night before; he had hidden in the ceiling of the bathroom waiting for the store to close. He brought nothing in with him. The store merchandise would be enough, to use to load the building for burning. He strung balloon full off camping fuel on the ceiling and poured lamp oil on anything that was combustible on the selves. A paintbrush worked for trailing accelerants across open areas and up walls, to the balloons on the ceiling. He had noticed during earlier visits to the store that a magazine rack was too close to the steam radiator that heated one area in the store. This night was picked because the weather forecast had predicted cold weather coming in from the big lake and would likely drop the temperature down to 50 degrees, causing the heating system to come on. He took a Coleman stove used for camping and placed it under the magazine rack, this would work for a time delay and to enable him to get clear before the fire started. The stove was lit and with the flames directed onto the bottom of the metal rack he figured about a twenty-minute lead time was just about right to get clear before the magazines caught fire and started the chain reaction. He had taped off the smoke detectors for the alarm system thinking that the tape would burn off and trigger the system well after the fire had started giving it ample time to do major destruction.

At 2:10 a.m. the alarm was triggered and the dispatcher sent out the call to the local fire department. The department would arrive to late the chain reaction was already doing its dirty work the fire crews would be in a defense mode of operations.

The electrical system had already shorted out, and the structure was fully engulfed in flames, the fire had used up all the oxygen inside and was starving the temperature was climbing inside the store to 1200 degrees and the large windows in front were beginning to crack as the fire sucked for the much-needed oxygen to complete the burning cycle.

It was sucking air in and around the doors and windows showing small streams off smoke as it breathed in and out. Thick black smoke was coming out the roof vents and out around the eves.

The first engine company pulled up to the fire hydrant directly across the street, just as one of the large front windows breeched under the vacuum caused by the oxygen starved fire, superheated gases at the ceiling ignited causing a flashover, a rolling inferno filled the inside of the store as fire broke out through the widow opening and up the outside of the building.

The Incident commander on seen radioed dispatched for mutual aid from the L'Anse fire station and instructed them to bring one engine and, six addition personal and have them set up in the back of the store to protect to structures across the alleyway. The first engine was hooked up and the 1200 gallon a minute pump engaged, six firefighters consisting of two teams of three put on their S.C.B.A and drug two, inch and a half lines to the side of the structure opposite the side that the now arriving ladder company was setting up on. The ladder company Lieutenant order a ventilation team of four to see if they could ventilate the roof and a two-man forcible entry team to assist the attack crews waiting to enter the building through the large double doors facing the side street opposite the ladder company. The doors were breeched and the attack crews went to work two men per line entered the structure as two stayed outside feeding the attack lines in through the door opening to the men inside. The ventilation crew opened a large 8'by 8' hole in the roof allowing the smoke, heat and gases out making the inside atmosphere less hazardous. The inside crews were working on their hands and knees, because of the intense heat and smoke. The L'Anse engine company arrived and set up in the back of the store as instructed they placed two 2 ½ inch ground nozzles at opposite corners of the structure and sprayed a water curtain directly down the alleyway to protect the building behind the store. Two men from the ladder company circled the fire building shutting off utilities as they went and watching for any signs of structural collapse, to warn the crews inside, once around the building they were placed on opposite corners diagonal from each other for this purpose only, they could watch two sides if the building at once from this position. The work was intense and tiring in full turnout gear and the attack crews rotated duties from outside to inside sparing each other for a better part of an hour. The Chief arrived on scene and took over command from the incident commander. The Chief noticed the side the ladder company was set up on, had left the adjacent structures exposed and instructed the ladder company to set up their large monitor nozzle to protect them. He also instructed the vent crew to break out the remaining store front windows once the attack crews had knocked the fire down and were in a safe location from the flying glass. This would let additional heat and smoke out of the structure allowing a cooling affect. The store fire was being brought under control and the work environment was less hazardous. The Chief then order two 2 ½ lines to be placed in to the store front window openings and set on a fog pattern to increase the steam volume, with this done he ordered the two attack crews out and into a defensive mode, if they see fire building inside, they were to have the outside nozzles shut down so they could go in and attack it.

The fire was dwindling due to the large amounts of water being put on it the steam cloud was large and could be seen for miles. The Chief then order large fans to be placed out front and at the side entrance blowing into the structure this would increase the chimney effect that the large hole in the roof provided for ventilation. The fire was reduced to a few hot spots that were being handled with smaller lines. The exposures were saved and the crews went to work packing up the L'Anse engine and the ladder company equipment, the attack firefighters were taken to a waiting EMS unit and were given liquids and their vitals monitored for exhaustion, the temperature they were exposed to had reached at least 350 degrees or hotter, with proper hydration they would recover quickly.

The salvage and mop up had started, using the L'Anse engine company and the Baraga ladder crews. It was almost 4:00 a.m. when the Chief decided to send some of the personal back to the station to get the returning trucks and engines ready for service. One engine remained and six firefighters to watch for hot spots and to help the Chief with the investigation. The fire had basically destroyed the inside completely burning all of the contents but the structure was still intact.

The arsonist had watched with great joy in his destruction, no one even noticed him as he watched from his vantage point he even went to the scene on foot, going as far as asking a couple of firefighters if it was a total loss. No one suspected him.

I was up at 6:00 showered and shaved, grabbed a cup of coffee and went out to the bench by the water to enjoy the morning. A wind had come up during the night and was causing the waves on the bay to white-cap. It was maybe sixty degrees but felt cooler by the water. The seabirds were gliding around looking for any dead fish or scraps that the waves may have deposited on the shore during the night. I sat watching two Gulls fighting over a dead fish, as the sun stated to come up more casting long shadows onto the lawn. I looked across the bay towards Baraga and noticed a steam column billowing up into the morning sky and being swept back inland by the offshore wind. That reminded me I was going to stop by the fire station and why hadn't the Chief given me a call on my cell phone, maybe he didn't need any help or maybe the investigation was all done. I went into the cabin and got my keys for the storage trailer I hauled here with all my furnishings and fire gear inside I found the green tote and put it in the back of my Yukon and decided to go to Baraga and see if the Chief needed my help. I wasn't sure where the fire was so I kept looking out the windshield up at the steam cloud trying to get my bearings as I drove this was rewarded by a few honks from unfriendly drivers that were behind me as I stepped on the brake every so often.

I found the fire scene and pulled right in behind the Chief's car, a young rookie firefighter came over and told me I had to move because this is a restricted area for fire personal only. I flipped my old badge open and told him who I was and requested he get the Chief. The rookie relayed my request to the Chief who was filling out a preliminary fire report using his car hood for a desk he looked up hand waved me over.

"Good morning Chief how are you doing today?"

"Not worth a shit, why does everything have to start burning at two or three in the morning?"

"That I don't know Chief, but it does seem to happen a lot."

"Yah it sure does can't get any sleep, so what brings you to our little barbeque Dalton?"

"I was having my morning coffee out by the water and I noticed the steam cloud, so I thought I would come over and see if you needed any help."

"Why not Dalton, I could use a hand, boys are just about ready for me to take a look see, you are more than welcome to join me."

"Okay Chief, I just have to get my gear on, do you have an extra helmet I didn't bring one?" The Chief sent the rookie for a helmet and I went to the back of my Yukon and put my coveralls on and a pair of Rocky boots I kept just for investigations the sole had a unique tread pattern and they were water proof, much lighter in weight compared to the big rubber ones used by the firefighters. The Chief and I walked over to the store that had burned and the rookie handed me a helmet by the front door. The Chief was giving me his idea of what he thought had caused the fire as we entered the burned-out structure, he was pointing to the back corner and something about a magazine rack and a heat radiator, when I interrupted him.

"Chief do you mind if I take the Rookie and do a walk around the outside first? I like to start outside then work inside."

"No not at all, knock yourself out. Rook go with Dalton and help him with anything he needs."

The Rookie and I went back to my Yukon and got out my cameras and clipboards with some blank pieces of paper on them. Then we went to the middle of the street in front of the store.

"Why are we out here in the street Dalton?"

"Okay Rookie, I'm going to give you a short lesson in fire investigation, if you are interested?"

"Sure, why not."

"The first thing you do is a size up or walk around outside. This will help you to get an idea of how the fire affected the outside and my give you a clue as to how the fire spread. You look for smoke stains around windows and door openings. The way the roof or walls held up during the fire are they burnt more in one area than the others. The locks on doors and windows should be check for forcible entry by someone other than fire personal."

As we both circled the structure, I was starting to get a few ideas on how the fire had burned. We walked up to the storefront and checked the glass from the windows for how much soot was deposited on them and if they had been knocked in or out. I didn't give the Rookie a lot of information just enough to keep his interest. I wanted him there for a witness as to what I was doing more than anything. We then entered the store through the front door; looking at the black residue on the walls left by the firewater was still dripping in a few spots and forming puddles on the floor. The Chief was over in a corner where the checkout counter had been and was explaining something to another fireman. I noticed a V pattern on the wall directly behind where he was standing, possible point of origin, but the fire appeared to have burned hotter at the ceiling. There wasn't as much damage near the floor or to the dry goods on the shelves.

"Well Chief what do you think? Did you find a cause?"

"I think so Dalton come and take a look. I was talking to the firefighter here and he said he remembers a magazine rack that used to set right here when he shopped here. I think that is what this wire thing is of course it's all bent up. The heat radiator set right behind it and he said on several occasions that he told the storeowners that they should move it because he thought it was to close. The radiator is this thing right here."

The Chief was pointing to a mangled-up piece of copper tubing and sheet metal.

"Take a look on top see the paper residue from the books?

"Yes, I see it Chief, but what are these square gallon cans over here from?" I was looking at an area between two shelving units.

"I think they are camping fuel cans, looks like they all ruptured from the heat."

"Yes, it does, do you feel confident that the fire started over here by the magazine rack?"

"That's what I'm going with, a combustible to close to a heat source."

"Yes, I'm pretty confident that it started here also. The V pattern on the wall, the white ash and the paint peel on the outside block wall damn near matches the pattern in here. I would say the fire burned here the longest no other area outside shows as much heat conduction through the walls. Yes, I would go along with your theory."

Then I noticed something sticking out from under the magazine rack.

"Hey Chief what is that right there, under the rack?"

"It looks like a Coleman stove there are a few more across the aisle right there on the shelf that's tipped over, maybe it got knocked under there by the attack crews, they came in right on the other side of the shelving units. The other side of the shelf had lanterns on it probably a display area for camping stuff. The shelf has collapsed from the heat."

"Yah I see what you mean, the shelf collapsed and the Coleman stuff just fell off, fuel lanterns and whatever."

The Chief was making a good assessment of the fire, but he hadn't mentioned the circle burn patterns that I noticed on the ceiling. The alligator of the tongue and groove pine ceiling wasn't even. The term alligator is used in the fire service to describe the way the charring looks on something burnt, as the wood burns it checks or creaks leaving a charred surface that looks like alligator skin, the longer the burn the deeper the creaks.

There were several circular patterns on the ceiling that had deeper alligator patterns.

"Hey Dalton did you notice how the ceiling has those deeper circles in the burn pattern?

Yes, I noticed what do you think caused them?

"I was thinking about them when I walked in the first time and I had one of my guys go up on the roof and measure the ventilators and there are six of them just about in line with the circle patterns, I figure the fire must have tried to vent through them that is why they show more burn."

"Yes, I see your point Chief." I couldn't disagree with him it was possible. "Do you think you are done with the investigation?"

"I think so I'm leaning towards accidental on this one but I'll take few pictures and look at them back at the station, but right now I'm going home to get some food and rest, my ass is dragging, I've here since about 2:30."

"Chief I can take some pictures for you and drop of some copies at the station, if you want to get out of here I kind of wanted to look around some more if you don't care.

"That sounds good to me, I'll leave the Rookie here to help you. All I have to do is tape off the area around the building with some crime tape and my ass is out of here, thanks again Dalton."

The rookie was looking around and trying to see if he had any ideas on how the fire started.

"Hey Rookie do they have a hardware store around here anywhere close?"

"Yes sir, just up the street about a block, go out the front door and take a left."

"Good I'll be right back don't touch anything until I get back." I went out to my truck and got the camera out of the tote tub and checked the picture counter, only four left I snapped them off with lens cap on and rewound it then put it in my glove box. I didn't really want to get in my truck with my dirty boots so I decided to walk. The hardware was more like two blocks and I was noticing some things seemed familiar as I got closer to it. The buildings were set close together and I noticed that I was standing in front of Jessica's office just as she pulled up to the curb in here Lexus.

She got out and came walking towards me smiling. My god was she gorgeous, she was wearing a buckskin colored denim skirt with a slit up the front that came midway up her thigh, knee high moccasins lased up front, and a white silk blouse low cut just showing the top of her cleavage around her neck she wore a gold chain with a small stone pendant shaped like an arrow head, it's point resting in the crease of her sensuous valley, raven hair was pulled back into a pony-tail that hung below her hips, in each ear she wore gold hoops with the same arrow head as the necklace. She walked with a confident stride her hair swaying with each step.

"Hi Dalton." She said, flashing me a smile that made the corners of her ice blue eyes wrinkle a little.

"Hi Jessica, how nice to see you."

Dalton, what are you doing downtown, are you looking for a car to fix?"

"What, a car what are you talking about?"

"Your get up, are you fixing cars or what? You look like a mechanic with those coveralls on." Now she was teasing me, beautiful and a sense of humor, how good could it, get.

"No, I'm working the fire scene down the street, kind of helping out the fire Chief, I'm on my way to the hardware store to pick up a few tools I need for the investigation."

"I was wondering what was going on down there. Is it the department store?"

"Yes, it wasn't a complete burn but the inside is pretty trashed."

"Do you know what caused it or of somebody did it?"

"No, not yet." I was lying I didn't figure it was my place to give out information it was the Chief's.

"Dalton what are you doing for lunch today?"

"I ah, I ah, I'm not doing anything as far as I know. Why?"

"I have something to talk to you about and I didn't really want to do it in my office. So, I thought we could do it over lunch."

"Okay, what time and where at?

"How about the Italian restaurant in L'Anse, say around 12:30?" "Sounds good to me, I'll be looking forward to it, see you there."

"Good I'll see you there."

"Goodbye Jessica."

"Goodbye Dalton, oh there is one more thing, you might want to change your clothes, they might not let you in with coveralls on." She chuckled as she pulled her office door open and went inside. I gave her a wave and started walking toward the hardware. The guy at the hardware was very helpful in getting me everything that I needed, a D handled shovel, brick layers trowel, multi tool, four rolls of 35mm film, and clean empty paint pails. I walked back to the fire scene carrying my gear and looking like a homeless person dragging my stuff along. The Rookie was sitting on the window ledge in the front of the burned-out store.

"Hey Rookie, I see you are still here, sorry I took so long I ran into a friend."

"That's okay, what are you going to do with all that stuff?"

"Come on, I'll show you, grab this shovel and come over to the Yukon; I have a few more things you can help me with."

I loaded the film in the camera and got out a few sheets of paper and put them on a clipboard and handed it to the Rookie.

"Here take this clipboard and I'll tell you what I want you to write down. Draw two parallel lines near the bottom and write the street name or number between them. This will establish the front side of the store, and be our fire scene diagram. Now draw a rectangle on the paper like the store is facing the street, got it?"

"Yes sir, like this?"

"Yep, very good, now letter the sides of the rectangle A B C D, A is facing the street and B is on the right, C in back and D on the left. Okay now I'm going to start taking pictures and you are going to right down the photo numbers as I give them to you. The first side is the front or a side now start in the left corner and write them in the order I give kind of space them out, all set?"

"I think so, just write them as they are given, got it."

I stared taking pictures of the storefront from the street and relayed the numbers after each one was taken

"Okay Rookie, start with 24, 23, 22, and so on as I move across the front, when I get to the corner I'm going to try and get a shot of it so I get two sides write that one down in an angle across the corners of A and B."

We circled the building taking pictures of all the sides and corners and writing down the numbers as we went along. I snapped the last few pictures on the second roll and labeled the outside of the film case. DEPT. STORE OUTSIDE. I then reloaded the camera with a fresh roll and told the Rookie what we were going to do next.

"Okay go grabs the paint cans and meet me inside the front doors."

The rookie returned and I had him put a new sheet of paper on the clipboard, told him to draw another rectangle and letter the side to match the first one he drew, with IA in the front, the letter I meaning inside. We took pictures of the interior walls and ceiling numbering just like the outside and the ceiling shots were writing down in the locations inside the rectangle. The next thing we did were some measurements of the burn patterns on the ceiling again the rookie used a new sheet of paper and drew the rectangle with the lettering system we used earlier. On the side where the fire had started, I had him write the dimensions down of the burn pattern on the wall. Once all the photographing and measurement were done, I took the paint cans and began putting samples of some of the burnt clothes and pieces of different items from the store shelves placing them in bags first, writing a date and time on each one before placing it in the cans. Then I began cleaning the floor of all the ash and wet material, down to the hardwood covering using the flat shovel, samples of the burn patterns in the ceiling were taken and placed into a can. The floor was in near perfect condition not much for signs of burning, but when I started to clean directly under one of the ceiling patterns the floor showed signs of some burning. The floor hadn't show me what I was looking for, no trailers or tracks from someone using an accelerant. The Rookie was asking question and I was trying to answer as discreetly as possible as to what I was looking for. I then began checking the numerous fuel cans scattered around the room all of them had ruptured due to the heat from the fire. Working our way out from the point of origin and noticing that most of the cans had blown the bottoms out when they ruptured. They must have exploded and flew across the room spewing their contents as they went causing rapid fire spread. Looking over the area where the clothing had been displayed and I noticed one of the fuel cans lying. The can was different than the others we had seen, it was missing the cap and the sides of it were collapsed slightly. The other cans had all bulged the sides out before separating the bottom, this one still had the bottom intact. I took some photos of the can and instructed the Rookie to right down the exposure numbers on the inside drawing. The can had sparked my interest but I said nothing to the rookie about it and I moved it over from the clothes it had been sitting on and using the blade from the multi tool I scrapped some of the charred material into a zip lock and handed it to the Rookie to put in a paint can. The under lying layers of the clothes seemed to be in pretty good condition so I cut some small pieces and put them into a bag and them into a separate can. The evidence was all loaded into my Yukon and I thanked the Rookie for all of his help.

"Is the Chief usually at the station in the morning?"

"Yah he gets there around nine, I'll tell him that you are going to stop by if I see him sooner."

"Okay, tell him I'll bring the evidence and the pictures by then, see yah later rookie and thanks again."

I raced back to the cabin showering and dressing in a hurry, having to stop by the, one-hour photo before my lunch date was going to cut it close for making it on time.

I told the photo shop that I wanted double prints and that the exposure numbers were to be kept in order with it printed on the pictures. They said I could have them any way I liked them. With that done I went to meet my lunch date at the Italian restaurant.

The parking lot was about half full and I hadn't noticed Jessica's Lexus anywhere so I parked and decided to wait for her on a bench by the front door. The day had turned out sunny and bright with the temperature rising to the mid seventy mark. It wasn't long before the black Lexus came pulling in and my heart started to beat a little faster in anticipation of seeing her again, I wonder what it is that she has to talk to me about?

The door of her vehicle swung open and a set of long tanned colored legs appeared below the open door. The buckskin skirt slid up slightly as she got out exposing more of them. The white blouse she had on was cover now with a vest that matched her skirt it concealed some of the cleavage I had noticed before. I wondered if she was modest in public or if the absence of the vest earlier was for my benefit. Gus had told me to be careful around her and now I guess I was being a bit ridiculous, why would she do that?

She had a graceful stride to her walk more like gliding than walking, her black her showing a hue of dark blue as the sunlight glistened off it. The sunglasses had concealed her blue eyes and she was smiling at me when she realized you it was sitting on the bench.

"Hi Mr., are you waiting for someone or would you like to have lunch with me?" She was trying to do her best Mae West impersonation.

"Yes, I am waiting for someone, but I think she is late, so I guess you will have to do."

She started to laugh, loud and unrestricted. This woman just might be a good time a sense of humor and good looks.

I held the door for her as she passed through my sense of smell noticed the perfume, she wore making the tiny hairs on my arms stand up. Man, she was heavenly. She greeted the hostess and we were shown to a small table for two in the back corner away from the rest of the lunch crowd. The conversation she wanted to have with me must be on the private side. The hostess took our drink orders and told us the waitress would be with us shortly. I sat down across from her as she had already started to look at the menu. The rest of the restaurant patrons were stealing glances at us and I noticed on the way to the table every guy in the place was checking her out.

"I think I'll have the chicken fettuccini, Dalton what are you going to have?"

I hadn't even looked at the menu I was too busy looking over the top of it at her lovely face.

"I don't know is it good?"

"Oh yes, very good some of the best I have ever had, I highly recommend it."

"So, tell me Jessica, is this lunch discussion business or pleasure?"

"Actually, it is a little of both but I don't want to start until we get our food. It's not very often I get to have lunch with a handsome gentleman like yourself so I'm going to enjoy it, before we get down to the business part."

"Oh, thank you for the compliment. My face started to blush slightly and she was giggling at the sight of it, her nose wrinkling a little as she teased.

"I see you don't take compliments very well a bit modest, are you?"

The waitress came and took the food order and we, each order another drink, as we made small talk about the weather and the fire at the department store. The food was excellent and we were nearly finished when she ordered another drink this one was stronger than the wine she had with dinner. I could tell whatever she had to talk to me about wasn't going to be easy for her.

CHAPTER SEVEN

"Dalton do you remember last week when we talked on the phone, I told you someone else was looking at the forty you bought and if you didn't want it, they did?"

"Yes, I remember I figured it was the tribe or something like that, why do you ask?"

"It wasn't the tribe, it was a land consortium, by the name of Keweenaw Land and Water."

"A lands consortium, what would they want with my forty acres?"

"They called yesterday and wanted to know if the deal went through and I told them it had. Then they wanted your address and phone number they said they wanted to make you an offer that you couldn't refuse. I told them I couldn't give out that kind of information."

"Thank you, for that, because I'm not interested, I have already lined up the contractor to build me a house, but you still haven't said why they wanted it or didn't they tell you that?"

"That's the part I didn't understand either, I assumed it was because it has an old growth forest on it, did you know that?"

"Yes, I was told that, by someone the, other day."

"You see Dalton that forty is very sacred to my people, particularly the canyon and bluff above it."

"Yes, Scream Canyon. The same person told me the legend about it."

"Oh, they did, what did they tell you?"

"He said, that an Indian princess jumped from the cliff and died something about bringing shame to her family or something. It was a great story. I thought it just added more appeal to the place."

"Listen close Dalton. It is not a story it's the truth. The princess was one of my ancestors, after she jumped, they searched the canyon floor and couldn't find the body, but at night her screams could be heard."

"That also was part of the story I was told, they thought it was her spirit and they got spooked and left."

Jessica started to become emotional and the tears were beginning to well up in her blue eyes as she tried to continue the conversation.

"Dalton, my family has been the guardians of that canyon for hundreds of years. When ford owned it, he built a small fishing cabin on it."

"The cabin I was told burned down after Ford got rid of the property.

"William Whitehorse burned it. He was Ford's fishing guide and the caretaker of the canyon for the tribe."

"Is he your grandfather?"

"No, he was my great uncle my grandfather's brother. He would go there with Ford and kind of keep him from venturing into the canyon to far, he also asked Ford not to build a permanent cabin there and to no cut the trees they are sacred to us. Ford agreed and when he got ready to get rid of it, he deeded it to my uncle, for all those years of service and because it was so important to him. My uncle never had children, so in his will he gave it to my grandfather because he was the next of kin. My grandfather lost it to the county for back taxes and the paper company bought it for the timber in a tax sale. They were going to cut it but the tribe somehow got it stopped and the paper company ended up putting it on the market that is how you ended up with it."

"So, what can I do for you do you want me to not build my house there is that what you are asking?"

"No not exactly, I'm just asking that you only cut enough trees to build and that you don't build it to close to the bluff that overlooks the canyon. I am now the guardian of it for my people, even though I can't force you not to I am asking just the same."

"Not a problem, I have to meet the contractor this afternoon out there and begin staking out the spot for my house. If you want you can come along and make sure that we don't get it to close to the bluff or canyon."

"Oh, thank you Dalton that is a big relief to my heart."

We finished our drinks and talked about her career some.

"Tell me Mr. James what is it that you do for a living? Cheryl Johnson told me you were some kind of investigator."

"That's about right." I was trying to skirt the question.

"That's about right on what? Asking in her, cross examination tone of voice.

"That I'm some kind of investigator, I used to work for the Detroit fire department in their arson task force division. Now I'm retired."

"What exactly did you do then?"

"I used to go to fire scenes and investigate whether it was arson or an accidental cause, I also used to teach other firefighters and give classes at colleges on the subject."

"Hmm, sounds interesting, sort of like a fire cop."

"Yes, like a fire cop, I would study how the fire acted or spread and determine if it burned naturally or if someone or something had helped it along, using scientific fact and reason along with forensic science you can narrow the cause of fires done to the very starting point. More like a detective than a cop."

"Like a homicide detective?"

"Yes, same principal, but instead of bodies I looked at fire scenes."

"Do you ever or should I say did you ever do a scene where bodies were involved?"

"Yes, many times, we call them fatal fires in the business."

"So how come you retired? You don't look old enough to be retired."

"Let's just say I got burned out, tired of seeing what people did for profit and to each other."

"But you were helping the fire Chief this morning when I saw you on the street. You must not be tired of it all together?"

"I told him I would give him a hand if he needed one."

"That's great we don't really have an investigator around here, I think they have to call out for one when needed. We usually don't have many fires around here and even fewer fatal ones."

Wanting to change the subject of conversation from me to her I asked.

"Jessica why is your family the guardians of the canyon?"

She sighed before answering, knowing I didn't want

to talk anymore about myself.

"The princess that died gave birth to a child, before she made her fatal leap. You may already know this. This child had blue eyes, and the princess thought her secret affair with the black robe would be discovered, so she killed herself to keep her family and the village from having to deal with her dishonor."

"Yes, and the Jesuits raised the child, right?"

"No, that's not right. The father of the princess was also the shaman or medicine man. He had seen the child was not of pure blood, so to save face and his power with the tribe he concocted a story that the Great Spirit had blessed the child with the power to see as the white man by giving him their eyes and he still possessed the heart and spirit of the people so he would be able to understand the white man ways but act in a manner to benefit his people. When the search party returned with the news about the screaming and no body being found he played off of this also he told them, that the Great Spirit had taken the princess in body and spirit to live with him."

"So that is why you have those beautiful blue eyes."

"You mean these cursed blue eyes, not everyone would agree now a days with the mystical reason why my family tree has people with blue eyes or why the baby had them, but whoever is born with them most be the guardian of the canyon. My great uncle William had them but my grandfather didn't nor my father, my uncle had seen that I had them before he died so that is why he gave the land to his brother so he could pass the torch to me when I became old enough."

"You have a very interesting family tree Ms. Jessica Whitehorse."

"Yes, interesting and cursed." She said flatly. Well Dalton I must get back to the office I have a ton of work to do. Thank you for listening to me and for having lunch."

I reached for the check and she insisted on paying it because she had invited me. I told her that I would get the next one if there were ever a next one, she assured me there could be. We walked together out to her Lexus I held the door for her as she got in.

"One more thing before you go Jessica would you mind looking into that land consortium and did you want to go with me this afternoon out to the building site and help decide where to put my house?"

"That's two things, No I wouldn't mind doing a little back ground check and yes, I will go with you this afternoon, say around five I'll meet you at your cabin. Okay?"

She drove off leaving me standing in the parking lot before I could answer.

Hmm, witty intelligent and beautiful, what in the hell have you done to deserve this Dalton James, my mouth saying out loud what my mind was thinking. I was on cloud nine as I got into my Yukon and drove to the photo shop.

I stopped at the photo placed and picked up the pictures of the department store fire scene. There wasn't time for me to take them to the fire station in Baraga I had to get back to my cabin and get some things in order before Jessica came this afternoon. The Chief would have to wait for the pictures tomorrow. I pulled into the driveway leading up to my cabin and noticed Gus' truck parked beside it, he had a look of impatience and anger on his old wrinkled face as he walked over to my driver's door when I pulled up. I thought I don't have time for this. He yanked open my door before I shut the engine off and started to nag on me.

"Where the fuck you been! Dalton, I have been here three times today looking for your sorry ass?" He went on bitching at me. "You think I got nothing better to do with myself, just because I'm old?"

Well yes, I thought, but didn't say it. Instead, I tried to calm him down.

"Whoa, whoa, Gus, take it easy what's the matter, you trying to have a stroke? What have you so fired up?

"There was a fire in Baraga last night Dalton."

"Yes, I know Gus; I was there most of the morning conducting an investigation."

I walked around him to the back of my Yukon and dropped the tailgate.

"See Gus, tools evidence cans and dirty clothes."

"Oh, Dalton I'm sorry. What are you going to do with the evidence?"

"I'm going to give it to the Fire Chief in Baraga first thing tomorrow, but for right now I'm going to lock it up in the trailer. So, grab some shit and help out instead of bitching at me, like old women."

The last comment brought a slight twinkle to his eyes and he started to lighten up some.

Now Gus tells me why were you so concerned about me, knowing there had been a fire last night?

"If you have a beer in that shack of yours, I'll tell you."

We both went into the cabin and I grabbed two beers from the fridge and sat them on the table.

"Have a seat Gus. You are going to have to talk while I clean up a bit."

"Clean up, what for?"

"Because I have company coming over at four o'clock, and that's about two hours from now so get talking.

"Company, what kind of company?"

I didn't have time for this shit and I let him know it.

"Goddamit Gus I don't have time for this, so get talking and quit asking. Okay?"

"Okay, okay, you don't have to get all pissy about it. I wanted to make sure you knew about the fire." He was finally getting to what he had to say. "Because I wanted to know if you were going to look at it, you know investigate it."

"Well, I did, is there anything else? Why did you want me to look at it?"

"Because the old Chiefly don't know if his ass is bored or punched."

The statement about the Chief's ass, made me grin and I started to lighten up some. The old man was humorous at times.

"Why do you say that Gus?" I asked as I went into the bedroom to change clothes. I slipped off my shoes, pants and shirt, grabbed a pair of jeans from the dresser and a tee shirt, put my pants on and went back out to the kitchen to hear Gus' answer. I hadn't even thought about my scarred back when I walked out shirtless.

"Because he handled those other fires, that I told you about and he couldn't figure them out."

I was standing facing Gus and nodding my head in understanding, I turned around to go get some cologne from the bathroom. That's when I heard Gus take in a big breath and choke a little on his beer he hadn't swallowed yet. I turned around quickly and put my tee shirt on, before Gus had a chance for a longer look. He just sat their kind of wide eyed.

"Damn Dalton what the fuck happened to the hide on your back?"

I knew the question was coming before he said it

"I got burned at a fire, it is a long story.

"That's alright Dalton I got time"

"Well, I don't right now, but maybe some other time, okay? Now is there anything else?"

"Yah there is, but I can't remember what it was." He was looking at the floor trying not to make I contact with me. "I guess that's all I got to tell you right now Dalton I'll let you go about your business, maybe I'll remember what the other thing was, and I'll be at the pub tomorrow around one if you want to stop by. See yah later." Gus walked out the door and left me standing in the kitchen wondering if I just scared the hell out of him or if he was being polite and had noticed my embarrassment and decided to leave so I wouldn't have to talk about it anymore.

Ah shit! I just scared the hell out of him. I said out loud. What the hell was Jessica going to do when she found out about my injuries? "Fuck, Fuck, Fuck!" I screamed.

No way to back out of our date she was probably on her way over right now. I finished getting dressed and tiding up the place. When she arrived, trying to hide my feelings of shame I didn't want her to think I was uncomfortable around her. She walked up to the door and knocked. I let her in.

"Hello Mr. James." She said cheerfully. "Arc you ready for our excursion?"

Hi Jessica, come in, I just have to call the contractor

and let him know, that we are on our way out there. Have a seat, I made a hand motion toward the dining chairs. I see you changed your clothes too.

"Yah, I didn't think a skirt and silk blouse were appropriate for walking in the woods."

She was all eyes, taking in the small cabin, and my attempt at decorating as I excused myself to make the phone call. I made the call and returned to the kitchen, she stood up as I entered.

"You look real nice Ms. Whitehorse, would like to accompany me to my humble homestead?"

I said in a southern accent. Making a grand gesture as I opened the door for her. She giggled and in a prim and proper voice with a British accent she answered.

"Yes, I would dear sir."

I was enjoying this as I opened the door of the cabin and she strode by in a very upright and courtly fashion, her chin up, back straight, eyes looking straight ahead.

She was trying to hold back another giggle but her eyes were giving it away, she started to giggle as I opened the passenger door of my Yukon and made a sweeping motion with my arm and bowed lowly.

Your carriage awaits you madam.

"Why thank you, sir." She was into a full-blown laugh as I went around and got in behind the wheel.

"What has gotten into you?"

"Oh nothing, I guess I'm just happy, I enjoy your company."

We drove along having small talk about the weather; good food likes and dislikes, clothes, things we enjoyed for relaxation and recreation.

"No work talks." Is what she said when we started to leave the cabin? She was looking out the passenger window as we drove along. I was trying to drive and sneak a glance at her every so often, sometimes finding I had wandered across the centerline when I looked back at the road, catching my glance several times but saying nothing about it. She had her black hair braided and pulled up in the back, revealing her petite neck, no earrings or makeup, the oversized flannel shirt was tied in front of her waist and the top few buttons were undone, showing some of her cleavage. The cuffs of her jeans were tucked into a pair of rag wool socks that came up mid-way on her calf and a pair of Rocky hiking boots. She was having a good time.

"Dalton this is fun, we should do this again. STOP!" she yelled.

I slammed on the brakes, nearly throwing her into the dashboard.

"What, what's, the matter?" I was all excited and wondering if I just hit something. Jessica undid her seatbelt and jumped out as soon as I came to a stop she ran back behind the Yukon and down into the ditch. I was still wondering what the hell was going on, when I began to back up to where she was standing in the ditch. She walked up to the open passenger door smiling and laughing, holding a big bouquet of wild flowers.

"What the hell you trying to do give me a heart attack? I thought I ran over someone, and what's so funny?"

She was laughing hard the tears were running down her tan cheeks.

"Oh, don't exaggerate Dalton, you aren't going to have a heart attack, you are in perfect shape."

"Well then could you please tell me what's so funny?"

"The look on your face when I yelled STOP! You looked like a scared deer, your eyes were wide and looking around, your mouth hanging open, ha, ha, it was classic."

She put the flowers in the back seat and I made her buckle up before I would move again.

"I'm glad you think I'm so amusing, but you scared the hell out of me I thought I hit somebody."

"Oh, I'm sorry Dalton please forgive me?" she laid her left hand on mine and a current of energy rush through me, that made the little hairs on my body stand up. I sat up straight in my seat, the touch of her hand, making a spark of desire ignite in my manhood. I quickly broke her touch and reached for the radio, not that I wanted to listen to any music but I did want to break the spell she was casting over me.

"You are forgiven, there isn't a damn thing on this radio."

"Dalton do you have anything to drink in her my throat is dry from all of this laughing and talking?"

"As a matter of fact, I do it's in the cooler on the back floorboard, behind your seat."

I was trying to reach the cooler lid and drive at the same time, but wasn't able to get at it.

"I brought some beer and a few wine coolers I didn't know if you liked beer or not. But I'm going to have to pull over, I can't get the cooler lid open from over here."

"Here, I'll get it." She said undoing her belt and turning around in her seat as I drove.

"I think I'll have a wine cooler would you like something?"

She was curled around the back of the bucket seat, her body between them and her most divine ass about six inches from the side of my face, hell yah I wanted something but it wasn't I a beer, I thought.

"Yah I'll take a beer."

"Here you go enjoy." She said handing me a beer and then buckling her seat belt. I took the beer and placed it between my legs, I did need some cooling off before we had to get out at the building site. My god I felt like some kind of pervert I lost all control around this woman; she took a drink of her cooler and placed it in the drink holder. The act of me putting mine between my legs hadn't gone unnoticed with her, the corners of her mouth curled up slightly as she glanced sideways at me.

"Ah, that's better, why did you pull your hand out from under mine Dalton?'

"I ah, didn't pull my hand out I was checking the radio."

"Yah right," she rolled her eyes at my response. "Do I make you uncomfortable Mr. James?" she asked turning in her seat to face me and looking directly into the profile of my face. "Don't lie to me because I can tell when you are, I come from a long line of shamans and we are taught how to tell when someone is lying." She moved over closer, leaning over the armrest with her lips close to my ear and her breast was pressing against my right arm as I tried to drive. In a low erotic whisper her husky voice asked again. I could feel her warm breath on my neck when she spoke.

"Do I make you uncomfortable Dalton, don't lie."

The sweat was running down my back and I was trying to take in a rattled breath through my nose and exhaled a sigh of pure tension, the sweat was forming on my brows and I took the beer in my right hand and moved my arm up gently trying not to bump into her breast, she sat back down in her seat as I took a drink before answering. Her voice changed into a cross-examination tone and she asked again before I could answer.

"Well Mr. James?"

"No," I squeaked in a nervous response, "I mean yes."

"Well, what is it? Yes or no, please answer the question."

"Yes, you make me nervous." There I said it.

"How so?"

She wasn't going to let me go, I was walking done the plank of embarrassment and she knew it. I took a long drink of beer and placed the bottle in the cup holder before responding.

"Yes, you make me nervous, when I'm around you I am afraid I might say the wrong thing and I kind of loose control of my thought process, I'm very attract-ed to you, you are intelligent, funny witty, and drop dead gorgeous. How can a bum like me not be nervous around you? I thought I was going to drive in the ditch back there when you whispered in my ear."

Her facial expressions changed as I talked, from happy to sad to contentment, then with a smile she placed her hand on top of mine. I took my left hand and wiped the sweat from my face. She patted the other, re-assuring me she was adhere of how hard it was for me to be so candid about my feelings.

"That is the truth Jessica, and I'm sorry if I offend-ed you by being so candid."

"Yes, I believe you Dalton and no I'm not offended, as a matter of fact I'm flattered."

"You are?"

"Yes, very much so. I don't remember the last time I had this much fun with a man, usually all they want is sex, they take me for what I look like and not who I am. Do you understand what I'm saying Dalton?"

"Yes, I think I do."

"I know you do, that's why I was playing the tease game back there I wanted to see what you would do, first with my hand on yours and then with my butt in your face and last but not least the whisper and the boob press, and you didn't even act like you noticed. Most men would have tried something, probably pulled over but not you, you just kept on driving and sweating, that showed me that you respect me and if I want to play a little you won't get all testosterone on me and try and force something to happen. I am very attracted to you Dalton James."

"You don't know how I was sweating through that back there."

"That's why I'm flattered, I aroused you sexually but, you had enough respect not to read into it for anything more than what it was, just a tease. I want to take things slow, I'm not really a tease and it seems like every time I go out with a man he wants to get in my pants. I haven't dated very much since my husband died and that is why, I haven't been able to find a man who respects me. You are different in a good way Dalton and I hope I haven't made you feel cautious around me."

"Thanks for the sincerity Jessica, does this mean I can ask you out on a real date?"

"Yes, you can, but I'm having a wonderful time right now."

Just then the driveway to my property came

apparent and the contractor's pickup was turning into it just ahead of us. I parked on the edge of the road just past it and Jessica got getting her bouquet of flowers from the back seat.

"Hi Derrick, this is Jessica Whitehorse." I said introducing the two of them. Derrick shook her hand gently and smiled.

"Hi Jessica, I'm Derrick Johnson, Cheryl has talked about you and her doing business together, nice to meet you."

"Dalton you never said Cheryl's Husband was your contractor."

"I didn't? I guess it never came up."

"Okay Dalton shall we get started?"

"Yah, sure what do you need me to do, Derrick"

"I'll grab a few things out of the truck and we can get started."

Derrick went to the back of his truck and got out a spray can of paint, the kind they use for marking the ground, a hundred-foot tape measure and a hammer. He handed me an armload of short wooden stake that he would use for marking out the building site.

Jessica led the way twenty yards ahead of us down the old trail. Derrick was spraying a stripe every now and then as we walked, marking the driveway and putting a paint mark on the trees that would have to be removed for widening, so he could get his equipment into the building site. Derrick was talking and giving me verbal estimates of how long the different stages of the project would possibly take, like the well and septic systems, the building site excavation and foundation work. I was nodding and humming replies, all the while checking out Jessica's backside as she glided along in front of us. We had arrived at the big hemlock trees and were standing below them admiring their size.

"Holy shit Dalton, those are big trees, and I don't think four adults could reach around them."

"Yes, they are big."

"Derrick could we make a left here and go through the smaller stand of pines? I think I would like my house to be somewhere down that ridge."

Derrick was marking the trees for removal and Jessica had changed positions and was now following us as I made my way to the new building site.

"I was going to originally build out there closer to the edge of that high bluff, but I think this may be just as nice a spot."

"Whatever or wherever, Dalton it's your house just be sure that is where you want it."

Derrick was marking the area around the location for the yard and septic asking me what way the house would face and if I wanted certain trees and rocks to stay for landscaping. Jessica had noticed my decision to move the house back from the edge of the bluff and seemed delighted and thankful. Derrick was telling me he thought the excavation would be fairly easy because the area was flat and the ground appeared to be sandy. He and I began the task of staking out the building site and Jessica walked over to the edge of the bluff. We had finished the measuring and staking, Derrick said he could start in the morning, he shook my hand and said he would bring the site plan with him in the morning and I could look it over before he went to get the permits. He said his goodbyes and waved to Jessica as he walked back to his truck.

I walked up the ridge, and stood next to Jessica who

was peering over the edge of the canyon with a sullen look on her face. I put my arm around here and her body trembled slightly.

"What's the matter Jessica?"

"I heard you tell Derrick that you were going to build up here originally, but changed your mind. Was that because of the discussion we had today?"

"No, not because of today, it was after I heard the story about the legend, told to me the first time."

"You never did tell me who it was that told you about it."

"It was Gus Jorgensen, the old lumberjack. I brought him out here the other day and he explained to me why he thought the trees were so big. Then today he seen me at the cabin after we had lunch and I mentioned to him that there had been another party looking to buy the property. His theory on that was that they probably wanted the timber, so I told him that I wouldn't sell it and that I would respect the sacred ground of your ancestors. Do you know Gus?"

"No, not personally, I know of him. What was his theory on why some land consortium would be interested?"

"He told me that this is a virgin stand of timber and worth a lot of money, the idea of cutting it was not favorable with him and he was glad to hear I wasn't going to let it be cut. He said there are not enough places like this anymore."

I was still holding Jessica around the shoulders and I pulled her back from the edge of the cliff.

"What are the flowers for?"

"They are an offer for the princess' spirit. Would you like to help me do it?"

"I would be honored Jessica, what do you want me to do?"

She reached back and took the braid from her hair and shook it loose, it hung down nearly to the back of her knees. She reached out and took my hand and led me to the edge of the cliff, with her toes barely sticking past the edge she bowed slightly, I was holding onto her belt from behind helping to keep her balance. She spoke in her native language, what I assumed was a prayer, the wind from the updraft caused by the cliff face was making her hair fly straight up as she leaned out over the edge. She tossed the flowers out over the edge and they began to rise riding the updraft and then they were carried out from the edge and slowly sank to the canyon floor.

"Did you see that, how those flowers rose and just hung there in midair?"

"Yes, my people believe that the princess is holding them before she blesses them and cast them back to the earth."

"That is wonderful belief." I said squeezing her hand slightly.

"Dalton thank you, let's go for a walk." She pulled on my hand slightly before letting go.

"Where are we going?"

"For a walk in the woods."

We walked along the edge of the canyon and down to the mouth and alongside the small stream that ran out of it. I followed behind her, noticing her footsteps were making no sound as they fell on the forest floor. The treetops were swaying from the slight wind but once you were down on the canyon floor it was fairly quiet. We walked through the canyon and towards the spot where the flowers had fallen to the ground beneath the cliff.

We had found the spot and she bent down picking one of the flowers up and placed it in her hair above her ear, she smiled at me and I thought my god she was heavenly. She had not made a sound the whole time we had walked and I had respected her silence. The slight breeze on the canyon floor was blowing directly into the cliff face where we had stood moments ago. I looked up at the treetops and noticed they were bent in the opposite direction, pointing out from the cliff face, looking at the different rock formation on the cliff, I noticed a small ledge sticking out about thirty feet down from the top and a small crevice just above it. Jessica took my hand and led me back out of the canyon not speaking a word or making a sound until we reached the old trail that led back to the Yukon. She turned to face me her expression was somber and her eyes watery, she encircled my waist with her arms looking up into my eyes, studying my reaction to this embrace. I placed my arms around her lightly stroking her hair as it lay against her back, she felt so frail and small under my hands.

"Thank you, Dalton." She said tipping her chin up our face's mere inches apart, she pressed her lips to mine and gently kissed me, she slid her hand up under my shirt and pulled us closer pressing our chest together and kissed me again. I froze the moment I realized she had her hand on my scarred back I became rigid, reaction was embarrassment, my arms releasing her, trying to pull myself from her. She released her hold and grabbed my hands pulling them down between us, with a questioning look on her face.

"What the matter Dalton, did I do something wrong?"

I was humiliated and it showed I hung my head and would not answer her, holding one of my hands she led me back to the Yukon, I spoke not a word.

I let her into the passenger side and we turned around in the road heading back towards town, she took a drink of her wine cooler.

"Dalton why did you pull away from me back there, did I do something wrong? Remember no lies."

"Could you get me another beer from the cooler, please?"

She turned around in the seat, her body not coming close to mine as she did it.

I took the beer downing half of it before placing it in the drink holder.

"What I am going to tell you Jessica I would like to stay between us and not be shared with anyone else, okay?"

"Okay Dalton, no secrets, right?"

"That's right, I used to be an investigator for Detroit fire department. I was one of the best, my books on fire investigation tactics are used in classrooms, and I have taught at ATF, FBI and numerous other enforcement agencies, the whole works, they respected me for my abilities and reputation."

She reached over and took my hand entwining her fingers with mine, and listening intently.

"I was investigating a series of arson fires. They appeared that the same person was setting them. I was sure of it and then I screwed up. The great Dalton James fucked up bad."

My eyes began to water as I told her the story

and she never made a sound squeezing my hand for encouragement.

"The investigation was going smoothly I could tell I was closing in on him, however the fires seemed to be getting more destructive, he went from simple fires to putting explosives in the mix. We were working the last fire I was called on. There were four firefighters helping me with the evidence gathering. They were looking for hotspots as I worked the scene. They were pushing up the ceiling tiles and I was on the floor looking at something. Do you know what a drop ceiling is?"

She nodded in understanding.

"They had worked down the one side of the room and were almost too where I was bent over looking at something under the desk. Evidently, they had lifted a tile that the arsonist had booby trapped with explosives. The two firefighters closest to the explosion were killed and one of the others was thrown over the desk I was under, my coat had been blown up over my head as the blast threw me under the desk exposing my back to the fireball. That is what you felt, when you put your hand under my shirt it's scar tissue and I'm not over the feeling of never being able to go without my shirt or letting someone see it, I'm embarrassed about it and ashamed because every time I see it in the mirror or think about it, I get the feeling that because I wasn't paying attention two very good firefighters lost their life and two families are going to grow up without a father or husband."

"I don't think it was your fault Dalton. The firefighters had to have some training on how to notice hazards. The job they do every day has dangers and the chance of something like that happening to them is a very real possibility. I'm just glad you made it and that two other firefighters were not killed. How did the other two make out were they injured?"

"I'm sorry Jessica but I still feel it was my fault. The other two only had minor injuries. The one that saved me and the other firefighter, was a woman by the name of Sarah Johnston she was blown off her feet, but had held on to the hose and was able to spray some water on me and the other one even though she was on fire herself a pretty gutsy gal if you ask me. I thanked her many times during my recovery period."

"It wasn't your fault it was the arsonist who did it. So that is why you pushed me away, you were embarrassed I would notice your back?"

"Yes, that's it basically and when you did it, I knew you were going to ask about it and I didn't know if I could tell you. My back is one big section of scar tissue I look like Freddy Kruger from the movie Nightmare on Elm Street. The only people to see it are the doctors and nurses that cared for me. However, Gus got a glimpse of it today, before you came over. I think it startled him a little bit, but he didn't say much."

She leaned over and put her head on my shoulder. I noticed she was trying not to cry. We were sitting in the driveway by my cabin, just sitting there in silence and thought.

"Dalton, you could have been killed, you wouldn't be here right now and I wouldn't be here right now either and I wouldn't have met you or been able to fall in love with you, like I may do some day." She rubbed my chest and gave me a kiss before getting out. I got out and walked her to her Lexus and opened the door for her.

"Thank you, Jessica, can I see you again?"

"I'm counting on it, come by my office tomorrow."

I stood there in the drive watching her until she turned onto the street.

"Tomorrow it is, my Indian princess." I said out loud and walked over to my cabin.

CHAPTER EIGHT

I met Gus at the bar around 1:00 in the afternoon. He was sitting at the same table we had used a few days earlier.

"Hey sonny how is, you?" He asked smiling from ear to ear. "Have a seat, how did your date go last night?"

"Hi Gus, good I was home by nine. How did you know I was on a date?"

"Did you take Jessica out to the canyon?"

"How did you know I was with Jessica?"

"Because I came by around eight and I see her Lexus parked by the cabin." He answered grinning again. "Do you think I'm some kind of shit head I notice them kind of things you know?"

"What were you doing spying on me?"

"No nothing like that. I remembered what I was going to tell you after I left the bar last night and I was on my way home so I thought I would stop by and tell you."

"Well, what is it?" I asked impatiently.

"What is what?"

"What is it that you wanted to tell me?" I motioned to the bartender to bring two beers before Gus could start telling me what it was, he had to say. Gus didn't start to talk until the bartender had brought us the beers and returned to his place behind the bar.

"I was digging through my dad's old records again after we talked the other day." He said reaching into his shirt pocket and laid an old piece of paper on the table for me to look at.

"Remember, how I said my dad never cruised that forty for Ford?"

"Yah, I remember."

" Well, he didn't cruise it for Ford, but he did cruise it for the paper company about thirty-five years ago. It was one of the last times he worked. The paper company hired him to do the surrounding area plus your forty."

"Why did they need him to cruise it?

"Because the old man still had his grid maps from when he did the surrounding area for Ford. He didn't have to chain it again, he just walked it off and refigured the cordage, because the trees had grown some in twenty years."

"Chained it, what is that?"

"Chaining is a process of measuring that was used by timber cruisers and surveyors, now they use GPS and string counters. Chains are an increment of measuring, there are sixty-six feet in a chain and eighty chains in a mile, therefore a forty would have twenty.

The old timers would carry enough chains to measure a forty or an eighty if they were strong enough you have to remember they are called chains for a reason. The chains were carried in a backpack or held in a holster type thing on their belt. The cruiser would attach one end to a tree and walk off the distance then using his compass or following the lay of the land such as a creek or something, he would change directions and walk off another line until he created a square or rectangle this would be recorded on a grid sheet like this and inside the grids, he would mark down the cordage or board footage by one-thousand increments. See these numbers in here?" Gus was showing me on the old grid map.

"The species of tree was also abbreviated and wrote down. The cruiser would make up a bid sheet with the cordage of each species in the selected parcel for the timber sale or so the company would know where the trees were located and how many cords or feet they could expect to harvest."

"Did you say a string counter is used now, what's that and did your dad do a cruise on my forty?"

"A string counter is a box that attaches to your belt, it has a spool of biodegradable string in it and when the cruiser hooks one end to the tree and starts walking, it has a counter that measures, so he can tell how far he has walked. When he gets done, he just breaks the string and he doesn't have to lug those heavy chains around. I have one at the house if you want to see it sometime. My dad did do a cruise and I also went out there yesterday morning before I seen you at the cabin, and did one of my own."

"I thought you were all worked up about the fire, you didn't tell me that you had been out at the forty. What did you come up with?"

Gus reached into his other pocket and placed a new piece of paper on the table.

"Dalton do you see these numbers right here? This is my dad's figure and this is the one I came up with."

"Holy shit Gus, is that dollars or board foot?"

"That is dollars estimated of course, veneer hard maple is about eight hundred to a thousand dollars per thousand board feet. I would guess that you have somewhere around three hundred thousand of hard maple and some veneer birch and other select tree species, so that number of five-hundred thousand dollars is quite reachable."

"You think that is why the land consortium is so interested I never would have guessed that trees were worth that much.

"Oh, you better believe it, and the more prime the forest the more they get for the wood, but if you don't know its value there are some, out there that will stick it to you."

"Gus you never seize to amaze me, I thought you said you were too old to do this stuff."

"I didn't say that, he growled, I said my back was fucked up not my brain."

He had taken the comment the wrong way, and I had offended him. I quickly tried to smooth things over.

"Would you like another beer? I didn't mean to offend you Gus."

"Yah sure, I'll drink another."

I motioned to the bartender to bring, one beer and Gus quickly gathered up the papers from the table and stuck them into his pocket. The bartender brought the beer and when he returned to his post behind the bar. Gus had kept his eye on him the whole time.

"What did you do that for Gus?"

He hooked his big thumb towards him. "Old long ears can't only hear well he can see well too."

"Gus I was out to the canyon yesterday with Jessica."

"I knew it." He said it like he had caught me at something. "I told you to be careful around her." Pointing his finger at me.

"I was careful and I don't see what the problem is that you have about her. Now are you going to listen or just bitch at me?"

"I'll listen, what's the story?"

"Remember I told you about a land consortium that was interested in the property?"

"Yah kind of, what did you say it was again?"

"It's a company or group that buys up land to preserve it or keep it in a natural state."

"Fuck me it is, that's bull shit bunch of bunny kissing, tree hugging, cocksuckers."

"Calm done Gus you are yelling and people are wondering what we're talking about best to keep it quiet don't you think? "

"Oh sorry, it's just every time I hear something about shit like that I get worked up, bunch of hypocrites. They preach and demonstrate about saving the planet and all that shit. Then you see them driving away in their big motor homes and buses. Where do they think the steel comes from and the wood for the insides? Do you remember that stupid bitch that lived in that big redwood out west for about a year or so, the fucking platform was made from wood and how do you think they fastened it up there with glue hell no they nailed it or screwed it into the tree that's how? Tell me, is some dumb bitch in a tree preserving something in a natural state?"

"Okay, okay Gus take it easy I'm the one that owns it not them. I'm having Jessica check into who owns them, you know a parent company or stock holding group."

"Dalton what is the name of it?"

"Keweenaw Land and Water, I think is what Jessica said."

"Never heard of it." The old boy was still worked up.

"This afternoon I am going to see Jessica again and maybe she can answer some of the question about them."

"You do what you want, but I still say people don't buy something and expect to get nothing in return, they are up to something."

I left Gus at the bar and went to Baraga to see the Fire Chief. I wanted to drop off the evidence cans and pictures I had from the department store fire. The Chief, I hoped had decided on whether it had been arson or an accidental cause. The station was a typical pole barn structure that most rural communities used for a fire barn. The rookie was out front polishing on the ladder truck and appeared to be working up a sweat. It didn't matter what fire station I had visited before; the rookies always were polishing the trucks.

"Hi Mr. James, you here to see the Chief?"

"Yes, is he here?"

"Yep, right inside, probably in the front office or in the lunch room."

"Okay Rookie thanks."

I entered the front office and the Chief was there so I went down the hall, to where the rookie had told me the lunchroom was. The Chief was stretch out with his feet up on the table watching the television. I set my paint cans down and he turned abruptly in his seat, he hadn't heard me come into the room.

"Hi Dalton what brings you by here?"

"Hi Chief, I thought I would bring by the evidence I collected at the department store, and give you the pictures I took"

"Oh, okay, what do you want me to do with the paint cans?"

I would like you to send them downstate to the forensics lab for analysis, the pictures you can look at then file them with your case file, in case something turns up from the lab.

"Dalton did you find anything out of the ordinary?"

"No not really, but the lab might."

I was playing dumb to see if he had come up with a different idea on how the fire had started.

"What are you going to call it accidental or suspect?"

"Not either yet, I went back over there this morning and had another look. There was a fuel can lying on top of one of the shelves and it was missing the cap. The sides were sunk in, all the other ones I found had their caps on and the sides were bulged out. It might mean something, I was going to run it by you, maybe go over and have you help me collect some evidence, but I see you already have, so I guess I'll send it what you have in the cans."

"Okay Chief, let me know what they find out, here is my address and cell phone number if you want to call me. I can't stay I have another appointment to get to. See you later and give me call no matter what."

I left the Chief standing in the lunchroom, when I returned to my Yukon the rookie was backing the ladder truck into the fire barn and he honked the air horns at me when I left. The day was beginning to warm up, so I took my flannel shirt off and decided Jessica wasn't going to mind if I had on a tee shirt when I met her in her office. The weather up here was never the same for more than two days in a row it seemed. The lake was like an air conditioner in the summer and a snowmaking machine in the winter.

Jessica had parked her Lexus across the road from

the office so I pulled in front of it and got out. I wondered if she had found out any information on the parent company yet.

The receptionist was talking on the phone when I entered, and she waved me in to Jessica's office. Jessica was sitting behind her desk staring into the computer monitor with a look of concentration on her face. The light from the screen casting odd shadows making her faces look older. The clothes she had on appeared to be from some professional women's line. The jacket and skirt combo, which most successful executive types seem to have. She probably had a court date today.

"Hi Ms. Whitehorse how are you today?"

"Just the man, I have been waiting for, how are you?"

"Good because you are just the woman I've been looking for." My Gaucho Marx impression needed some work, but she enjoyed it.

"Come around her I have something to show you."

"All right I hoped you would say that" My response was a bit more like Gaucho as I made my way behind her desk. She was giggling at me.

"No not that, this." She said pointing at the monitor. "It's the backer of the land consortium, it's a small corporation from Houghton. I'm trying to see if it has a parent company." She was tapping the keyboard and scrolling down through the different documents that popped up on the screen. I wasn't familiar with what they were but she seemed to have a handle on it.

"What is it that you are looking at?"

"It's a list of corporations and subsidiaries

Here it is, the corporation is owed by K.B. Enterprises."

"K. B. Enterprises, do you know of them?"

"No, but it says here that they are worth 62 million dollars."

"That seems like a lot for a small company from around here."

"Not really, it says they own a motel chain, a restaurant, a food supply company, department store, and a timber harvesting company. Which is the one backing the land consortium."

"Amazing, the old man was right."

"What old man?" she asked with a puzzled look.

"Gus. He and I were talking about it today and he wondered why someone else would be interested in my forty. He figured it was for the timber on it. He found his dad's old timber cruisers maps and he went back and refigured them and he came up with a value of around a half a million just for the trees."

"Holy shit Dalton, just for the timber?"

"Yah that's what he said. He didn't believe that someone would buy something and get nothing in return, he was sure there was some way for a profit or the consortium would not exist."

"It sounds to me like this Gus fellow is pretty sharp. I'd like to meet him sometime."

"Yah, I'm sure you would but I don't think the feeling is mutual."

"What does that mean?"

"I don't know he has some sort of hang up about you, says that you are dangerous. I think the old coot is afraid of you."

"Why do you say that?"

"He was the one who told me about your ancestor and the legend I think he is superstitious."

"Well, I never heard of such a reason as that, but I

would still like to meet him sometime."

"I'll see what I can do, but no promises. Okay? Now Ms. Whitehorse it's time to get back to work."

She was pecking away at the keys again, her face contorted into a scowl across her brow intently studying what was on the screen. I moved in behind her chair and began to massage her shoulders and neck. She moaned softly enjoying the therapy of my touch.

"Oh, that feels good." She whispered, rotating her head slowly.

I leaned in close placing my mouth by her ear and whispering, my breath caressing her neck. She sank down in the chair slightly then sat straight up and giggled.

"Don't! Dalton that tickles and I can't concentrate."

I leaned in close again on the other side of her neck and began to whisper.

"How would you like to go out to dinner with a good man who will treat you right?" her eyes began to drift shut then she sat up straight again with a wide smile.

"Sure, but where would I find such a man?"

She could be a smart ass; I'll have to add that to her list of things I liked about her.

"Where would you like to go?"

"I don't know, we can decide on the way, let me load this information onto a disc and we can get out of here." Jessica loaded the disc in the computer and hit the intercom to her receptionist and checked if there were any last-minute messages she had to answer before she left for the day, there wasn't any so we followed the receptionist out and locked the office behind her. The wind had picked up again and was dropping the temperature. Jessica wrapped her arms around herself as we went across the street to my Yukon, I held the passenger door so she could get in and when I got in, I turned the heater on full blast. Turning around in the street I headed for the restaurant district.

"Well, where to, Italian, Chinese, family style or bar food?" I asked her as we drove, the inside of the vehicle had warmed up and I reached over and turned the temperature down. "Have you decided yet Ms. Whitehorse?"

A wicked little smile appeared on her face making the corners of her eyebrows point upward in a devilish manner. Then her face changed to a sultry half opened eyed look, like you would see in a playboy magazine. Leaning closer, placing her right hand on the inside of my thigh, long slender fingers stroking my leg, the pouting lips barely touching my ear she whispered in a low husky voice.

"I've decided." She purred. "I would like a large piece of meat."

My breath caught in my throat little beads of sweat formed on my brow, I damn near swallowed my tongue, trying to respond.

"What, what did you say?"

She lightly touched the tip of her tongue to my ear. "You heard me." She purred again.

This sent a shiver through my body. She quickly moved back to her side of the vehicle.

"I said I want to go to the casino. They have an excellent prime rib and it is cut very generously." She was beside herself, knowing she could push my buttons.

"Oh, was that what you were talking about? I thought I was going to get into a head on collision."

She was putting on the innocent look now. "What

did you think I was talking about? I just told you what I wanted for dinner."

"If I didn't know any better, I would think you were a tease.'

"Is that what you call it? Teasing, I seem to remember someone in my office today asking me to dinner in the same way."

"Okay, but why are you so much better at it then me?"

"Who said I was?" she said smiling.

"You did, you said it tickled."

"I didn't say what it tickled, did I? Dalton you have to learn to loosen up around me. I'm not going to bite you."

We turned into the casino parking lot and the atmosphere between us had become less edgy. I was really beginning to like her. We walked into the restaurant and the hostess recognized Jessica and she led us to a table for two in the back away from the bar area. The male patrons I noticed were gawking at Jessica as we strolled through between the tables. She didn't even notice. We ordered the prime rib and drinks.

"You know Jessica I would like to look into that corporation some more kind of see what they are all about."

"I knew you would that's why I saved it on a disc at my office, you will have to wait a couple of weeks until I get back."

"Get back? You didn't say anything about going away.'

"I'm going to Chicago, it has to do with Indian affairs and I represent the tribe, some kind of seminar so I have to be there for it. I'm sorry I didn't tell you sooner."

"That's okay don't think anything of it."

"Dalton you could go with me."

"No that's okay, I have plenty to do around here until you get back. Derrick is starting my house and I told him that Gus and I would help so he would be able to get more done and have to more people he won't have to pay. He said he would probably have the walls up in two weeks."

"Wow that's fast."

"Yah, I'm looking forward to it my cabin is starting to get that small feeling and derrick said that log homes go up fairly quickly until you get to the utilities and inside finish work."

"Dalton you have only been at the cabin for a week, how can you be getting tired of it already?"

"I don't have any phone, there's no place for my computer let alone hook up to the Internet."

"Why do you need the internet?"

"I like to log on and talk to the guys in the forensic lab to see how they are coming along on evidence that I send them, plus I have access to different investigation tools and resources that I can't get up here in a library. The scientist that I talk to can give me a heads up on certain aspects of the case to see if there are similarities and I can be aware of them ahead of time."

"Oh, I see sort of like knowing ahead of time what the arsonist might be using or how he's using it."

"Yes exactly, I might be able to help the Chief out on the department store fire, I collected some evidence and he was sending it to the crime lab."

"Dalton do you think that someone may have set fire to that store?"

"I don't know that is why I would like to get the info from the lab scientist, without having to wait for the results to be mailed back. There seems to be a few things that don't look right to me."

"Dalton have you shared your views with the Chief?"

"No not in so many words. He is still in charge of the scene. I don't work for his department. Besides he says it still is under investigation and he has his ideas that it is a suspect fire."

"How do you know that?"

"Because, I stopped in there today and gave him the evidence I collected and he is going to send it down-state for the forensics lab to look at."

"What did he say that made you think he knew what he was doing?"

"He found some of the same evidence or question-able things that I found. He said he was going to call me, so we could go and collect the same evidence that I already found and that because I had done it, he would just send down what I brought to him today." "Oh bullshit!"

"Why did you say that Jessica?"

"Because he doesn't know if his ass is bored or punch." She was getting a bit worked up and I didn't have a clue as to why?

"Interesting terminology councilor, is that fact or speculation?" I asked grinning at her change of emotion.

"I'm sorry about the language, but it is a fact he couldn't find water sitting in the middle of a lake."

"Oh, think nothing of it, as a matter of fact, that makes twice so far that I have heard about the Chief's problem recognizing his ass."

Jessica smiled at my comment and at the same time wondered what I was talking about.

"Gus had said the exact same thing to me earlier

about the Chief."

"Gus said that? I think I might like him already."

"Yah, well just remember what I told you about Gus."

Our food arrived and Jessica wasn't kidding about the prime rib it was enormous. We sat and ate in silence enjoying our meal. She was even beautiful when she ate.

"Dalton?" she interrupted my thought, her face showing lines of apprehensiveness.

"What Jessica, do have something you want to tell me?"

"I have something I want to share with you, but I'm a little worried it might bother you it's something about my past."

"Remember no lies, now what is it I'm confident that I will think no less of you, be as candid as you like."

"Did you know I was a widow?"

"Yes so, what does that have to do with us?"

"Please Dalton let me finish. I was married to a sleaze ball of a man. We got married when I was in law school. I was young, he was older said all the right things you know. I was naive and wide-eyed at the world outside my home. We married and moved back here. It wasn't a big hit with my parents. My father didn't like or trust him from the start. He said he was a weasel, but I defended him he was my husband I thought I loved him and things were going okay for a while, with work and the relationship. Then he decided he needed more money and started running this insurance scam. He would sell the property for an inflated price and give a kick back to the seller to keep his mouth shut. Then he would insure it and have it burned down also collecting the payoff from the insurance company. He and the adjustor would split the money nobody found out because the adjustor was also the investigator for the insurance company. This worked out pretty well for them until somebody killed my husband and torched the last place.

The police started to investigate the insurance adjustor when they couldn't find him, they turned to me, because my former husband had taken out a million-dollar life insurance policy on himself naming me the beneficiary."

Jessica reached across the table taking my hand and looking me straight in the eye.

"Dalton believes me, I didn't take any of the money. My husband was so far in debt, that by the time I paid everything off there was nothing left. I didn't kill my husband."

"Jessica, I know I never thought you did."

"How did you know I was a widow?" she was nodding before I answered and we said it at the same time.

"Gus told me, you guessed it. Why did you tell me this Jessica?"

"I didn't want you to hear it from somebody else, plus I wanted your opinion on how the fire Chief missed everything during the investigations."

"Well jess I can't really tell you that maybe he was inexperienced in how to work an arson fire. That is part of the reason I wanted to have access to the Internet, I was going to see if I could get a look at the reports from the incidents surrounding your husband's death."

"You can do that?"

"I know the people in records that file the reports when the fire departments send them into the state offices, I'll just tell them that I have a suspect fire up here I'm working on and I want to use them for comparison. It might take a while but I don't see a problem with it."

"Dalton you could use my home computer."

"Nice of you to offer but, I have to use my own I have software built into it that does comparisons and data analysis to other fire reports I have entered for the last twenty odd years. I think old Gus will let me use his. Besides he is like a walking history book of this area."

"I'm sorry Dalton but we have to go I have to pack yet for Chicago "

I waved the waiter over and asked for the check, gave him the money plus a tip.

We exited the restaurant Jessica took my arm and leaned her head on my shoulder as we walked to the car.

"That was an enjoyable dinner Dalton thank you."

"I enjoyed it too."

I held the door for her as see got in and we drove back to her office, she was trying to make a mental list of the things she had to pack for her trip to Chicago and I was trying not to think about how much I enjoyed her company and would miss her while she was gone. When we arrived at her office I pulled in behind her Lexus and she leaned over and gave me a long kiss, holding the side of my face in her palm, I put my mouth close to her ear as she hugged me and whispered into it.

"I hoped you enjoyed yourself."

"I did, thank you." She answered quietly.

"Hope that big hunk of meat was satisfying." I

SCREAM CANYON

teased as she got out.

"Not as much as the next one I hope." She was standing outside the open-door giggling. "I'll call you when I get to Chicago, good bye Dalton.

I watched her get into her Lexus and I headed for the cabin I needed a cold shower.

♦ 129 ♦

CHAPTER NINE

Gus came by at around 8:00 am. I swear the old coot knew when I was cooking something. He sat down and talked in between mouthfuls as I cooked another breakfast for myself.

"Hey Gus I have to ask you something."

"Shoot, Dalton what do you need?"

"I have a computer and I was wondering if I could hook it up at your house."

"What for, can't you hook it up in here?"

"I don't have a phone line in here and I need to get on the internet."

"I don't see why not; we can go as soon as we are done eating."

We loaded the computer into my Yukon and I followed Gus to his place.

It was a big farmhouse probably built around the early twenties. The exterior was wood lap siding and the front porch was full glass, the kind seen on most farmhouses built in that era. It was set back from the road and a large fruit orchard could be seen in the back yard area. The old barn had seen better days. The sidewalls were leaning away from the prevailing wind side and the tin on the roof was blown off in a few spots. The yard around the house was kept up but lacked that feminine look of a flower garden and the little lawn ornaments that usually go with them. Gus had just mowed the yard and kept the branches picked up from the two large maple trees that were in the front. The orchard had been mowed between the trees and a few showed signs of pruning, probably just the variety of apples that Gus preferred. The grass around the barn had been left to grow on its own and an old steel wheeled tractor could be seen sprouting up from a location to one side and a couple of old implements had been taken over as well by the weeds and small brush encircling the old structure. The winter supply of firewood was stacked neatly along one of the old fencerows between the house and the barn. Gus entered through a side door holding it open so I could pass through with the computer. Once inside Gus lead me up a few stairs and through the kitchen into what I believe they used to call the parlor, which was just beyond the large dining room. The kitchen also had a small dining table and two chairs. The main dining room was used for guest and family gatherings it had a big beautiful three leaves hard maple table with eight matching chairs. Gus had kept the place in immaculate condition. The table he had for the computer was an old hard wood desk where he kept his phone and it was almost too nice looking to set anything on. The interior trim was all wood and had been what looked like hand carved with a diamond pattern. There was a set of sliding solid wood doors that could be pulled out of the wall where they were hidden to close of the parlor from the dining area. The stairway leading upstairs was done in maple and had a birch handrail a narrow hallway lead past it towards what I assumed were the bedrooms and a bathroom. There was a doorway under the stairway that Gus said lead to the basement.

"Here you go Dalton will this desk work for you?"

"Oh yes of course but are you sure you want me to set my stuff on it? It's beautiful and your house is very nice, the wood work is astounding, how did they afford all of this hand carved wood trim and these solid doors that are recessed into the walls this is great."

"Thank you, Dalton, but they didn't have to afford it they done it in their spare time. My grandfather and my dad done it, they didn't have television to watch back then so when they came in at night or in the winter, they would carve wood and build doors sort of like a pastime."

"Well, they did a great job, I couldn't even imagine what craftsmanship like this would cost nowadays, and do you carve too?"

"No, I don't have the patience for it and besides I have a television and that's my pastime."

I hooked up the computer and put a splitter in so Gus would be able to use his phone and not have to unhook the computer every time I wasn't using it.

"It looks like this will work."

"Whatever you say Dalton, I don't know a damn thing about those contraptions."

"I think I'm all set Gus. What do you say we go fishing?"

"Sounds good to me just let me grab my shit and a few beers, fishing is dry work. He, he," Gus giggled as he went to get his fishing equipment.

We spent the day exploring some of Gus' fishing spots. I told him what Jessica had told me the night before about the land consortium and that got a rise out of him.

"I told you there was something funny about them fucking tree huggers."

"Jessica wasn't able to find out who the parent company is, she said she would work on it while she was in Chicago and let us know when she got back in two weeks."

"What you going to do until then?"

"I'm going to help build my house, that's why I'm fishing today, probably won't have much time for it later."

"I can give you a hand if you want."

"That would be fine, what can you do trim work or rough in?"

"No nothing like that Dalton."

"What is it that you had in mind?"

"Supervisor."

"I'm afraid that Derrick is the super on this job." I was going along with his joke to see what he would come up with.

"Well then Dalton I guess I have to do what I do best."

"What would that be?"

"Drink beer and talk smart. HA, HA, HA." He was cackling at his own joke and he took a gulp of beer after he caught his breath.

"You are hired old man."

We ended up at Gus' secret trout spot on the Sturgeon River, somewhere west of L'Anse. We caught some nice Brown trout and Gus caught the biggest Speckled trout I have ever seen, somewhere around twenty inches and he was bragging and ribbing me about it.

"See Dalton, I told you, you couldn't catch the big ones using that bullwhip and a gob of feathers for bait."

"Yah, yah, I hear you, old man keep bragging."

We drove over to my house in process and talked to Derrick to see what time in the morning he wanted us to start and Gus was showing off his fish to the guys working and he was bragging about how it fought. I think it might have been the biggest one he ever caught but he wasn't going to tell me that. We got back in the truck and decided to go to Gus' for fish dinner.

"Come on old man let's go, and quit your bragging."

"I'm coming, I'm coming. Hold your horses."

We pulled out onto the road and I hadn't noticed any traffic coming in either direction when we had gone about two miles I looked into my rearview mirror and there was a large log truck coming up behind us and it wasn't wasting any time in closing the space between us. The truck was loaded with some large maple logs and they were sitting on the trailer length ways and the driver had pulled right up to my rear bumper so close that all I could see was his Mack hood ornament and some of the chrome grill.

"What the fuck is he doing?" I said out loud.

"What you talking about Dalton?" Gus asked sitting in his seat half dozing.

"That log truck behind us he's climbing up my ass, look how close he is."

Gus turned in his seat to see what I was talking about.

"Holy fuck Dalton step on it!"

"I'm going sixty now."

"I don't give a shit if you are going eighty, he's going to give you a push." Gus was yelling and I mashed my foot down on the gas pedal. I sped up to seventy and the truck closed the gap again.

"What the hell is his problem?"

"I don't know Dalton but there is a spot just up here a bit you can turn into but you are going to have to hit it pretty square because it's not real wide it's on the right."

I sped up to eighty and Gus was instructing me on where the small driveway was. He was right it wasn't very wide so I swung to the left and tried to get my Yukon to slide sideways so I could hit the driveway straight on. The loose gravel on the road made it feel like I was on ice at that speed and I over shot the turn off slightly. Gus was yelling as he looked out of his side window at the truck coming for us, I had hit the four-wheel drive button the Yukon lunged ahead with a force sending us into the ditch with a jolt I thought the airbags were going to release. Gus banging his head on the doorpost when we hit the far side of the ditch. The truck sped past blowing his air horn, just missing the rear end of my Yukon. The mud and water had flown in the air and completely cover the windshield. I took a deep breath my adrenaline was pumping, everything that had been in the back had been thrown into the back seat and up behind our seats. Gus was all piled up against the door and I was having trouble getting mine open because of the angle that we were sitting at, I used my feet to get the door open and went to find a stick to hold it open so I could get Gus out.

"You all right Gus? I'm going to get something to hold the door open and then you can climb out."

"Okay Dalton but hurry up, it's starting to get wet in here."

When I returned Gus was standing on the inside

of the passenger door holding the driver's side open. I could see blood trickling down the side of his face.

"Here Gus let me prop that open then I'll help you get out, you sure you are okay? There is some blood running down your face."

"Yah, I'm all right, what the fuck was that all about stupid cock sucker tried to kill us."

Gus had to use the armrest for a step and he was able to pull himself out without much trouble and he was bitching the whole time about what he was going to do to that truck driver once he found out who it was.

"Well, what do we do now?" I said to no one in particular. I think we are fucked; I can't back out because it might roll over." The Yukon was leaning so much that the driver's door was facing almost straight up.

"Gus do you think you can walk?"

"Yes, I can walk, I just got a bump on the head everything else seems okay."

"How far do you think it is to town maybe we can get some help?"

"I would say about eight miles, but it's only a couple back to your place maybe Derrick can give us a ride."

Gus and I started to walk back towards my place we had only gone about a mile when we saw Derrick pull out of driveway and headed our way. He pulled up with a questioning look on his face.

"I thought you two were headed to Gus'?"

Gus was fired up now, after the shock of the crash had worn off from our walk.

"Some fuckhead just ran us off the road and now we're stuck."

Gus and I got in with Derrick. "Do you guys have any idea on who it was?"

"I don't fucking know but if and when I find out, I'm going to beat the shit out of him." Gus answered.

"All I know Derrick is that it was a log truck and I was busy trying not to get Gus and I killed by it."

We drove up to where Gus and I had left the Yukon in its off-angle position.

"Holy shit! Dalton you're lucky you didn't roll that thing; I have a nylon tow strap in the back off the truck maybe I can give it a jerk and at least get it up on the road. We are going to have to take it easy so we don't roll it over any further."

Derrick backed up to the Yukon and fastened the strap to it and then to his truck I got in the Yukon and Gus was giving directions and watching for any signs of a rollover as Derrick applied pressure. He had to try several different angles, before he was able to get the Yukon back onto the gravel road. I had basically let Derrick do all the pulling as to not spin the wheels or make the thing lunge in the wrong direction.

"Fire it up Dalton let's see if it'll run pop the hood if you can."

I pulled the hood release and Gus gave the hood a few good hits with his fist and it popped open. I tried the ignition and it started right up.

"It seems to be okay Dalton no signs of anything leaking, I'll see if Derrick wants to follow us to my house in case it quits."

Gus asked Derrick and he agreed, the trip to Gus's was okay, I don't think anything major was damaged, just some sheet metal and maybe a front-end alignment was all it was going to need to get fixed.

Gus and I went into his place and he went to the task of preparing supper and I went to the computer to do some work. Gus came out to tell me supper was ready.

"Supper's ready, what you working on Dalton?"

"I'll tell you over a plate of trout."

CHAPTER TEN

The first week of Jessica's absence was rough enough but halfway through the second I was really beginning to miss her. Gus and I had helped Derrick with the house project. Gus was true to his word. He was really good at drinking beer and talking smart. We had driven there every day without ever seeing another log- truck.

"I sure wish we would have seen the name on that truck Dalton."

"Why is that Gus?"

"Because I would like to kick the shit out of somebody my head still has a bump on it."

Gus was about seventy or so and in pretty good shape, both physically and mentally. At one time he was probably a force to be noticed. He was about six foot one or two, probably a couple inches taller before his back started to bend forward from too much manual labor. Weight wise I would guess two hundred pounds, in his prime probably closer to two fifty. But what stood out most of all was the size of his hands I had never seen anyone with such big mitts on him, all knotted up and the onset off arthritis beginning to push some of the digits out of alignment on his sausage sized fingers. I could just picture the old man swinging those to sledge hammers in a bar fight and doing some major damage to some smartass that tried to cross him and ended up with a broken face for a reward. When you shook his hand, it felt like you were ten again and shaking hands with your father. I didn't see the ability there for fighting anymore the will was there but the body wasn't, he just talked rough and tough.

"Gus, I got something I want to do."

"What is it Dalton?"

"I'll tell you when we get to the bar."

"Why are we going to the bar?"

"Because I'm getting tired of cooking for your ass all the time." I said joking with him.

"Good because I'm starting to get tired of your, cooking. You couldn't boil shit for a tramp. If I had a dog and he ate some of that stuff you call food he would have to go and lick his ass for three days just to get the taste out of his mouth." He sat there full of himself after his last comment and I was laughing at him, where did he come up with this stuff.

"You are quite the philosopher Gus."

We pulled into a parking spot in front of the bar and Gus and I got out laughing and carrying on as we went in. Gus chose a table in the back corner away from the ear-shot of the bartender. I went to the restroom to clean off some of the days dust while Gus ordered the drinks, he had a beer waiting for me when I returned to the table.

"You Know old man you are going to turn me into an alcoholic."

"Why, do you have a beer before breakfast?"

"No, I don't."

"Well then you aren't even close, so drink up I hate drinking alone. What was the something that you wanted to tell me?"

"I was thinking about those fires that Jessica's husband had been involved in and I've been reading the reports on them that I retrieved off the internet hook up at your house. The only problem is that they are too general I need photographs and maybe site map of the building or plans and I don't really want the fire Chief to know about what I'm doing."

"What do you have in mind Dalton?"

"I'm thinking you should go fishing tomorrow."

"What for?"

"Because I'm going to the fire station and have a look at the files and you are going to take the." Gus held up his hand to stop me in mid-sentence, hooking his thumb towards the bar.

"Hold on Dalton old long-ears is trying to listen."

Gus waved him over to the table.

"Hey why don't you go in the kitchen and fix us up two burgers and fries, and when you get them ready bring two more beers with them. Thank you."

Gus leaned in closer to me when the bartender headed for the kitchen.

"Okay Dalton, what were you saying about the files? You planning on stealing them?"

"No, I just want to take a look at them, maybe borrow a few pictures."

"So why do you want me to go fishing, can't I help you with it?"

"Yes, you are going to take the Chief fishing and I'm going to get the rookie to let me see the files and I don't want the Chief to stop by unexpectedly."

"How are you going to do that?"

"I'll figure something out, maybe tell him some bullshit about checking for a haz-mat report whether it was filed or not."

"You don't think the rookie is going to tell the Chief were in snooping around in the files?"

"I'll bet on it, that's why I'm going to put a haz-mat report in the department store file. Then I'll just take a quick look at the other ones and put them back."

"Then you aren't going to steal them?"

"No, I don't think so maybe lift a couple pictures is all."

The burgers and beers arrived and Gus and I ate in a hurry. I had to get back and make up a bogus report and he had to call the Chief before he went to bed. It was already eight and I didn't want the Chief to think it was strange that Gus was calling him too late to go fishing.

"We better eat up, I have to get back and make a report and you have to give the Chief a call, before he goes to bed."

"Okay Dalton, I'll call him and then I'll give you a call if everything is okay for tomorrow."

"Sounds good Gus, I'll see you later tomorrow."

"You thinking that those other fires are connected to the department store fire?"

"I don't know but I'm going to try and find out."

Gus and I left the bar; he had left his truck at my cabin so I didn't have to go all the way out to his house. I offered for him to call the Chief from my place but he said he wanted to try and think up a story for why he was calling the Chief so late to go fishing.

"I'll call you later Dalton maybe in an hour or so."

"Okay Gus I'll be listening for it, see you later,"

Gus pulled out of the driveway and I went into the cabin to take a shower first. Then try and make out a false report for the department store. The days grime and sweat came off in a refreshing and relaxing wave I stood under the water stream of the shower for a long time just letting the flow wash away the days' work and my aching muscles. The house project was coming along nicely and I was starting to get tired out from it. I must have sweated two gallons of water out today, and it didn't help that I wore two shirts all the time. Most of the guys that worked for Derrick went shirtless after ten in the morning because for some reason the temperature decided to climb up to the mid-eighties and the humidity was high. The two-shirt thing was going to have to go pretty soon or I wasn't going to be much good in couple days I would be to exhaust. Gus had never brought up the fact that he had seen me with my shirt off and he never asked me why I worked in it every day, he was a good guy and I was grateful to him for respecting my modesty, someday I would tell him about how I came to getting scarred. Gus called just as I got out of the shower and let me know everything was all set for tomorrow. I took out a haz-mat report form from my briefcase and made up some stuff about the fuel cans and the other hazardous material that may have ran out of the building as the water from the hose-streams were applied to it may have washed some of it into the storm drains and how the fire department had put drain blocks in and done everything according to procedures blah, blah, blah.

The next day I woke up with a terrible stiff neck and shoulders my back was tight and the scarred skin tissue was tight feeling, I was afraid to bend over for fear I might tear something. A few stretching exercises and I was good to go. I hadn't slept very well, tossing and turning, dreaming off Jessica standing on a cliff in a white buckskin dress, with beadwork and feathers her hair was blowing straight up as she peered over the edge. She looked over to me then stepped off floating in the air like some kind of magic trick before stepping back onto the edge again, at that moment I woke up, with the soreness of yesterday's work.

I got dressed, made a cup of coffee and went to the fire station, just as planned. The rookie should be there if the Chief had went fishing with Gus. The day appeared to be starting out with a humid haze slowly lifting above the tree line and off the big lake. The humidity was going to be high again and I wasn't looking forward to it again, maybe sometime today I would be able to go with just a tee-shirt, but for now I would wear my double layers. There was an old Ford pickup parked in front of the fire station and I assumed it belonged to the rookie. I parked alongside of it, taking a clipboard and my report as a prop for my charade. I entered the building with a certain air of authority. Maybe if the rookie noticed that I was all business he would leave me to my task and not ask too many questions.

I found him in the lunchroom making a pot of coffee.

"Hi rookie, is the Chief around?"

"Hi Mr. James, no he isn't, he called last night. Said he was going fishing and that I was to hold down the fort, if I got in a bind, I was to call him on his cell phone. Do you want me to give him a call?"

"No, I don't think that's necessary. I would hate to bother him if he's fishing."

"What can I do for you?"

"I was just doing some follow up work on the

department store fire and I wanted to take a look at the files, I think we may have forgot to put in a Haz-mat report. I want to make sure everything is okay."

"Haz-mat report what for?"

"It's should be filed if any of the run off from the firefighting procedures carries contaminate into the storm drains then the public works is going to want to know where it came from. So, we file one of these to cover our ass, if you get my drift."

"Oh, I see but we had gutter block in how could anything get past them?"

"I know, that's why we file the report. So, could you show me where the files are kept please and I'll get out of your hair."

"Yah sure, right down here in the Chief's office, top drawer of the file cabinet, or maybe the second one. Here I'll take a look for you."

"No that's all right I can get it."

The rookie was being a little too helpful. How was I going to get him out of here so I could look at the files?

"Hey rookie would you mind going out to my Yukon and getting the envelope that's on the seat I forgot to bring it in with me it has some picture of how the storm drains were blocked. They should go in the file with the report."

"Sure, you said they were on the seat?"

"Yep, right on the back seat, drivers' side, and while you are out there. Take a look at my Yukon. I got in a fender bender the other day, maybe you could recommend a place I could get it fixed."

"Okay I'll do that; I know a couple of buddies of mine that can fix just about anything they have a shop just down the street from here."

"Sounds good, go take a look and I'll pull out the file."

The rookie left the office and I hurriedly opened the file cabinet, not really sure what to expect of their filing system. The department store file was cataloged in the top drawer by date of fire. The rest of the files were in order the same way. I pulled it out and set it on top opening it up. Then I went through the rest of the drawer pulling out the files that were for the old fires, only sliding them up far enough to open them for a quick look I didn't want to get them out of order in case the Chief got suspicious and went to see what I was doing in his cabinet. The first one had only a few shots of the outside if the building after it was totaling burned to the ground. The second and third were basically the same. One of them had a good angle on the one remaining wall that was left standing, not much good for comparison purposes. The four was the fatal fire that Jessica's husband had been found in, bingo this one had multiple photographs and they were at different angles. They mostly were of the body but you could still make out the majority of the inside of the structure. I looked them over quickly. Then a bell rang it must have been hooked to the front door to let someone know if anybody entered the fire station. I quickly put the pictures back and grabbed the file, sitting open on the top of the cabinet just as the rookie return.

"Thanks rookie, I don't see any Haz-mat report so it was probably a good thing I decided to drop one off, isn't any pictures either. You can never be too careful or thorough anymore, to damn many lawyers to try and stick you with something."

"That's for sure, do you think the fire was set?"

"I don't know maybe the Chief will when the reports come back from the lab. What did you think of my Yukon, can your buddy fix it for me?"

I was talking and walking, trying to get out of the office in case something caught the rookie's eye.

"Well rook thank again; I would like to stay and visit but I have an appointment in a few minutes. Tell the Chief I stopped by and let me know if he needs anything else."

"Okay Mr. James I'll do that, and my buddy won't have any trouble fixing your Yukon. Just stop by and he will give you an estimate, tell him I sent you maybe he will give you a discount."

"I'll do that and thanks again, see you later."

I was out the door and in the clear, driving back towards my cabin. I would have to get a hold of some better pictures but how? The few I had seen had shown the late professor lying in the fetal position on the floor, but they only showed some of the interior, enough for me to see the little bomb blast marks on the ceiling and how the fire may have spread. I needed some better shots. Maybe Gus would come up with something or somehow. Just then I realized I wanted to go to Houghton when I had left the fire station, and I was headed the wrong way, after making a U-turn my brain was in rapid fire mode and I was trying to figure out how I could get my hands on some better photos of the fatal fire, damn I know there has to be more pictures somewhere. The drive to Houghton went by quickly I couldn't tell you about anything that was alongside of the road I was in my own world thoughts and memories running rampant through my mind. The trip to Houghton was for some mountain climbing gear and I found it at a small

sporting goods store that specialized in mountaineer-
ing and skiing, thy offered ice climbing gear some scuba
stuff and other various sporting equipment and clothing. I bought some rope a helmet, repelling harness,
headlamp, and some climber's gloves. I had something
else on my mind and Gus was going to help me with it
before jess got back. Driving back to L'Anse I picked up
a pizza on the way and headed straight for Gus' place, it
was almost seven and Gus was looking out the kitchen
window as I pulled up, he had the door open and was
waiting for me. Before I walked up.

"Did you get the pictures Dalton; did you find out
anything?"

"Yes, I did, here take this pizza and I'll explain what
I found as we eat." I handed Gus the pizza box and he
hurried around the table and kitchen getting plates and
beer.

"I'll take a soda if you have one." I had to lay off the
beer for a while my midsection was starting to show
some growth that I didn't need.

"Yah. I have a soda in here somewhere, so tell me
what did you find out?"

Gus sat down and started to dissect the pizza, stuff-
ing half a piece in his mouth and chasing it with a long
drink of beer.

"I found some of the pictures if the fire that Jessica's
husband died in., they weren't really good but I did see
enough to get me thinking."

"What did you see that got you thinking?"

"There was a similar burn pattern on the ceiling, I
seen it in just one of the pictures they were mostly of
the body. The angles were all wrong to get a good look
at the ceiling. I wish I could get my hands on some of

the fire scene photos."

"What did you say? Something about similar patterns, what does that mean?"

"Like I said they weren't really good but it did look like the same circle or pattern was on the department store ceiling."

"You thinking they are related to one another, show me what you mean by burn patterns."

"Come on in here where my pile of photos is on the desk we can finish eating and maybe you and I can figure this out."

Gus and I went into the other room and sat down at the old dining room table first he put some towels down so we would hurt the finish with or cans and the greasy pizza box.

"Here put these down I don't know where my table clothes are right of hand."

"That's fine, here take a look at these pictures." I was sorting through the fire scene pictures and passing them to him.

"Do you see those kinds of circular patterns on the ceiling, they are burned in deeper than the surrounding area."

"Yah, I see them, what does it mean?"

"I think that somebody loaded that place up for a quick burn, that's why the whole place was burning when the trucks pulled up."

"How does he load up someplace, I don't get what you are telling me."

"The arsonist take balloons and fills them full of gas or something that is an accelerant, then he hangs them from the ceiling. Once the fire starts all the heat accumulates at the ceiling the balloon gets weak from it and they break. The first ones break and increase the size and temperature of the fire causing the rest to go off in a chain reaction."

"Okay, now how does he get the balloons to burn, if they are all blowing up how does he get out?"

"They use something like a time delay anything a candle or a book of matches with cigarette stuck in it, a stove or a furnace anything that will give time to get out."

"What does the circle patterns have to do with the balloons?"

"Let's say the arsonist has put the balloons up on the ceiling like I explained earlier and they start going off one right after another, even though everything is burning the area where the balloon was has burned just a little bit longer because the fuel inside erupted and caught the ceiling on fire first or the gas burned in the atmosphere directly below it where the balloon was hanging, thus making a deeper burn pattern in the ceiling."

"So, you are saying that this was done at the department store and maybe at the fire that Jessica's husband was in, but why aren't the clothes on the shelves in these pictures all burned, it looks like some of them on the bottom shelves are still okay."

"Now you are getting it Gus. This is what I look for when I go to a fire scene, first you ask why. Why didn't some things burn and others do, the pictures of the store show an unnatural burn cycle."

"Burn cycle what's that?"

"The burn cycle is how a fire consumes the surrounding area or fuel source. The fire started low on the floor in a corner and it burned up the wall and the ceiling first before any of the fuel down by the floor caught on fire."

"But isn't that how fires burn, up toward the ceiling?"

"Yes, it is, but as a fire burns it goes up and out, this is true, the thing that bothers me on this one is that the wall that the fire went up first is made of cement blocks and you know damn well that they don't burn very good, so why didn't the floor burn more in the store first the fire is only going to follow a fuel source and cement isn't one of them, the magazine rack was the original fuel source but according to the people familiar with the place nothing else was close to it."

"Oh, I get it now Dalton, you are thinking because the fire couldn't burn up the wall and start the ceiling it would have to go across the floor and start maybe a shelf of clothes or something before it made enough heat to get the ceiling burning."

"Yah exactly, that's why I'm using the balloon theory. The fire burned a lot longer at the ceiling then it did at the floor. It also flashed over from the looks of it and I don't see enough of the dry goods being burned to create enough heat for that to happen."

"Flashover what's that?"

"Flashover is what happens in a fire when the combustible materials reach an ignition point all at the same time. The fire creates so much heat in such a short time that it doesn't actually touch the fuel it just heats it to its vapor point, or flash point. When it ignites the vapors burn not the material itself. The whole atmosphere of the room becomes one big fire- ball a very violent one at that. Sometimes firefighters are caught in them and usually don't survive. The smoke doesn't kill them it's the heat, you're talking somewhere around twelve hundred degrees or more, melts plastic helmets face shield everything, it cooks them in their coats."

"Holy Christ Dalton, is that what happened to you?"

"No, not exactly it was more of a firebomb then a flashover. That's why I'm thinking that somebody started it. The floor should have shown more burn or at least some of the stuff on the shelves."

"So, what do we need to prove that they used the same trick on both fires?"

"I would like to see some more picture for one thing and maybe report that wasn't edited, after it was put into the computer."

"Well, is there one at the fire station, or did you get a look at one today?"

"I don't know I didn't have time, but if there were more pictures, I might be able to figure it out, even some of the outside of the building might help."

"Shit Dalton why didn't you say outside right off the bat, I got some from the newspaper, they are just articles but some are taken outside showing the building I'll get them they are in my old trunk upstairs."

Gus went upstairs and I cleared the table of the pizza remains and empty cans before he returned.

"Here you go Dalton this is all of them, it doesn't really show too much but it might help."

"Let's see Gus is this all the fires or just the one Jessica's husband was in?"

"I think it may be all of them I'm not sure, can you see anything worthwhile?"

"No not really but, I think we just found a source for some more pictures."

"A source, what are you talking about?"

"You ever seen a news photographer, take just one picture?'

"No, they take a whole bunch, what are you getting at?"

"That's the source the photographer might just have a whole roll of pictures on each fire we can go ask him if we can figure out who he worked for."

"He probably worked for the paper, it's not that big of a publication."

"It has his name in the side bar of the picture here, John Sutton photo local news."

"Well maybe we should go see old Johnny boy in the near future, but right now this old fuck is going to bed, lock up when you leave, and thanks for the pizza and the fire lesson, good night."

I had only stayed at Gus' for another hour, studying the reports and photos from the old newspaper clippings. My thoughts of the fires turned toward Jessica, I wondered if she could maybe give Gus and me some insight on them after we had some pictures from the news photographer. The evening drive home from Gus' was short I had not realized that I had drove past my cabin until I was only a half of a mile from town. The thinking process had made me unaware of my surroundings as I drove. The night air was warm and humid. The smell of the big lake when I got out at my cabin was hanging low and thick. It had a dead fish smell, with a hint of sweetness from some of the flowers that were growing around the resort property. I had decided to sit outside for a while the inside of the cabin was too hot for sleeping and the absence of air conditioning had raised the room temperature to uncomfortable sleeping. I opened the windows and doors leaving the cooler night air to filter through the cabin. The bench out by the water was a good place to sit and catch a cooler breeze coming off the lake. The dark stillness of the night was only broken by an amber glow coming off the street lights in Baraga across the bay. My mind once again turned to the Indian princess and the sight of the flowers that Jessica had tossed from the bluff and how they floated in the air before falling to the canyon floor.

A movement along the lakeshore caught my attention, the changing shadows and sounds of the water as it lapped against the shoreline made it difficult to determine what it was that I was seeing. Some grunts and rattling sound could be heard in between the waves. Whatever it was it was on the prowl and looking for a meal. I got up from the bench and moved closer my curiosity getting the better of me. The creature was going about its business not even aware of my presence. The distance was only mere feet know and I was straining to decipher what I was looking at. It came at me with a lunge and a snarl, the rattling sound followed as it stopped short of me. I jumped, startled at this offensive movement. The realization of what I was looking at came into the picture, it was a raccoon I had been watching, and the night was more of a familiar place for him than me. Leaving the Raccoon go about his business I returned to the cabin. The temperature inside had dropped a few degrees; however, it was still warm I decided to take a cool shower and turn in for the night.

The opportunity of a night of restful sleep eluded me again. I woke up tangled in my sheets and sweating. A quick shower and into my clothes before eight I was pulling into Gus' driveway.

Gus hollered from the kitchen window, for me to come in.

"Come on in, breakfast is almost ready."

Gus was standing at the old stove cooking bacon and eggs a pile of potatoes occupied a cast iron frying pan in one corner. He was wearing his boxer shorts and a white tee shirt that had small grease spots on it from the hot grease spitting out of the pans. His bare legs though muscle well for a man of his age had not seen the sun in many years they were white as parchment.

"Morning Gus, you're going to burn your legs with that grease if you don't get some clothes on."

"Why am I bothering you?"

"Yah, I'm afraid of what I might see."

"Not to worry my boy, the horse is in the barn for good." He remarked a small smile turning up the corners of his mouth.

"I'm not worried about the horse I'm worried about the barn door flying open." I said with a smart-ass tone in my voice. That comment got his dandruff up.

"Here, smart-ass take the spatula, and watch the eggs, I'll go get some pants on if it bothers you that much." Gus retreated down the hallway towards his bedroom, bitching as he went.

"I don't know what the big deal is, if the horse can't get up it can't get out."

I stood there flipping the eggs over in the pan and snickering to myself. He returned to the kitchen with his pants on the suspenders were hanging down alongside his legs.

"What's so funny?"

"You, what you said about the horse not being able to get up, so it can't get out."

"You think that's funny you young fuck? Well, I don't, it's been a long time since I woke up and seen the one-eyed cobra staring at me from under the covers. We used to have a lot of fun in town." He said with a devilish grin. Remembering his younger days.

"Here you go Dalton' would you like some coffee?" Gus slid a plate full a food in front of me and grabbed the coffee pot off the stove, before sitting down across from me.

"Thanks Gus, it looks great."

"Yes sir, me and old one eye tearing up the town on a Saturday night, those were the days. This one time I met a set of twins over in Baraga."

"Whoa! Gus that's enough I hate to tell you, but I'm not interested."

"All right, all right, what brings you out here today so early? You didn't say anything about it last night."

"I was wondering if I could see your barn for a while."

"What for, it isn't much good anymore, a guy could throw a dead cat thru the wall just about any place he wanted to."

"Are the beams in good shape? Do you know if they are sound enough to hold up a man?

"Yes, I think so, what the hell you up to now?"

"I need to practice my mountain climbing, well mostly repelling."

"Repelling, what's that?"

"I'll show you after breakfast."

Gus and I finished breakfast; I cleared the table while he was finishing getting dressed.

"I'll meet you out at the barn Gus." I hollered as I went out the door to get my gear out of the truck. Gus met at the barn and stood there with a dumb-founded look on his face.

"What the hell are you going to do with all that rope and why do you need the barn beams?"

"I'm going to climb up there and tie one end to the rafters and then slide down using this harness." I climbed the old wooden ladder that led up to the hay loft, tied off the rope, snapped it into the repelling harness, leaned out and slid down the rope using my hand as a brake, setting myself down smoothly next to where Gus was standing, shaking his head.

"You look like a big spider coming down that rope. What did you say you had to do this for?"

"I didn't say yet, but you are going to help me." I said pointing at him.

"No, fucking way, Dalton I'm not sliding down some rope."

"You don't have to, but I still want your help. I have something I've been thinking about and we're going to check it out." I climbed the ladder and slid down again, after six more practice runs, I thought I had the feel for it. The suspense was killing Gus and he was asking questions and trying to guess what we were going to do next.

"Come on Gus, let's go I'll show you when we get there."

Gus helped me load my gear back into the Yukon, then he went into his house to get some beer for my cooler, I told him I would be drinking water today. I didn't think it was a very good idea to have alcohol in me for my repelling task.

Gus and I drove out to my house site Derrick and his crew were in the process of shingling the roof. Gus was still trying to guess what I was up to.

"Okay Dalton cut the suspense shit and tell me what you have in mind."

"I will, I will, grab some rope and follow me."

We walked over to the edge of the cliff where Jessica had made the offering of flowers. I started to get my harness, helmet and gloves on. The whole time Gus stood there with a puzzled look on his face.

"Gus tie the end of this rope off to that big maple over there, make sure it's a good knot my life depends on it."

"Not until you tell me what the fuck you're doing."

"Remember the legend of the Indian princess?"

"Yes, I remember, what about it, it is just a legend?"

"You said they never found the body, right?

"Yep" he answered,

"Well, I got an idea on where it might be."

"We don't even know if it was a true story, so how do you know if there ever was an Indian princess?" he exclaimed.

"Well, I don't but it's important to Jessica and she said," that there was" so I'm going to have a look."

"I don't know Dalton this don't look really safe to me, and how am I supposed to help you if you get in trouble?"

"I'll show you grab that other coil of rope. Gus you are in charge of the safety line whatever you do don't let go. I'm going to tie one end to myself and you take the other end and go around that tree. It has to work like a brake so wrap it around twice, now I'm going to slid down this other rope and I want you to hold tension on the one wrapped around the tree let it out as I need it, once I'm where I need to be, I'll tie it off to the cliff face, you should feel some slack. When I'm ready to come up I'll give a shout and two good tugs. I will be climbing up the anchored one but you can give me a hand by pulling on this one. Okay?

"Yep"

I did a small demonstration on how I wanted him to pull on the rope using his legs to do most of the work.

"Looks simple enough, so you think you'll find her? He asked.

"I got a hunch is all and I want to see if its right, here we go."

I eased myself out over the edge leaning back against the rope, using my legs to walk backwards down the cliff face until the undercut was at too much of an angle, this is where I had to use my repelling technique. Gus was keeping good tension and I was able to slide smoothly down. The updraft was trying to lift me and push me into the cliff face. Using me feet to spring of the rock wall I was able to maneuver around the rocks and small brushes. The small ledge was off to my left about twenty feet so I had to swing back and forth running along the rocks to get my momentum up once over the ledge I dropped down onto it. Placing an anchor into the rocks I tied off the lines. The ledge was only about three feet by five feet square. With the wind blowing up the rock wall it made for a precarious perch, the tied line was shortening so if I fell it would catch me. Another anchor went in just for good measure. There was a small crevice that led in from the ledge. The squeeze thru was tight, it was wider at the bottom than the top, I had to lie down and wiggle thru, my back scrapping against the sharp rocks. The chamber in side was long and narrow looking. The ceiling was only about four feet from the floor, which was covered in slimy stinking goop.

"What the hell is that smell, ammonia?" My answer came in the form of a squeal, and small wing beats.

"Bats! Ah shit I hate bats."

The cave dwellers had only used the front part of the entrance, there were only fifteen or so. They didn't completely cover the ceiling. I kept working my way deeper into the cave, about twelve feet in the cave ceiling made an upwards turn enabling me to stand a little hunched over making it easier, to move. I unhook my safety rope and proceeded into a larger room of about ten by ten feet, the floor was covered in a residue of dust a couple of inches deep, no bats on the ceiling and no shit on the floor. I was scanning the floor area using my helmet lamp, when I noticed something white in color protruding up thru the dust. "What the heck is that? It looks like a pelvic bone. I gently brushed the dust from the floor in the area surround it using my glove like a small broom the full skeleton started to take shape. The leg bones, ribs, shoulders, arms, and skull all the soft tissue had been gone for a long time. The small bones of the hands were crossed over the chest plate. I began to study the skull closer and noticed the teeth, were wore done more in the front then I had seen on other bodies, that I had looked at in the past. From what I could judge the person was short maybe five foot tall, the pelvic bone looked female, not sure would need forensics done to be sure. The light cast from the helmet lamp wasn't bright enough to pick out details. I turned on a small halogen flashlight and began to scrutinize the skeleton more closely. The femur or thighbone of the left leg was broken it appeared to be a compound fracture when the bone broke the two pieces had slid past each other. The right ankle was fractured in two places and some of the small bones of the right foot showed fractures also. The right forearm had a break as well as the collarbone. Whoever this was they had suffered excruciating pain, probably dragged themselves into the back of the cave. The hands looked to be intact. My light caught the glimmer of something in between the hand bones and the chest plate or sternum. "What the heck is that?" I didn't want to disturb the remains any more than I had to. The pliers on the multi-tool worked as a set of forceps. I began to remove the layers of small hand bones to reveal the object. Taking care to remember how to put them back in place. There were some small black stones about the size of a pea, laying on top of the sternum, and a gold cross about one inch wide by one and a half long. The beads looked to be polish onyx or something similar. I placed everything back, trying to make sure it was in the correct spot. The cross and stone were from a rosary used mostly in the Catholic faith. I would have to do some investigating as to whether the native peoples were given them by the Jesuits during the conversion ceremonies.

Trying not to disturb anything else I exited the small cave and crevice. Retying my safety line and hooking into the other I gave the rope two good jerks and Gus started pulling up the slack as I climbed. I was convinced that the body or skeleton I had seen in the cave was if fact the Indian princess. Gus was pulling pretty well, so the climb up went almost effortless.

"I'm almost to the top Gus, just keep the rope tight and I'll climb over the top edge."

"Well Dalton did you find anything? What the hell is that smell did you fall in some shit?"

"No, I crawled in it, its bat shit to be exact."

"Where did you find the bat shit?"

"I'll tell you, grab those ropes I have to get out of these clothes I stink and it's starting to gag me."

"Yah no shit it's gagging me too. What you going to do drive home naked?"

"No, I brought another change of clothes they are in the back of the Yukon."

"Good, because I didn't want to be seen riding around with a naked guy, especially one who stinks."

"Throw that stuff in the back and I'll go get changed."

I grabbed my duffel bag, opening the back door and the front one I began to change standing between the two.

"I think I found the Indian princess Gus, Gus are you listening?"

"Yah I'm listening." He answered with his back to me.

"What did you say Gus? Turn around so I can here you."

"Are you sure Dalton?"

"Yes, I'm sure it isn't anything you haven't already seen."

He turned around and came closer.

"Did you say you found the Indian princess?"

"I think so. The other day when, Jessica and I were out here to see Derrick. I was talking to Derrick and Jessica was standing up there on the bluff making an offering to the spirit of the princess, she tossed some flowers over the edge of the cliff."

"What the hell does that have to do with this?"

"I'm getting to it hold your horses. When Jessica tossed the flowers. They didn't fall right away instead they rose up in the air and out away from the cliff before falling. Then Jessica and I walked around to the bottom of the canyon to check it out. While I was looking up at the cliff face, I noticed a small cave or crevice in the face about forty feet down. That cave is where the princess is or at least her skeleton."

I turned my back to Gus as I put on my clean pants, exposing my shirtless back to Gus.

"Holy shit! Dalton."

"Yah I know Gus its ugly."

"No not that you are bleeding, you cut you back on something."

I turned my head trying to see the cut. "Damn skin is so thin you just bump it and it bleeds, that's why I always wear a tee-shirt, it gives me some protection." How bad is the cut?"

"Not too bad, maybe some cleaning and a band aid or two should fix it up."

"There is a first aid kit in the back end would you mind getting it and doctoring me?'

Gus got out the kit and preformed the first aid I needed.

"Okay Dalton I think that should do it. Where are we going now?"

I tossed the bat shit clothes into an empty garbage bag and then into the back of the Yukon.

"We are going to your house; I need to look at those newspaper clippings again."

"But I thought you figured out who the photographer was the other night?"

Gus took a beer from the cooler before getting into the passenger seat.

"Did you want one?"

"No thanks I have a water here some place. I want to give the newspaper a call and see if the guy still works for them or if they have any copies on hand of all the fire scenes."

We drove back to Gus' he decided he was hungry and that he would fix some lunch while I dug into the news clippings.

"You want some lunch Dalton?"

"No thanks Gus, I'm getting to fat." I said rubbing my belly.

"Oh shit, you're not, you look fine."

"I don't know if I like the sound of that coming from a guy who just seen me naked."

"Fuck you Dalton, you know what I meant." Gus snapped and grunted in disgust as he went to the refrigerator.

"Yes, I know I'm just messing with you, maybe I will have a sandwich. The newspaper clippings are they in the desk drawer?"

"Yah I didn't move them."

I brought the papers back to the kitchen while Gus was making sandwiches. I gave the news office a call.

"What did they say Dalton do they have any of the pictures?"

Gus was asking in between mouthfuls of sandwich and gulps of beer.

"Yes, they have some but we'll have to get there before they close, if we want to get them ordered for coping. So, grab your food and let's get going. They close in one hour.

We took the food and some of the old clipping and drove to Baraga. The news office was small and only employed six people the editor met us in the front office where the photographer worked. He had already told him that we were coming and he was in the process of trying to find his negatives of the fires he had stored in his cabinet.

"Hi guys, which ones do you want and for which fire. I have them all."

"Can we have them all? I'll pay for the copies if that's going to be a problem."

"No, not at all Mr. James, just let me have the first scoop on the story if you find something out. Would you like them in 5x7 or 8x10's?"

"Will they be clear in the 8x10's, if so, I would prefer that size, and as far as the story, you get first scoop."

"Great, I won't have these ready for a couple of days, maybe Tuesday if that's all right. My tech is gone. I'll tell him to make both sizes in case they come out to grainy."

"That will be fine, thank you very much and I'll see you on Tuesday."

Gus and I headed back to his place.

"Dalton what time you got?"

"7 Pm why? You have some place to be?"

"No just wondering. Wasn't Jessica going to call you?"

"Oh, shit I forgot all about that. My cell phone doesn't show I missed any calls. Maybe her flight was late."

"What do you have in mind for supper?"

"Damn Gus all you think about is food and beer."

"Yes, that's because I'm old. When I was young all I thought about was pussy and beer." Ha! Ha!

"Gus you are terrible, all right what did you have in mind for a place to eat?"

"I was thinking steak a big thick rare T-bone steak, and I know just the place when we get to L'Anse, I'll show you."

Gus gave me directions to a small family style restaurant. The steak was wonderful, Gus was right they did an excellent job of preparing it.

"You were right Gus this is good; I'll have to remember to bring Jessica out here sometime."

"Yes, sir they know how to cook a steak. Do you think we should get going you don't want to Miss Jessica's call?"

"Yah you're right, I wonder why she hasn't called."

Gus was content to take a nap while I drove him back to his house. The cell phone rang as we turned into Gus' driveway.

"Hello Dalton speaking."

"Hello handsome, what are you doing?"

"Hi Jessica, I'm just turning into Gus's driveway. How come you are so late, it's nine o-clock?"

"I had a delay in Chicago, weather or something. I'm leaving Marquette and I probably won't be home for another hour or so."

"Do you want me to come over?"

"No not really I'm really tired. Is Gus with you?"

"Yes, the old coot is napping in the seat." That little comment got his attention and he sat up rubbing his eyes."

"Watch who you call and old coot."

"I would like you and Gus to come over for dinner tomorrow, my treat is there anything Gus doesn't care for I don't want to cook something he doesn't like."

"No, I think he'll eat just about anything."

"Dalton, would you please ask him, you shouldn't

pick on him like that."

"Yah, Yah, Yah, Gus? Jessica wants to know if there is anything you wouldn't like for dinner tomorrow."

"Why would she want to know that? I'll eat just about anything as long as it doesn't have rice or spinach in it."

"Did you catch that? No rice or spinach."

"Yes, I heard, then I'll expect you boys to be at my place around five."

"Okay five it is, do you want us to bring anything?"

"No, I'll take care of everything, talk to you tomorrow Dalton good bye."

"Good bye Jess."

"Why did she want to know if I didn't like something to eat?"

"Because we are going over to her house for dinner tomorrow at five o-clock sharp and she is looking forward to meeting you."

"I don't know Dalton, why would she want to meet me?"

"She said you sounded interesting and intelligent; besides she has some information about the consortium she wants to share with us. So, you're coming."

"She said all of that about me?"

"Yes, more or less."

Gus started to puff out his chest.

"I may be old but I still got it. Do you want to come in for a while?"

"No, I think I'm going to go back to the cabin, I need to get some sleep, and my back is starting to tighten up."

"Okay Dalton, I'll be ready for tomorrow, just give me a call so I know what time to meet you."

"Okay Gus good night." I watched Gus make it to his back door before backing out of his driveway.

The day of rock climbing and cave searching, made me tired and I had all I could do to stay awake while taking a shower. The cuts on my back seemed to have quit bleeding, so I didn't have to worry about trying to bandage them before bed.

"Oh, what a day the skeleton discovery and the newspaper photos. This is starting to turn into regular detective mystery. I wonder what Jessica found out about our consortium questions."

Talking to myself was becoming a frequent occurrence for me. I slid into bed and was out before my head hit the pillow.

CHAPTER ELEVEN

I woke up Sunday to a sunny sixty-five-degree day the big lake was flat and tranquil looking. Gus had mentioned that if the water was calm in the morning, following a hot spell. Get ready because a storm was coming. He was right by midafternoon the temperature dropped off to forty and the wind began to blow. The waves on the lake seemed to be about eight to ten feet in height, slamming onto the break wall and showering the lawn in front of the cabin with their spray. How could the climate be so erratic in one day? The large freighters using the Great lakes for shipping had started to come into the bay trying to find shelter. The waves in the bay were high, but out in the open water they probably exceeded twenty feet. I couldn't blame them for playing it safe. If they go down the chance of survival is very low. The trees were swaying with every gust, sand began to swirl in small whirlwinds and a waterspout was seen cutting across the bay.

I was on the cell phone talking with Gus about this evening's dinner date. "What should I wear Dalton?" "Nothing to formal, I talked to Jessica earlier and it sounded like she was going to try and have something outside like a barbeque, but I don't know now with this weather starting to kick up.

"Yah it's starting to blow pretty good out here, I lost

some of my old barn roof, and a couple of pieces of tin went flying across the yard. Do you want me to meet you there "Where, Jessica's or my place?" "Your place."

"That sounds good we can ride together. Is there anything else?"

"No, I just wanted to know what I should wear and if I was riding with you. Okay Dalton I'll see you at four."

"See you then Gus good bye."

What on earth was that all about, it had to be only about one o-clock. The old guy was really excited about this dinner. For someone who started out not wanting to meet her, he sure changed his mind in a hurry.

It was only one o-clock and I was getting bored sitting around the small cabin. I decided to clean my Yukon out I had accumulated some garbage and beer cans from the past two weeks. Taking a garbage bag and some armor all cleaner out of the cupboard. I set out to perform the task at hand. When I opened the backend, a stench hit me square in the face that nearly knocked me down.

"Ah shit, what the hell is that? The bat shit clothes in the back must have did some fermenting from the warm weather this morning. I had forgot all about them last night. Now what was I going to do? I hurriedly cleaned the inside and went into the cabin looking for something I could use to mask the putrid smell. I began to try every cleaner I owned and settled on pinesol it seemed to mask it the best. Just then Gus came pulling into the driveway. The doors of the Yukon were all open and I had not had a chance to change.

"Damn Dalton you aren't ready, get your ass moving we don't want to make her wait for us. Didn't anybody ever tell you not to be late when it comes to a woman?'

"No, they didn't, come in the cabin and I'll be ready in a flash."

I hustled inside carrying my assortment of cleaners. Gus came in behind me bitching about not ever being late blah, blah, blah. I quickly took a shower, putting on a pair of khaki pants and a polo shirt, fifteen later minutes we were heading out the door. Gus had sat at the kitchen table drumming his fingers and checking his watch every two minutes.

"Okay Gus I'm ready let's go."

We got into the Yukon, then Gus got out.

"What are you doing Gus?"

"I forgot something in my truck hold on."

Gus climbed back in, wrinkling up his nose as he buckled his seatbelt.

"What did you forget?"

"What the hell is that smell? It smells like a bat shit out a pine tree."

"Just open your window and quit bitching. What did you forget in the truck?"

"This, it's some wine from my cellar I thought Jessica might like to have it with dinner."

"That was thoughtful of you, it looks pretty old, and how much do you think its worth?"

"It's not worth a shit if you don't like wine and I don't, it was my mother and grandmothers supply. I would say it was about eighty years old give or take ten years. Do you think she'll like it?"

"I have no doubt, she'll enjoy the gesture. You sure are being generous, and you look pretty sharp too."

Gus had on a white long sleeved, blue pinstriped shirt with matching blue pants, wing tip shoes and a bola around his neck instead of a tie, clean shaven with a hint of cologne.

"Do I detect a hint of cologne in the air coming from you?" I was teasing him. "I thought you didn't like a man to wear perfume?"

"Who the fuck could tell in this bat shit buggy we are riding in, and I didn't say that. I said that a young boy with an earring shouldn't have on perfume. Now shut up and drive we're going to be late."

I left Gus alone, not real sure of where it was that I was driving to. I called Jessica for directions. I had missed the turn for her drive and had to turn around. This made Gus a bit more unnerving.

"What the fuck? Don't you know where you are going now, we are really going to be late?"

"Don't worry she knows we missed the turn and I have never been to her place before so settle down."

We pulled into the drive and we were only fifteen, but according to Gus it might as well been an hour.

"I told you that you should never be late it is all right if you have to wait on a woman but they should never have to wait for you."

"I heard you now quit bitching and grab the wine; I want you to behave in here I'm kind of fond of this woman and don't say any of those colorful little phrases of you like to come up with."

Gus got out straightening his coat and pulling up his pants, he even checked his hair in the side mirror. What was this old coot up to?

"Don't worry about old Gus." He said pointing at himself. I know how to act around a lady."

He had just finished his sentence as the door opened with Jessica standing there smiling.

"Come on in you two and quit talking about me. Hi

Dalton, how are you?" she leaned forward and gave me a kiss.

"Please come in, you must be the famous Gus I've heard so much about." She said sticking her hand out for Gus to except. "I'm Jessica Whitehorse."

"Gus Jorgenson, nice to meet you miss Jessica, nice house you have here." He said looking around the room. "And what a lovely hostess. I have a gift for you." He was laying on the charm and gave her the old bottle of wine.

"Oh, why thank you, this looks wonderful, where did you get it from?"

"It's from my wine cellar."

The old man was soaking in the response to his gift and holding my ladies hand the whole time. What was up with that? The old hound was moving in on my woman. I was starting to think the story about the horse was bullshit.

"Do you know how old this bottle of wine is Dalton?"

"No Jessica I don't, but I'm glad you like it."

"I hope you enjoy it Miss Jessica."

"Thank you I will." She stretched up and planted a kiss on Gus' cheek.

That made him straighten up his back, he looked like he gained two inches in height, his face a shade of crimson. He finally let go of her hand and she led us down the hallway leading into the kitchen and dining area.

"Would you gentlemen like a glass of wine or a beer?"

"Beer please." Gus and I answering at the same time.

"Okay, I'll get it just go into the study and I'll be in

with the drinks. Go down the hall and take a right."

Gus and I went into the study. There was a desk on the far side, with a computer center and fax machine. The walls were covered in oak a small bookshelf on one wall full of law books and different reading material. Some wildlife paintings and Native American decorations covered the others. The furniture comprised of two Victorian style high back chairs upholstered in a dark green velvet with a matching sofa, two cherry wood end tables with wooden lamps placed on them. I was standing next to Gus and leaned over and gave him a light elbow to the ribs.

"What do you think you are doing, you old hound?"

"What are you talking about?"

"I saw you putting on the charm."

"I was just being polite, I thought that's what you wanted me to do?"

"Yah well behave you old Casanova, besides you told me she was dangerous."

"She is, a woman who looks like that, could make a man do dangerous things. Hell, she is fine enough to make a dog break his chain."

"Gus enough, with the insight." I lightened up some after Gus' last observation.

Jessica came into the room carrying the drinks on a tray.

"Here you go, now please sit down I have something I want to show you."

Motioning with her hand to the two chairs, passing in front of Gus and giving him a little wink with those beautiful ice blue eyes. Gus was grinning as she glided across the room stepping behind her desk, she sat the glass of wine down and began typing on the computer.

Gus and I slid the chairs closer so we could see when she turned the monitor towards us. I gave him a knock that shit off look as he sat down, he returned the innocent, what do you mean one back.

"This wine is wonderful Gus. Someone in Baraga owns the conglomerate that we found the other day. I went into the file that Dalton and I had looked at in my office. I made a copy of it and did some digging while I was in Chicago. I took my lap top and did it when I was in my room at night, all there was to do was work no pleasure." She said giving me a wink, which made Gus grin and look at me. She started to point out something on the screen turning it so Gus and I could see.

"It says here that the controlling shareholders live in Baraga. They have multiple interests in several other companies. See here?" she began to scroll down the page and pointed them out to us. They have holdings in Canada, Mexico, and the Cayman Islands also." Gus interrupted

"These the same people who are backing the land consortium that was after Dalton's property?"

"Yes, that's right, they were formed in 1995 and sold shares to power brokers, then slowly bought them off. The family here in Baraga owns sixty percent of the stock. "

"Gus do you know anyone that rich around here?"

"No Dalton, but that doesn't mean there isn't someone."

"There could be, we just have to find out." Jessica offered. "They are hiding it well. The holdings in other countries are probably for tax purposes."

"Why do you say that miss Jessica?"

"The holding in the Caymans is usually there for

a reason, it is one places where the banks almost out-number the other buildings. It has the most banks per capita than anywhere else on earth. The people hide their money in them so the IRS doesn't find it and tax them on it."

"But how do they get it down there?"

"They run it through a business or dummy corpora-tion, show that they didn't turn a profit or regain the dividends when in fact they skimmed it off the top and wire it to the Caymans. Once it is down there it pro-tected. The IRS will do an audit but if they have a good bookkeeping system, they won't catch it for a long time and before they do, they company files bankruptcy and it becomes a wash. The IRS ends up with a company that isn't worth anything."

"Did you say1995, Gus isn't that when the first fires started?"

"Yah, I think so isn't that what the photographer said yesterday?"

"What photographer?"

"The one Gus and I visited yesterday; he works for the newspaper. We were looking at your late husband's case report."

"But he died in 96?"

"I know but the fires started in 95, so Gus and I thought we could figure out if they were somehow related to the department store fire if I could get my hands on some better pictures. Then Gus showed me some old newspaper clippings he had and the name of the photographer is always in the sidebar of the pic-ture, so we went to the paper yesterday and he is mak-ing us copies of everything he took of the fire scenes."

"Dalton what are you thinking?"

"I'm not sure yet, but doesn't it seem strange that a conglomerate that you found started business at or around the same time the fires occurred? You also told me one time that he had holdings in the Cayman Islands."

"Yes, I did but so what?" she answered slightly annoyed by the memory.

"But they never found the insurance guy either." Gus said.

"Yes, that's right, what was his name." She was looking up at the ceiling trying to remember. "Oh, hell I can't remember, it will come to me. Excuse me gentlemen, I have to check on dinner."

Gus stood up when she did as she left the room. She gave him a smile to show his gentlemen's politeness hadn't gone unnoticed. We both turned and watched here exit the room.

"Damn Dalton that is one fine looking woman and she is smart as hell too. You better hang on to that one."

"I'll have to agree with you, old man. Do you think we should tell her about the princess?"

"Not just yet Dalton, it may upset here let's wait until after dinner."

Jessica came to the doorway of the study; neither of us heard here coming and we both looked at each other guiltily.

"You boys talking about me? She said making a face. Then in a sultry voice, she said, dinner is served. Turning on her heels she went back towards the kitchen leaving Gus and I standing there with our mouths hanging open. You could hear her giggling as she walked down the hall. I started to follow and Gus just stood there his wide-eyed with his mouth hanging open.

"Come on Gus put your tongue back in, it's time to eat."

We followed her into the dining room as she directed us where we were to sit.

The table was set in a country look with family style serving dishes. The main course, grilled ribs with corn on the cob, a vegetable tray, several types of salads, Jell-O, pasta and tossed. The drinks consisted of the wine Gus had brought, beer, and iced tea. The dinner looked fabulous, as did the hostess.

"Okay you guys dig in, before the food gets cold. I was planning serving this outside, but the weather is getting nasty, my patio table tipped over from the wind."

Jessica was still standing; Gus stood up and gestured for her to sit as he slid her chair in for her. Then he returned to his seat.

"Ladies first I insist." Gus said

"Why thank you, Gus you are quite the gentleman."

I took the comment to be a slight for me not getting up to get her chair and Gus made a mental note which I was able to decipher from the grin on his face.

Gus was having a good time, lots of fine food and conversation with a beautiful woman. If things kept going, I would never get him out of here he would want to come over to Jessica's house every week.

We finished eating and Jessica suggested we take our dessert into the study where she would bring in some coffee to finish the evening.

"I think we should go into the study for dessert. Dalton takes this tray of cake in and I'll bring in some coffee. I have some more questions to ask you about the fires and I can tell that you have something to tell me."

"How did she know that we had something to tell

her Dalton?" Gus asked me as we entered the study.

"I don't know but women have that extra sense about them. I want to wait until she gets comfortable, then we can tell her, okay?"

Jessica came in carrying a tray with a small coffee cache and three cups. Gus turned down the coffee, deciding that beer went with chocolate cake. Gus took the chair and I sat on the couch next to Jessica.

"Well did you two gentlemen enjoy your dinner?"

We both answered her with enthusiastic yeses.

"Jessica what did you want to ask us about the fires?"

"I think you two have something to tell me that is more important, so why don't you go first."

Gus gave me a reassuring nod and I took Jessica's hand before I began to speak.

"Jessica, we have something to tell you but I'm not real sure if it is going to upset you or not so bear with us if we sound foolish."

"Okay Dalton, go ahead." Her lovely blue eyes looking directly into mine for answers to what I was about to tell her.

"You know Gus and I would never hurt you right?"

"Yes, I know, now quit beating about the bush and spit it out."

"Okay, to make a long story short Gus and I think we found the Indian princess."

"The Indian princess?" she looked at me with a puzzled expression.

"Your ancestor, the one you made the offering to the other day out on the bluff above the cliff. We think we found her and we thought we should tell you because you looked so distressed when you were there."

"Oh Dalton! That's great news, but how did you find her and why do you think it is her?"

"I'm glad you are happy." Gus and I let out a sigh of relief.

"The other day when you and I were out there we walked down to the canyon floor." she was nodding her head in recognition. We walked through the canyon and you were picking up the flowers. I was looking at the face of the cliff and noticed a small crevasse about thirty to forty feet from the top edge. Then I got to thinking about how the flowers had floated up in the air when you tossed them over the side."

"I don't quite understand what you are getting at Dalton?"

"I had a dream about you the other night and that is when it came to me."

"Oh, you did?" she said raising her one eyebrow with a slight smile on her face. Which caused Gus' face to blush a little.

"No not that kind of dream, well maybe but this one was different, anyway getting back to the story. You were standing on the top edged of the cliff, dressed in this killer white buckskin dress. I began to walk up to you and you just smiled and stepped off the edge, but you didn't fall you floated up and then gently stepped back onto the ground, much the same as the flowers did when you tossed them."

"So that's how you know where the princess is, I still don't see how you know?"

"The updraft in the canyon is what makes the flowers float and I figured if the wind was strong enough the day, she jumped that she may have landed on that small ledge, so Gus and I went out there and did some exploring, I was able to lowered myself down to the ledge and the small crevice I could see from the ground is actually a cave. I was able to wriggle my way in and I found a skeleton a very old skeleton. The hands were clutching a small golden cross and there are some small black stone beads laying around it, I figured it might be a rosary like the catholic church uses for praying."

Jessica was still bewildered, but delighted to hear the news. "Why were you so reluctant to tell me this?"

"Because I thought it might upset you, the other day you seemed so sullen I didn't know how you would take the news."

"I wasn't sullen, I was listening to her scream that is why I told you that I'm cursed. When I go out there, I can hear her pain and I don't know what to do for her."

Gus became interested now and leaned closer towards her. "Did you say here her scream, and did I hear something about a curse, Miss Jessica?"

"Yes, that's right, remember Dalton when I told you that anyone in my family with blue eyes is cursed and is supposed to be the caretaker, that's why because we can hear her screaming."

"You didn't tell me, you could hear her, why do you think your family is able to hear her?"

"Because she didn't receive the proper burial ceremony. My people believe that when someone dies, a ceremony has to be given so the Great Spirit can accept the soul of the deceased. Now that, you may have found her I can perform the ceremony and she will be able to rest peacefully. This is really great news. When do you think I can see her?"

Gus looked at her with some apprehension.

"Well, Miss Jessica I don't know, that might be a problem."

"What kind of problem, Gus?"

"You have to slide down a rope like a big spider and then you have to go into a cave full of bats, then I have to pull you up. I don't know if that's such a good idea."

"I'm sure Dalton could show me how to slide down the rope, as far as the bat's go, I'm not to skittish of them." She got up from the couch and knelt down next to the chair where Gus was seated, her facial expression couldn't have been more pitiful. The large eyes took on a look of grief, while her bottom lip protruded out into a slight pout. She took one of Gus's big hands into both of hers.

"Oh, Gus please? I'm sure you could pull me up."

He folded before the second word was out of her mouth.

"Yah, I'll do it but just once and I want you to know I'm going to be really nervous. I don't want anything to happen to you, so Dalton you better make sure you know what you are doing with that rope."

"Oh, thank you Gus." She stood up and gave Gus a kiss on the forehead leaving a lipstick mark. He about had a seizure.

"When can go see her Dalton, tomorrow?"

"I don't know about tomorrow, the weather has to change, before we go hanging over the edge of a cliff. The updrafts in that canyon are pretty strong; if we aren't careful, we could get slammed into the rocks face first."

"You two guys talk it over; I'm going to go get Gus another beer."

Jessica left the room and I started to laugh at Gus sitting there with a big lip mark on his forehead and his mouth hanging open.

"What the hell you laughing at?"

"You, your mouth hasn't closed since she gave you that kiss and there is a big red lip imprint on your forehead."

"Oh." He said wiping his head with his shirtsleeve.

"What do you think Dalton, do we have time to do it tomorrow or are you going to have to give her some rope training?"

"I don't know, we can ask her if she knows anything about repelling."

Just then Jessica returned with Gus' beer handing it to him and then returning to her spot next to me on the couch.

"Did you two decide yet?"

"I think we can go tomorrow if the weather breaks and only if you have every repelled down a rope, if not I'm going to have to teach you some techniques. Have you ever climbed before, I'm mean mountain climb or repelled on a rope?"

"Not mountain climbing, but my one brother and I used to go ice climbing up by Big Bay. We would use ice axes and climb up maybe fifty feet and then let ourselves slid down the rope after we reached the top."

"Good that should work, how long ago did you do this?"

"Maybe five years ago, but I think I should be able to remember how to do it. You can give me a quick study program when we get out there tomorrow."

"If we go tomorrow, good then first thing in the morning we can drive up to Houghton and get you some gear at the sports shop."

Gus and I stayed until around eleven O-clock. Gus was telling stories of the old days when he used to work in the logging camps and Jessica and I were getting a chuckle out of them.

"Jessica, I think it's time we left, I have to drive Gus home yet and we should be on the road tomorrow by nine. The sports shop closes at noon."

Gus and I got up simultaneously and Jessica showed us out getting Gus's coat out of the closet by the door and holding on to mine while Gus went out the door.

"Come here Dalton, and get your coat."

I encircled her with my arms and she gave me a long passionate kiss.'

"Thanks for the wonderful evening Jessica I wish I could stay."

"There will be other nights, thanks for telling me about the princess. I'll see you tomorrow now go take that sweet old man home before he falls asleep in the driveway."

"Okay I'll see you in the morning good night."

Jessica opened the door and waved to Gus who was seated in the Yukon waving back at her while she stood in the door opening.

"Are you ready to get going? The wind is blowing something terrible and I think it might rain."

"Yes, I'm ready Gus, so how did you like Jessica?"

"I tell you what Dalton I can't remember when I ever seen a woman that was that beautiful and she can cook too."

"Yah I know, she's smart as hell too."

"That voice she does, sort of a bedroom whisper my god I thought I was going to pass out."

"I noticed; your mouth was hanging open like some degenerate." I laughed as I kidded him.

"Talk smart wiseass, you better hang on to that one or old Gus might sneak over and sweet talk her."

"I'll be careful, I thought you said she was dangerous?"

"She is, a woman that looks that good could make a man do bad things. Now shut up and let me sleep, wake me up when we get to my house."

Old Gus leaned toward his door and tilted his head forward with his eyes closed. The heater in the Yukon was on full blast and it wasn't long and I could hear a slight snore coming from him. The dinner had been a success and I think Gus was impressed with Jessica. I drove to Gus' dodging small tree limbs that had been knocked down by the wind that was becoming stronger. The rain was now blowing sideways across the road and I kept my speed down. The visibility was a mere fifty feet and sometimes less. When the lake decided to kick up a thunderstorm it did it with a vengeance. The usual fifteen-minute drive to Gus' took thirty on account of the storm. I wasn't looking forward to driving back to my place, but I decided Gus shouldn't drive his truck home. He slept through the whole trip to his house and when I pulled into his driveway, I had to wake him.

"Gus get up, your home."

"Home? Why did you bring me home? My truck is at your place."

"Yah, I know. I didn't want you driving home in this storm, you seemed pretty tired, and you can get your truck tomorrow."

"Sounds good to me, see yah tomorrow Dalton thank you."

"Gus, do you want to go to Houghton with me and Jessica in the morning?"

"No thanks, Dalton this old man is going to sleep in. I'll see you tomorrow."

"Okay Gus, I'll be by around noon or shortly after. Oh, one more thing, do you have any more of that wine you gave Jessica tonight. I would like to buy some from you. I want to have some; you know for when the time is right."

"I'll check, can't promise anything ask me tomorrow."

I stayed in the drive until Gus made it up to his house. The drive back to the cabin was uneventful; I had to steer around a few downed trees, the visibility was getting worse just as I pulled into my parking space by the rental.

CHAPTER TWELVE

I was at Jessica's by nine sharp remembering what Gus had told me about being late for a date with a woman. I went up and knocked on the door. A voice from within said "Come in Dalton." She was standing in the hallway wearing jeans and hiking boots, with only a sports bra on the top half.

"I'm not quite ready come in and have a seat in the kitchen, I'll only be ten minutes."

Jessica was talking as she went down the hall towards her bedroom.

"That's fine, do you have any coffee?"

A voice from behind the bedroom door answered. "Yes, it's in the coffee maker there are some travel mugs in the cupboard to the left."

I negotiated my left and right and found the mugs filling two for the trip. Jessica returned from the bedroom with a flannel shirt on the tails tied around her waist. She had pulled her hair back and secured it into a large bun it back. She looked good even when she wasn't dressed up.

"Did you want a coffee too Jess? I didn't put any cream or sugar in it."

"That's okay I take mine black, now let's get going I'm excited today and I don't want to sit around."

"Yes dear, I'm on my way, we taking your truck or mine?"

"We can take yours; I'll get mine when we come back, and I have some ceremonial items in mine already."

Jessica and I drove north towards Houghton; the day was beginning to brighten as the sun came up farther. The storm had passed as quickly as it came, the few scatted branches on the roadway were being picked up by the highway workers, we had to wait in one area where a large White pine had been blown across the roadway and the crews were busy cutting it into blocks and pushing them out of the way with a front-end loader. The sports shop was open. I had to find a restroom and Jessica went right in looking for a salesman to help her get outfitted. It was a fully equipped store having everything from fishing and kayaking to hunting and mountain climbing gear, along with snow skiing and bicycling equipment. I imagined the college students frequented the place regularly. I came from the restroom to find Jessica being helped by a young man of around twenty. He had on a sweatshirt and khaki pants the shirt had the MTU logo on it and he was somewhat of a cocky looking sort. His hair spiked up into a razorsharp flattop, a small diamond stud earring in one ear, from the looks of his build he may have been on one of the college sports teams. Jessica was putting him to the test, at first, he started out with, I know what you want attitude, which was him he thought but when she was thru with him, he was sweating and nervous. She was having fun with him, trying on different harnesses, then asking him to adjust her cheek straps, deciding if the fit was okay, after trying four different brands she went back to the one he had originally picked out for her. The poor kid would have to kneel down behind her and pull the straps that ran up between her legs and around the bottom curve of her butt cheeks.

"I, I, is that okay miss does it feel comfortable?"

The sweat was running off his forehead and Jessica was playing him for a fool.

"Yes, I think that feels okay, it has a few pinch points but I think it will be alright. Now do you have a helmet with a light on it?"

"Yes, right over here, there are several styles I would recommend this one."

He took a helmet from the self and placed it on her head, reaching way out in front of him so he wouldn't get to close to her breast.

"I think the chin strap is out of adjustment, Chad could you fix it?"

The poor kid tried to extend his arms to reach for the strap adjustment just as he did Jessica stepped into him pressing her chest lightly against his. I had seen enough and made a motion with my hand for here to hurry things up. The helmet fit and Chad got, the proper hardware that we would be using for her to, repel down the cliff. He then carried all the gear up to the counter and I gave Jessica what the hell are you doing look as she stepped in front of me, but she wasn't done with poor Chad just yet.

"Chad could you tell me if you have any adjustable sports bras?

"No, I don't think so, I thought those only came in spandex, I usually don't work the undergarment area, but I could ask one of the girls to help you."

"No that's okay, I think we have enough."

I paid for the equipment and Jessica and I walked back out to the Yukon she never made a sound until we were inside putting on our seatbelts. Then she broke out laughing.

"Jessica what the hell was that little show in there for?"

"Why whatever do you mean sir?" in a perfect southern bell accent.

"What I mean is that you are cruel. Old Chad was a basket case by the time you walked out."

"Did it make you jealous?"

"No, not after I seen him walk over to where you were standing by the harnesses. He had his eye on you as soon as you entered the door. I was watching him before I found the rest room. You walked by and his chest puffed out he even ran his fingers thru his hair, before he came from behind the counter. I thought wrong move buddy that isn't some college coed, you are going to go down in flames."

"Yes, I felt his eyes on me, I figured he would try putting the college boy charm bull on me. I noticed he had that look at me swagger about him and I thought I might have some fun with him."

"Excuse me Chad do you have sports bras that adjust? I think my butt straps are too tight could you loosen them for me?" I was mocking here exchange I had witnessed.

"Every time he knelt down behind you his hands would start shaking and more beads of sweat would appear on his face."

"Oh, Dalton I wasn't that bad. It will give him something to brag about back at the dorm. By the end of the week, he'll be telling his roommates that he had me right on the sales counter."

"Yah, probably so, but right now he's probably looking for some ice and next week he'll get his ass kicked."

"Why do you think that Dalton?"

"Because the next time he reaches between some little coeds' legs to adjust the ass straps on a harness, her 260-pound linebacker boyfriend is going to pound the crap out of him. That's why."

She was snickering.

"What's so funny Jess?"

"The Chad's of the world, they think they are god's gift to women, but one acts like I did back there with confidence, their macho bullshit goes right out the window. No confidence just bullshit."

"Aren't we just the little analyst?" I said teasing her slightly.

"No not an analyst, just observant. I have seen my share of Chad's already. The law school was full of them. Young good looking and rich, thought they had the world in the palm of their hand, could get any girl they wanted to sleep with them if they just told them how good they were or how much money they had, but when a girl comes along with good looks and brains with the confidence to call their bluff they blubber and make fools of themselves just like old Chad did back there. And that Mr. James concludes your lesson for the day. Now when are we going to go see the princess?"

"As soon as I drop you off. You can meet Gus and I out at the canyon, and bring a spare set of clothes you'll want to change when we are done. I have to stop and pick him up on the way."

I drove over to Gus', finding him sitting on his porch, all excited and ready for the expedition.

"Hi Dalton, where is Jessica?"

"Hi Gus, jump in she is going to meet us out there."

"Hold on, I have to get my cooler and gloves.'

Gus retrieved his cooler and placed it in the back with the rest of the gear, and we were on our way.

"Why is Jessica going to meet us out there? I figured she would ride with us."

"I told her to drive because, we still have to go get your truck later and if she was feeling upset afterwards, I thought I might go over to her place and help her deal with it."

"Dalton, do you really think that the skeleton is the princess?"

"Yes, I think so, from the looks of the bone structure and the teeth. The way it is laying undisturbed, not including the small rosary or what might be a rosary. Yes, I think there is a good chance that it is her."

"What do you mean bone structure?"

"Well, the large bones of the skeleton are small in stature which would indicate female. The pelvic region looked to be fully developed and I noticed that there were signs of resent childbirth indicated on the pelvic floor. The teeth were the giveaway."

"The teeth, why do you say that?"

"The teeth are key indicators to an anthropologist, when they study indigenous people. The lack of decay is one sign. How many people have you ever known to not have a bad tooth? I would guess not many. The northern peoples of Alaska and the artic circle went for many years without bad teeth, until the white man introduced them to sugar. The native peoples used their teeth as tools for tanning hides holding objects and for eating and chewing tough meats and plants. The teeth of the skeleton showed signs of heavy wear in the front, and a lack of decay. My guess is that she used them for tanning buckskin which is a known fact that they chewed on it to soften the leather after tanning."

"Yes, I believe I read that some were. The lack of decay is something I never thought about. Hell, old George Washington had rotten teeth and just about everyone else in those days. Why would you think that she wouldn't?"

"Because George Washington had a sweet tooth and poor dental hygiene, that princess was dead before George became president and the natives of this area lacked the sugar in their diets, other than some Maple Sugar or syrup, and occasional hand full of berries or fruit and they were pretty much sugar free. I also read that they did practice some form of dental hygiene whether it was brushing with a stick or just picking out the stuff between them."

"Well, I'll be damn Dalton you seemed convinced that it is her. Too bad you couldn't get an autopsy done on her."

"Yes, it is, but I doubt Jessica or her people would allow that to happen."

"Did you ever ask her, what she thought of the idea?"

"No, but maybe I will if need be, there's Jessica's Lexus turning into the driveway just ahead of us. Now remember Gus don't go making any of your off-color remarks, please?"

"Not to worry my boy, old Gus has everything under control."

Jessica had pulled up to where the front of my soon to be garage was under construction and got out asking Derrick who was up working on the roof. "If it was in the way."

Derrick shook his head and said something I

couldn't hear from inside my Yukon. Jessica came walking up to the driver's door as I parked behind the Lexus.

"Hi Dalton are you ready to go?"

"Hi Jess, yah I'm ready, but first we have to go over to the edge of the cliff and see how much of an updraft there is today the wind is calm but that won't mean a lot if there is a thermal coming up from the floor."

Gus and I took their gear from the back of my Yukon, Jessica carried her harness and helmet while Gus and I brought the rest. I had decided to try and get to a point that was directly above the small ledge and the cave opening. I didn't want Jessica, to have to try and swing herself over like I had done the first time down. Gus was standing back front the edge, with mix feeling about being so close. I think he was afraid of falling. I thought I should keep him calm and gave him a task to do while I checked the updraft situation.

"Hey Gus would you mind uncoiling the ropes and checking them for frays, I'm going to check the updraft, Jessica can get her harness on. Gus if you want tie up to that Big Birch tree, when you're done checking the ropes and then I'll throw them over the side."

Gus went to his task as Jessica put her harness on, the edge of the cliff directly above the small ledge had an outcropping sticking out and I wasn't able to stand and look over the edge far enough to see the small ledge, but I think we were in the right spot. Gus would have to give Jessica hand get back up and over the out-cropping when she came up.

"Here you go Dalton the ropes look good and I have them tied off on the Birch tree. You think the updraft is okay for this?"

"Yes, I think we are all right. How does the harness fit Jessica?"

"I think it's okay, but would you take a look to make sure I have it secure enough."

I noticed some apprehension in her voice. I wondered now if this was such a good idea.

"Yes, you look secure and what about the gloves and helmet are they okay?"

"Yes, they seem to be, but you are going to give me a few lessons first, right?"

"Yep, as soon as I get my gear on."

I put my harness, gloves and helmet on. Made sure everything was secure, putting some rock anchors in a small fanny pack and hanging two on my belt we were ready for the first lesson. I explained to her how to lean out and slid down the rope and not to worry about falling because I would go do first and secure the line while Gus held the safety line that was hooked to her harness. He would be the one that control her decent. Then I would help her on to the ledge when she came down. Then once we were done inside the cave Gus would pull her back up. She felt comfortable with the plan and tried some different hand positions on the rope so she could use them like a brake. Once she was ready, I got into position and stepped backwards off the top of the cliff. Sliding down the rope as I looked for the ledge, my guess of where it would be was a bit off by four feet so I was able to swing over easily and step on to the ledge, I then anchored the rope and gave Gus a jerk on the safety line, that was the signal for jess to start down. She stepped back over the edge and slid down without a problem smoothly landing on the ledge with a big smile on her face.

"Hey that was pretty smooth Jess, are you sure you haven't done this much?"

"It's been a while but I guess it's like riding a bike once you learn you never forget."

"Now when you get ready to go inside don't shine your light around a lot until you get back inside a bit the bats are just inside the entrance and if we don't scare them, they will probably stay put."

Jessica slid thru the opening easier than I had, I could hear her gasp a little when she came to the area with the bats. I tied the ropes off and wiggled my way into the cave opening, scrapping my back worse than I had the first time.

"Ouch that hurt! Jessica, are you in the back of the cave yet?"

"No not yet I have my light off, I'm off to the right from you."

"Go ahead turn your light on I'll be right behind you."

Jessica turned her helmet light on and duck walked in to the back of the cave I on the other hand crawled on my hands and knees. I entered the larger opening and Jessica helped me to my feet, she was able to stand up right I was slightly hunched over.

"Dalton, where is she?"

"Shine your light over to the left she is right along the back wall, be careful where you step, you will see her bones when the light hits them."

"Oh, Dalton I'm so nervous, I don't know if I can do this."

"You will be okay I'm right behind you, give me your hand."

We walked towards the back of the cave; my light

trained on the floor Jessica was looking at the walls.

"There she is Jess just like I found her, come over and have a look, see where the gold cross is and the little black beads, do you think it was a rosary."

The look of joy on Jessica's face was worth it all.

"OH! Dalton, I think you found her, see the little blue beads by her collar bones, they use to wear them on their garments for decorations."

"Yes, I see them I wondered what they were, are you going to perform the ceremony now?"

"Yes, I have all of my stuff in this fanny pack, but I have to do it alone."

"That's okay I'll just go over on the far side and give you some privacy."

"Okay, and thank you for finding her."

She gave me a kiss on the cheek and when she did, I noticed a small tear roll down her cheek. I went over to the far side of the cave trying to give her as much privacy as I could in such a small space. I was facing the wall and looking at the layers of rock when my light beam caught something odd sticking out from the rock about one foot from the floor.

"What the heck is that?" I began to move slowly towards it trying to figure out what I was looking at. It looked like a shoe, but how could a shoe get in here. I snuck a peek over to where Jessica was and she was performing the ceremony so I didn't want to interrupt her, but I would have liked a second opinion on what it was I was looking at.

I went to where the object was and to my surprise it was a shoe, the bottom of a shoe, and connected to it was a skeletal leg bone that led into a crevasse in to the rock wall. I knelt down and tried to look into the crevasse, the other shoe came into view and there were bits of clothing hooked to the bones, something like polyester, pants? Why would there be polyester pants on a skeleton inside a cave that contained the remains of a three-hundred-year-old Native American? I bent over the shoe that was sticking up and tried to slid my hand done the leg bone, I could feel the back pocket of the pants and there was something inside the right one, but I couldn't get it out my hand was too large to manipulate my fingers in the cramped space, man what I wouldn't give for smaller hands right now. I tried a different angle and still couldn't get into the pocket. My concentration was on my hand, I hadn't noticed that Jessica had come over she laid her hand on my shoulder and my heart stopped for an instant just before I let out a scream.

"OH SHIT!"

"Oh, I'm sorry Dalton, what are you doing with your hand down in the rocks?"

"I'm trying to get something out of this pants pocket."

"Pants pocket, what are you talking about?"

I stepped back from the shoe sticking up show Jessica could see.

"Dalton, is that another body, where did it come from and who is it?"

"Yes, it is, and I don't know, that's what I was trying to figure out, just before you scared the crap out of me, there's something in the back pocket of those pants but I can't get my hand down there and get the thing out, my hand is too big."

"Do you want me to give it a try?"

"Yes, if you wouldn't mind, or I can bring something

in here and try and pull the body up, but I'm afraid if I do that it might fall down farther, I don't know the depth of the crevasse."

"I'll try Dalton, but you have to hang onto my waist I don't want to fall in there with the body."

Jessica leaned over the leg sticking up and had her head resting against the side of it, stretching with her arm down into the hole, with a look of disgust on her face.

"Ah yuck this is really gross; I can feel it can you pick me up some I think I can reach it if you help me kind of stand on my head."

I lifted her by the climb harness and she wiggled down into the opening some more now her shoulder was completely inside the crevasse.

"Pull me up, I have it in my hand but I can't push myself back out."

I pulled her up and held her there until she recovered her balance.

"You got it, good job, what is it?"

"It's a wallet, let's see who it belongs to."

"No wait, put it in my fanny pack, I don't want to run the risk of damaging it before we can see better, we'll open it up at your house. When we get back up to where Gus is don't mention anything to him, Okay?"

"Okay, but why?"

"I'll explain later, are you all through with the ceremony?"

"Yes, all through."

"Then let's get out of here, remember don't say anything."

Jessica and I exited the cave, once we were outside, I hooked up to the rope and then hooked Jessica onto hers, I gave Gus the jerk signal and he pulled me up. I figured if I tied Jessica on then Gus and I could pull her up with ease once I was on top.

"Hey Dalton, how did it go was she happy?"

"Yes, all set, let me get unhooked and then we can pull Jessica up."

Jessica hung on and when she got to the out cropping, she leaned way back and walked herself up and over the top with Gus and me holding tension on her rope.

"Nice job on the climbing Jess."

"Thank you Dalton I think I could do some more if you want to go sometime."

"Sounds good, let's stow are gear and then we can change clothes in the garage."

"Well Miss Jessica was it the princess?" Gus was asking Jessica as he held the back of the Yukon open.

"Yes, she can rest easy now I performed the ceremony, thank you Gus." She leaned over and gave him a kiss on the cheek.

"Oh, you are welcome, but there is one more thing."

"What Gus?"

"For such a pretty lady you smell a lot like bat crap."

We all cracked up at Gus' remark and that was Jessica queue to go change. I grabbed my change of clothes and handed Jessica her bag from the back of the Lexus.

"I thought we could change in the garage, but I hadn't noticed the door wasn't on yet, let's go into the house."

I led the way in, Derrick had most of the rough in done the windows and doors were on but the interior was still in a shamble. I told her to go into the soon to be laundry room. I waited for her and then I went in. Jessica and Gus were standing by the back end of my Yukon when I came out, they were laughing and Jessica gave Gus a light hearted slap on the shoulder.

"Gus you are terrible, Oh hi Dalton, would you like a beer? Gus has some in his cooler."

"Yah sure, what's so funny?"

"Oh, nothing Gus was just telling me a joke, this is going to be a nice place when Derrick is finished."

"Yes, I'm looking forward to it, that little cabin I'm staying in is starting to cramp my style."

Gus had already loaded all of the gear into my Yukon and Jessica had put the dirty clothes into her Lexus.

"Well Miss Jessica you seem to smell better, would you like another beer?"

"No thank you Gus, I think we better get going I have some paper work waiting for me at home."

"Gus you heard the lady let's roll."

"I tell you what Dalton why don't you go with Jessica and I'll just drop your truck off and pick mine up at your place?"

"Sounds good to me, as long as Jess don't mind."

"Yes, that's fine, I kind of wanted to talk to you alone anyway."

Gus took my Yukon and Jessica and I went to her place.

"You sure you don't mind me coming over?"

"No not at all I was hoping that you would I missed you and besides I want to see what's in that wallet we found on the dead guy in the cave."

"Yah I feel a little crappy for not telling Gus, but I think it would be best if he didn't know anything right now, at least not until we find out who it is, he would be asking questions a mile a minute."

"We can tell him soon enough, by the way thanks again for finding her, I feel a lot better now that I know she is finally resting after Hundreds of years."

We pulled up to Jessica's she hit the automatic garage door opener and drove in hitting the button and closing it behind us.

"I'll unload the clothes and put them in the washer, go in I'll be in a minute, there's a beer in the fridge if you want one."

I went in and took the wallet from my fanny pack placing it on the kitchen counter then went and got out two beers from the fridge. I sat down at the bar placing two clean paper towels down on the counter and then the wallet. Jessica came in and stood behind me looking over my shoulder.

"What are you doing Dalton?"

"I'm getting ready to look into this wallet."

"Look what I found in the Lexus underneath the clothes in the back."

Jessica was holding up a wine bottle.

"Gus must have put it in there, he's such an old romantic, and would you like a glass?"

"Yah sure I haven't opened my beer."

Jessica took two stemmed glasses from the china cabinet that was suspended above the counter opening the old wine she was reading the label.

"I think this one is older than the one he brought last night; I wonder where he gets them from?"

"He has a wine cellar in his basement, something about his grandma or mother used to drink the stuff."

"Here you go, oh it has a wonderful smell."

Jessica handed me a glass and raised hers in a toast."

"Here's to the Indian Princess, may she rest in peace."

"Hmm this is good Dalton, what are you doing?"

"I'm going to try and open this wallet but I'm afraid I might damage the contents. Do you have a sharp knife maybe I can dissect it by cutting off the outer layer of leather, I'm afraid that it will crack if I try to pry it open?"

"Yes, I have a filleting knife will that work?"

"Yes, that should work, this is good wine, and I wonder how much of the stuff the old boy has in his stash?"

Jessica brought me the knife its long slender blade was razor sharp I began to carefully cut the stitching that held the two pieces of leather together.

"What are the chances that there is something inside Dalton?"

"I don't know but I think this is working, we may have to put some water on it in places to soften up the spots where the body fluids have dried things together."

I was working delicately, trying not to cut anything but string, when the knife slipped and cut a two-inch gash in my left hand.

"Ouch damn that hurt."

"Oh, Dalton what did you do, come with me I have some first aid stuff in my bathroom."

Jessica grabbed me by the elbow and led me into the bathroom that was off the side of her bedroom, I was holding onto my cut hand trying not to get blood on the floor.

"So, this is the bedroom of Miss Jessica Whitehorse I been wanting to get in here since I met you." I said looking around the room.

"Yah well you seen it now get in the bathroom before

you get blood on my rug."

The room had a king-size bed made of maple with matching dresser and headboard a large beau rough stood against one wall, the two large doors next to it must have been for a walk-in closet. The dresser had a large mirror fastened on the top and in one corner was an overstuffed chair with a brass-stemmed lamp for reading.

She pushed the bathroom door open with her hip and it was almost as big as the bedroom. There was a double vanity sink, which she led me to, and turned on the water, the two people sit down shower looked inviting. I could still smell a slight bit of bat droppings. In the corner was a two-person garden tub with Jacuzzi style jets, a full-length mirror was fastened to the wall above the sinks and a tall one fastened to the back of the door.

"This is a very lovely bathroom it looks like you could spend some a lot of time in here, you have it fixed up very nice." I said complimenting her on her choice of décor.

"Thank you, I do a lot of meditating in that big tub over there."

Jessica had a small first aid kit in her medicine cabinet and she cleaned and dressed my cut hand. Her first aid skills were pretty good.

"There you are Mr. James all fixed, but you may want to go to the clinic tomorrow and have a doctor look at it, just to make sure you don't get an infection."

"Very nice job Dr. Whitehorse I'm impressed."

"I think I could use a bath; Gus was right I still smell like bat poop."

"Okay I'll go out and see if I can get the wallet open."

"I think you could use a bath yourself; you stink too." She said pinching her nose with her fingers.

"I would like to, but I don't have any cleaner clothes with me."

"I have a robe you can wear or just wrap yourself in a towel. I have your other clothes in the washer and they won't take long to dry, go ahead get in the shower."

"I don't know Jessica I'm not real comfortable about showing off my scarred back."

She stepped in close, looking into my eyes.

"Whatever they look like, won't matter or upset me Dalton James now get in the shower, you smell." She giggled as she walked over to the tub.

"Alright but you are going to have to get out of here, until I'm done."

I started to undress; she had started to fill here big tub with water before she exited. I turned on the shower and stepped under its soothing warmth. The moisture brought back the smell of the bats in to my nose. I had washed my hair and was soaping my chest when I thought I had the door open. My anxiety level went up the glass doors on the shower I wondered how much of me they would reveal.

"Jess is that you?"

"Who else would it be, I brought you a fresh towel and a robe they are hanging on the towel rack by the shower. I'm' going to get in the tub before the water gets too cold."

In the tub, how was I going to get out of the shower without her seeing me? I quickly scrubbed myself and waited standing under the stream of water. Thinking I had given her ample time to get in the bathtub. I didn't want to see her naked just yet and I sure as hell didn't want her to see me. I shut the water off and opened the glass door just enough to retrieve the towel. I dried myself standing in the shower stall and wrapped the towel around me before I got out.

"Are we a bit modest Dalton?" she was lying in the tub with just her head above the water, she had brought in the bottle of wine and was sipping some from her glass. The sweet smell of jasmine coming from her bath water filled the air. I turned around quickly so I was facing her.

"Yes, we are and I'm still not convinced this was a good idea."

"How is your back?" she asked looking at me with her eyes half closed taking in the relaxation of her warm scented bath.

"My back, what do you mean?"

"Your back where you scrapped it crawling into the cave today. I noticed some blood on your shirt when I put them in the washer."

"Oh, that's what you meant. I think it's okay."

"Maybe I should put something on it for you. You don't want to get an infection in the scar tissue."

"I think it will be fine, now enjoy your bath I'm going into the other room."

"Not so fast, I think I should take a look." She said gracefully standing up in the tub. The water and small streams of suds sliding down her sensuous body a vision of pure sexuality. The water giving her tan skin a darker hue, her long black hair flowed down her back and front concealing her nipples, a small black diamond of soft hair below her flat stomach. My god she was a goddess, stepping out of the tub the vertical lines of muscle s moved in her tone thighs, not at all ashamed of her nakedness, bending down and taking a towel from the small stand next to the tub, letting her hair fall forward she wrapped it into the towel and tied it on top of her head, her ample breast lifting when she reached up, dark pink nipples hard and protruding from the air, she slid into a terry cloth robe. I was shaking, aching with desire, my towel unable to conceal my thoughts. She looked at me with comforting eyes, moving closer then stepping behind me where I stood frozen in place waiting for a gasp of horror to come from here mouth.

"Relax Dalton I won't hurt you I would never do that."

I could feel her breath on my neck, she began to kiss me there and on top of my scarred shoulders moving her soft delicate fingers over my back, kissing and caressing my scars, following the ugly lines the fire had caused. Moving her full pouting lips over my neck she began kissing me more warmly her tongue lightly touching my ear, whispering softly "it's okay." The robe she had on was gone her cool wet breast now pressing against my back as she reached around my waist removing the towel that had tried to conceal me. My knees were shaking and I wanted to bolt but I just stood there frozen, thinking I would burst from desire. I wanted her more than anything I had wanted before. Her long soft finger beginning to tease me I could feel her breath on my neck becoming hotter as she moaned softly. Stepping in front of me she led me to the bedroom, removing the towel from her hair she lay on the bed her long black hair fanned out above her on the blankets. Our bodies molding together perfectly, my body pressing down on her as she lifted her hips to accept me. The look of passion in her half open eyes softly moaning as I entered her the rhythm intensifying until release then rolling on to the bed. I noticed the small beads of perspiration that had developed on her skin as her chest softly rose trying to recover her breathing rhythm. Our first sexual encounter had been quick as most are with new found lovers I had hoped that there would be more, as I lay beside her holding her and watching her as she lay still almost asleep. This was someone I could definitely fall in love with. We had laid together for the rest of the night, she had awoken once in the night and covered us I hadn't even noticed. The last words she spoke before falling to sleep were "Dalton I love you, was it everything you had expected?" before I could respond she was sleeping.

The next morning Jessica was up before me and evidently, she had been up for a while. The door of the bedroom open and she came in walking with some authority and purpose in her step; she came to the edge of the bed holding a bundle of clothes in her arms. Placing them on the overstuffed chair she walked over and pulled the blankets off me exposing my naked body.

"Come on sleepy head get up its nine in the morning, I brought your clothes in and breakfast is waiting."

"Okay, okay, I'm moving, but what's the hurry?"

"I want to know who that wallet belongs to, so get up and get showered, I'll have a coffee waiting for you when you are done. Now hop to it." She reached over and slapped my bare backside.

"Ouch! You sure are bossy in the morning, but you look good."

"Thank you."

I got up with a bit more grumbling, showered and

dressed. Entering the kitchen Jessica had made a light breakfast of Bagels and fresh fruit coffee and juice. We eat out on the back deck listening to the birds fight over their morning meals of bugs and seeds.

The sun was making an appearance and it appeared to be a full showing today, with a cloudless sky and a soft wind from the west. The daytime temperature could reach seventy-five or eighty which suited me fine I didn't care for the high humidity we had been burdened with in the previous weeks, after breakfast we went back inside the kitchen to try and solve the mystery of who the wallet had belonged to.

"Dalton do you want a different knife, I have some smaller ones in the drawer to the left of the sink. I'll go get a white towel to put on the counter so you can see if anything falls out of the wallet while you work on it."

"Okay let's put it on the table I think the light is better and I can sit more comfortably."

I tried the shorter knives and was making some head way. Jessica was leaning over my shoulder watching as I worked.

"Are you getting it Dalton?"

"Yes just a few more stitches and I think I'll have it. There we go that's the top layer, now let's see what's inside." Jessica hurriedly sat down in the chair next to me as I inspected the contents of the wallet.

"Oh, the curiosity is killing me." She squeaked.

"Let's see, two twenty-dollar bills three fives and some ones, well he wasn't robbed. Some pictures that you can't see all stuck together, two credit cards and a driver's license."

"Who is it Dalton can you tell?"

"I can't see the picture really well but the name is?"

I was squinting trying to make out the letters thru the dried body fluids. "Clifford Adams is what it says, same as the credit cards, but I can't make out the pictures." I raised my head up to look at Jessica and her face had an expression of shock and bewilderment.

"Did you know him Jess?"

"Yes, I knew him, he was the insurance adjustor who was running the scams with my late husband. I couldn't remember his name until you just said it. I thought he disappeared; left the country they found his car at the airport in Marquette." She was trying to reason things out in her mind. Everybody assumed he had killed my husband, took the money and split."

"Jessica I can't make out the picture on this license, do you think we can pull something up on your computer?"

"Like what why do you need a picture?"

"Because I want to make sure this is the right Clifford Adams, before we call the authorities, we can use his driver's license number and maybe we can get a match with a picture."

"Let's go check." She headed down the hall and into the study taking her seat behind the desk she started hammering on the keyboard typing in a web address.

"Give me the driver's license and the credit cards Dalton."

She pulled up several State of Michigan sights and found that she wasn't able to retrieve anything with a picture.

"Any luck Jess?"

"No not yet, everything keeps coming up deceased or missing, nothing with a picture."

"When you bring up the death certificates do, they

have a social security number with them?"

"Yes, some of them do, why?"

"Give them to me and I'll write them down, I have an idea that the F B I may have something on file about this Clifford Adams. They should have a picture of him if he's missing or wanted."

Jessica dialed up a new server and punched in the F B I most wanted and the Missing Person's Division. The computer clicked and hummed the website came up with pop-up windows and boxes giving directions on where to go in their Data base to find what you were looking for. Jessica clicked onto the missing person's icon and nothing came back other than a description of a Clifford Adams, next she tried the Most Wanted catalog and got a hit off the driver's license number, she scrolled down and clicked on the little camera icon and a picture began to form on the screen the pixels filling in the frame. Jessica was watching with anticipation staring into the screen. The general description of a white male, blonde hair, blue eyes, height, and approximate weight, date gone missing and charges pending, followed by a picture that looked very much like a license photograph. Jessica sucked in a loud gasp. That's him, that's Clifford Adams! That's the guy who my husband was doing the scam with."

"Is there any other information about him, was he married, did he have any children?"

"I don't know you take a look."

Jessica got up from her place behind the desk and moved to the other side, pacing back and forth rubbing her forehead, trying to overcome the shock of finally finding out what had happened to her husband's former business partner.

"I can't believe this, but who killed him and who killed Mitch?"

"Who is Mitch?"

"My late husband. I guess I never told you his name."

"No, but I never asked either. It says here that he had a wife and one child a boy, but it doesn't say where they live or had lived, at least not and address."

"Dalton what are we going to do?" She asked trying to figure out our next move.

"I think we better call the FBI and ask some questions first, before we give them the whereabouts of Mr. Adams."

"Why don't you think we should just tell them, that we have found the body of Clifford Adams?"

"Well, we don't really know if it is him for sure, and I would like to ask some questions about where the family might be living. I want to tell the boy and the wife that we might have found him."

"Why do you want to do that?"

"Because I think it would be better if I could tell them how he was found. Would you want some FBI suit to tell you that your criminal dad was found rotted in a cave, after not seeing him for six years?"

"No not really, I can see your point."

I got on the phone and contacted the FBI field office in Michigan. I tried to ask them some questions on where I might be able to find the family of Clifford Adams. They responded by telling me that they wouldn't give out that information.

I was a bit disappointed in their response, but I went on to tell them of our discovery and that only three people knew about it. The third one was going to be Gus as soon as I would see him. They told me to keep a lid on the info and that they would have a couple of agents there by Wednesday at the earliest. I thanked them and hung up.

"They are going to send up a couple of agents by Wednesday, I guess we are supposing to just sit tight until they get here. That solves the mystery of what happened to Cliff Adams."

"No not really, in part yes, but what ever happened to the money?"

"Good question, maybe the FBI can answer that for us when they get here."

Jessica was still pacing, turning on her heels her face taking on a look of concern.

"Dalton what about the princess?"

"What about her?"

"My people aren't going to be very comfortable about a bunch of crime scene people poking around a sacred burial site."

"I see what you mean, I'll call the FBI back and explain to them that we have some concerns about the site and that you would appreciate it if they used some discretion, with the press and the recovery teams."

"Do you think they will go for it?"

"I don't know, but I can give it a try."

I called the FBI back and explained to them where exactly that Mr. Adams' body was and that the site also contained the sacred remains of a Native American princess.

"What did they say Dalton?"

"They didn't see a problem with it and that they had a team working a case in Wisconsin that would be here on Wednesday afternoon, complete discretion would be used, only the local law enforcement and the State Police would have to know."

"What do you want to do now, I don't think I can sit around here or my office all day. I'm to wound up."

"We could." The phone rang before I could give her my response, she answered and I could tell you it was on the other end before she handed me the phone.

"Hello Gus what can I do for you? Yah okay that's great, we can pick them up on the way, and do you need anything else? Okay we'll see you in a few, Bye."

"What did Gus want?"

"He said the photos are ready at the newspaper office, and he wanted us to bring them out, he said he is going to make some lunch and thought we could look at them together."

"Okay, then let's get going I'm going to call my secretary and tell her I won't be in to day."

Jessica called her secretary and I took the wallet and put it in a plastic bag along with the towels that had been underneath it while I had performed the dissection.

We went to the paper office and found that the photographer had come in on Sunday night and copied the photographs for me. He was leaving for Detroit, this afternoon and wouldn't be back until Friday. I thanked him for his effort and paid them for the copies.

Driving out to Gus' Jessica and I had tried to briefly look at the photos as I drove her Lexus, the photographer had done a nice job with the copies. The 8x10s were as clear as the smaller ones. He had even put them in order as the fires had occurred.

Gus was looking out the window of his kitchen as we pulled into the drive. The day was becoming bright and I wasn't looking forward to spending it inside, but Jessica had told me on the drive out that she wanted to know what I was trying to figure out by looking at the pictures. With that said I couldn't deny her and besides we still had to tell Gus about the body of Clifford Adams that we had found in the cave. I hadn't thought about how I would do that, somewhat relieved that Jessica had come along, he wouldn't dare make a fuss when she was near.

Gus held the door open for us as we entered his house.

"Hi, glad to see you Ms. Jessica, come in I have some lunch ready, hello Dalton, take the lady into the dining room I will bring in the food in a minute. We can look at the pictures in there."

"Okay Gus, come right this way Jessica." I led Jessica into the dining room she was complimenting Gus on his house and the woodwork that his relatives had done. I think she might have been trying to get another bottle of wine from the old boy, kissing him on the cheek when he greeted her at the door.

"You are terrible Jess." I whispered to her while Gus was in the kitchen preparing lunch.

"Terrible, what do you mean?" the look of innocence pasted on her face.

"If I didn't know any better, I would think you were trying to charm another bottle of wine out of him."

"I'm doing no such thing; I just like him and I'm showing my appreciation.

"Yah, whatever but I think I can see a bottle of wine in your near future."

"Please, sit down you two, lunch is served." Gus announced entering the room with a try stacked high with sandwiches and all the condiments, along with a large picture of something. We sat and began to eat or lunch. I wasn't sure what kind of meat was in the sandwich; Jessica beat me to the question.

"What are these made of Gus?"

"Venison, I hope you like them, do you want some iced tea?"

Gus poured her a glass and handed me the pitcher. I guess he didn't want to poor mine. He and Jessica were chit chatting and I was looking through the photos trying to sort the ones out that I thought might have something of interest for the fire investigation.

I had separated them into three piles, one with outside shots, one with inside shots, and the ones of the surrounding spectators and fire personnel at the fires. Jessica was asking Gus about the venison and how old the house was, laying on the charm as expected.

"Gus where did you get the venison from?"

"I shot it, last fall. My Father built the place him and my grandpa were the woodworkers."

"Oh no kidding, that's great it looks very nice." She said rolling those big gorgeous eyes and smiling.

"Would you like to take a look around?"

"I'd love too."

Gus and Jessica got up leaving me to my pile of photos and a half-eaten venison sandwich. She had taken Gus' arm when he offered it to her as they walked down the hall admiring the craftsmanship of over one hundred years. The basement tour would probably be last and I would bet a C note that she came back with a bottle of wine. Hell knowing how she could charm the old boy she might come back with the whole case. I chuckled at the thought and went back to examining

the photographs. Somewhere in them I believed was a
clue that would tie the fires with the department store
fire. I sat studying them not really knowing for how
long when I heard Jessica's laugh and Gus snickering as they came back into the dining room. She was
carrying two bottles of wine and she still had her arm
hooked through his, as she gave him a light slap on the
shoulder.

"Gus you are a scamp."

"I know that's why you like me." He said grinning with confidence. I think the old man was getting
younger just from being around her.

"I see you were able to find some wine to go with
your tour."

"Yes, I did, Gus has a wonderful place here and you
should see his wine cellar."

"I'm glad you enjoy the stuff, I can't stand to drink
it, so anytime you want some just let me know, but it
might cost you a dinner or two. Did you two enjoy the
one I gave you yesterday?"

"Yes, we did thank you Gus. Dalton did you figure
anything out by looking at the pictures?"

"Not really I have some questions. Why don't you
two join me and I'll explain what I am looking for, they
were separated in to the different fire scenes and I went
through them and separated them into what I thought
were the order of importance. The photographer has
a date and time imprinted on them of when they were
taken so we should be able to put them back according
to fire scenes."

We began looking at them passing them around
and asking each other about different aspects of whom
they knew and what was taking place in the photos.

Jessica pulled one out and looked at it. The picture was from the second fire and it was of the people standing around the scene spectators mostly with the fire trucks in the foreground.

"Here's one Dalton, take a look at the blonde headed guy in the background standing off to one side of the building. It just a profile shot but I think it is Clifford Adams."

I took the photograph and went to my briefcase that was sitting beside the old desk that Gus had let me use; taking out a magnifying glass I studied the picture more closely.

"I think you are right Jess, but what the heck is he doing there, they wouldn't see an insurance adjustor from down state at a fire scene up here. What are the odds of that? The other pictures of the second fire didn't have anything else to reveal as far as Clifford Adams went, but Gus had come across a couple of photos taken of the inside of one of the fires, basically an accident shot, the frame was of two firefighters as they worked a hose, but in the upper corner of the picture you could make out a circular burn pattern on the ceiling. I went to the desk again and brought back the photos of the department store fire I had taken and the old newspaper clipping Gus had shown me earlier. I compared the photos and there was a definite similarity in all of them. The one was the shot that appeared in the paper, the other was taken on a different side of the structure; it had been a shot of the fire crew doing a ventilation procedure on the gable end below the roofline. The photographer had incidentally got the ceiling in this one and it too showed the circular burn pattern.

"I think the one is the same as the newspaper clipping, but the other is from the other side of the building. The one from the department store has the same circle pattern as these do."

"What the hell are you and Jessica talking about? Who is Clifford Adams?"

"Have a seat Gus and I'll tell you all about it."

Jessica and I filled Gus in on the body we had found in the cave. He was a bit upset at first. Until Jessica explained to him that we didn't know who it was until this morning and that the FBI was contacted and is handling the recovery along with the press. We don't want a bunch of reporter or site seekers tramping around the place, we want to try and keep it quiet so don't tell anybody anything okay?

"Okay Dalton, but now that you found the guy where the hell is the money?"

"That is what Jessica, you and I are going to try and figure out, maybe the FBI can help us with some of the questions, but I still think there is a connection to everything."

"When are they coming, do you think that the old fire has something to do with the department store fire?"

"They are going to be here on Wednesday, and yes I think that somewhere we are going to find that this string of fires has a common link."

"I thought it was the same guy we were looking for Dalton, but now that you found old Cliffy, it can't be can it?"

"I don't think so but it has to be someone familiar with the old fires, a copycat I guess is what it's called, not the same person, just someone using the same technique."

"Then we have to find out who owns the department store."

"That's right Gus, Jessica didn't you say that you had a friend that worked at the county clerk's office?"

"Yes, but we will have to go back to my house I don't have her number with me."

"Okay then let's go to your house, you can drop Gus and I off at my place and I can pick up my Yukon."

Jessica, Gus and I were on our way to the rental cabin. Jessica was driving I took the passenger seat and Gus was in the back seat. Gus noticed a logging truck approaching us in the oncoming lane.

"Hey Dalton does that truck coming at us look familiar to you?"

"Yes, now that you mention it, the grill and bug deflector look really familiar. When it passes by us try to see what the name is on the side."

"I'll bet a dollar that's the same one that tried to kill us the other day."

"Okay here it comes."

"K B Wood Harvesting." Jessica blurted out loud.

"Yah, Dalton that's what I read too."

"I'll write the name down, when we get back to Jess' we can try to see who owns the company."

"Do you two really think they, were trying to run you off the road the other day, or were they merely playing around with you?"

"They weren't playing with us and I still have the bump on my head to prove it."

We arrived at my rental and I told Jessica to go on without us. I had a few things I wanted from the cabin and Gus was ready for a beer so I thought I would get some from the refrigerator. I told Gus to start the

Yukon, because he had hidden the keys the day before under the back bumper.

"I'll just be a minute Gus go ahead and start it up I have few things I want from the cabin."

I set my briefcase by the Yukon and walked up to the cabin. The door wasn't closed completely and the lock looked like it had been tampered with. Pushing the door open slowly, the reason for the broken lock became evident. Someone had broken in and trashed the place.

"Holy shit! Gus come over here." I yelled for him so he could hear me over the sound of the running engine.

"What is it Dalton?"

"Somebody trashed my place; they have everything turned upside down. The furniture the boxes of stuff I didn't get unpacked."

"What do you think they were looking for?"

"I don't know everything I have of value is locked up in the trailer."

"What do you want to do, call the police?"

"No, I think I'll wait until the FBI shows up on Wednesday. There isn't really too much I can do about it today. Let me get a few changes of clothes and a shaving kit together. Do you mind if I bunk with you for a couple of days?"

"No, not at all, whatever you want to do."

"Thanks Gus I'll get my stuff maybe you can get some tools out of the Yukon and see if you can fix that door so the caretaker won't notice, that it is broke."

"Okay Dalton, but first I'm grabbing a beer from the fridge."

Gus went to work on the door and I tried to find some clothes, searching through the mess that the intruders had made. I stuffed two changes into a duffle bag I found under the bed and grabbed my shaving kit from the bathroom. Gus was able to fix the door but it was going to open from the outside so we had to go out the door facing the lake on the front of the cabin. Tossing my bag and briefcase in to the Yukon we headed for Jessica's place.

"Who do you think broke into your place Dalton?"

"I don't know, but maybe we can find out something when we get to Jessica's, I still think that everything is connected somehow, but we just aren't seeing it."

"Yah, I'm starting to think that way too."

We pulled into Jessica's and parked by the garage doors. Gus got out and walked up and knocked on the door as I grabbed my briefcase from the backseat. Jessica answered, with a yell from inside for us to come in. we found her in the study staring into the computer screen on her desk.

"Hi guys come in and sit down. I just got off the phone with the clerk's office; she was able to give me the name of the department store owners. The name is of some local business group but they have a billing address somewhere else. I think if we bring up the list of businesses the conglomerate owns, we will probably find it listed along with the wood harvesting company that owns the truck that tried to run you off the road."

"Good work Jessica, you didn't waste any time when you got home."

"Yes, and the list is almost done being printed you two look it over while I refill my coffee cup. Would you like a cup?"

"No thanks, I'm all set."

"I'm good too, Miss Jessica I have a beer in my

pocket to finish before it gets warm."

Jessica left the room chuckling at Gus for carrying a beer around in his pocket.

"Well, you never know when a guy might get thirsty." Gus said looking at my reaction to his response.

"Yep, here it is, K B Wood Harvesting." I said looking up from the list Jessica had printed out. This conglomerate owns just about every business I the area."

"Now we know the" who," but how about the why?"

"I don't know maybe the Feds can tell us something when they get here. I'm planning on running every scenario by them that we can come up with. So, let's keep a lid on everything."

"What should we do until then Dalton?" Jessica asked as she entered the room overhearing my conversation with Gus.

"Why don't you go to work tomorrow, normal routine stuff? Gus and I can go out to my house I'm sure Derrick can find something for us to do. Besides, I want to keep an eye on the canyon."

"What about you r cabin Dalton?"

"What about the cabin?" Jessica asked looking bewildered.

"Somebody broke in last night they trashed the place."

"Trashed it, what do you think they were looking for?"

"I don't know, but I'm not saying anything to anybody until the Fed guys show up.

I'm going to bunk with Gus for a few days until this thing is over."

"No, you're not. You two are going to stay right here. I'm not staying here by myself if somebody is out breaking into places because of what we're working on. Gus can stay in the guest room and you can take the futon in the family room."

"But Jessica."

"But nothing, I don't want anything to happen to any of us, so we stick close together."

"Don't argue with her Dalton, I think she means it; besides you'll lose anyway."

"Alright, but Gus and I have to go out to his place and get the disc from my computer and I'm sure he wants to get a few things for himself. We can meet you back here in two hours."

"Okay guys go get your things and I'll go get some food for us, leave your cell phone on and I'll do the same if you aren't back in two hours I'm going to start calling. When you get back pull your Yukon into the garage and close the door behind you."

"Okay Jess. Come on Gus lets go to your house."

CHAPTER THIRTEEN

Tuesday was spent anticipating the arrival of the FBI. Jessica went to her office for a half Days' work, Gus and I went to the fire station to see if the lab report had come back on the Department store fire.

The sun was starting to warm the morning air, moving in from the big lake. The radio station Gus and I were listening to in the Yukon, said that it might reach eighty today.

We arrived at the fire station, parking in front and entered the building. The Chief was sitting in the lunchroom watching the morning news report on the television mounted on the block wall. He had a cup of coffee and a large cinnamon roll sitting in front of him on the table.

"Hi Chief, how are you this morning?"

He whirled in his seat slightly startled by the intrusion.

"Good morning Dalton, Hi Gus. What are you two doing, coming in here and scaring the shit out of an old man before his morning coffee?"

"I was in the neighborhood and I thought I would stop by and see if the lab report came back on the store fire."

"No, nothing yet. It should show up pretty soon.

You know it takes a while for things to get way up here. I tried to call you yesterday, but the resort owner said you weren't to be found."

"Oh, he didn't say anything to me, but I haven't seen him either. Gus and I have been fishing some and working on my house whenever Derrick can use a hand. Probably just missed you."

"If something comes in, I'll call you, same number?"

"Yes, if I'm not there try Gus' and here this one also if the first two don't get me."

I wrote down Jessica's number on a scrap of paper I had in my pocket.

"Where's this? It doesn't look like the calling are that you guys are under?"

"It's Jessica Whitehorse's home phone, but please only use it as a last resort. I don't think she has it listed."

"Okay Dalton, whatever you want. Have you two been going out?"

"Yes, for a little while now, some dinner dates that sort of thing."

"Oh, well good for you and good for her that poor women went through hell after her husband was killed. Nice girl and not too bad to look at either. I wish you the best of luck."

"Thanks Chief, well Gus and I'll get out of your hair. See you later."

"Yep, see you."

Gus and I started for the door and the Chief came down the hall behind us.

"Hey Gus, when are you going to take me fishing again?"

"Maybe Friday if the weather holds out that storm has the streams all muddied up and I think it will take a few days for them to clear. I'll call you on Thursday Okay?"

"Sounds good, see yah."

Gus and I left the fire station, and turned onto a side street that ran along side of the main highway.

"Where are we going now Dalton?"

"Just a little precaution, I don't want the Chief to see what way I'm going."

"Why do you think he is hiding something?"

"I don't know but we can talk about it later at Jessica's I have some questions I want to ask her. I think I'll give her a call and see how much longer she thinks it will be before she gets home." I punched her work number into the cell phone and was greeted by her receptionist and was told she had just left for the day. I hung up and punched in her cell number. She answered on the second ring.

"Hello Jessica, here."

"Hi Jess, this is Dalton. I was just wondering what you were doing."

"I'm on my way home, as soon as I do a few errands. What are you two up to?"

"I think Gus and I are going to grab a beer and then come over later if that is okay?"

"Sound good, I'll see you then. Oh, and Dalton same thing as last night park in the garage, Okay?"

"Yah, okay I'll see you later bye."

"Well old timer let's go find us a cold one, sound good to you?"

"Well heck yah, I'm drier than a popcorn fart."

Gus and I went to one of the bars in Baraga I didn't want to go to our usual place in L'Anse. Gus had two I had one. We chatted about the fishing season and the

upcoming fall hunting season, trying not to say anything about the case. We weren't really sure you were
involved and we didn't want to tip anyone off about
what we had found. Finishing the last of our beers we
left and drove over to Jessica's. I pulled the Yukon in
the garage and closed the door. The smell of food cooking from inside the house was pleasant and Gus noticed
it before he had taken a few steps towards the kitchen
from the garage entrance.

"Damn Dalton something smells good."

"Yes, it does, I wonder what she is making us?"

"I don't care I'm starving; you didn't bother to stop
today for lunch. I'm hungrier than a bitch wolf with a
batch of pups."

"Well come on then, you, old bitch let's go see
what the dear lady has prepared for your ever empty
stomach."

Gus and I entered after a soft knock on the door.
Jessica was standing in the kitchen stirring something
on the stove. She had her hair pulled back and had
changed in to a pair of shorts and tank top. She was a
vision of summer beauty. Something you might see in
one of those women's magazines, just a normal every-
day woman enjoying a casual afternoon in the summer
around the house.

"Hi Jessica, what are you making?" I asked as I
walked up behind her and gave her a kiss on the neck.

"Hi Dalton, Hi Gus."

"It smells wonderful, old Gus is weak from hunger."

"Go wash up and I will see if I can nurse him back
to health."

Gus and I went to wash, while Jessica began to set
the table.

"Have a seat you two I'll only have a couple of more things to set out, what would you like to drink?"

"A couple of beers will be all right." I said as I sat down.

Jessica came back with two beers and a tray full of steak fries, to go with the oven-baked sandwiches she had prepared. She explained to Gus that the sauce she had made could be used to dip the sandwiches in as well as the fries. He opted for just pouring it on everything and eating it with a fork.

"What do you call this thing, Miss Jessica?"

"Well, its call a hoagie, it has shaved beef and cheese mushrooms and fried onions, and the sauce is made like a thin gravy. Do you like it?"

"Yes, it's delicious and I can't say that I have ever had one before. Thank you."

"I'm glad you like it, how about you Dalton?"

"Yes, very good, I was thinking when we are done eating. I would like to look at the conglomerate some more and I wanted to ask you a few things about the incidents surrounding your late husbands' death, if that is all right?"

"Yes, I don't see why not, we can go into the study as soon as we are through."

Jessica, Gus and I went into the study after clearing the table. Jessica went to work on the computer and Gus and I took a seat on the couch.

"Let's write down what we know so far about the holdings that the conglomerate has in this are." I suggested.

"We know they own the Department store, KB logging and trucking, the land consortium and several other small businesses in the outlying areas. Jessica can you look to see if they have any interest in insurance firms or investment houses."

"Yes sure, it will only take a minute." She punched a number of keys and found what she was looking for.

"Here it is, Dalton they have several holdings in insurance and some in investment broker houses. Do you want me to print out the list?"

"Yes please, print two if it isn't too long."

"Not a problem, why are you interested in insurance companies?"

"I have a hunch and I want to see if I'm wrong or right."

Jessica handed Gus and I each a copy of the list.

"What are we looking for Dalton?" Gus asked.

"I don't know for sure but when I find it, I'll recognize the name. I have a hunch that the department store was covered by one of these companies on this list, as well as the old fires having a connection to names on this list."

"I thought the insurance company went bankrupt after the fires that involved my husband and Clifford Adams?"

"No not bankrupt, just changed the name, they don't close down insurance companies over a little that, if they can prove they had nothing to do with the misdealing. They probably pinned everything to Clifford and your husband."

"So why do you think they are related or connected, we don't have the name of the carrier for the department store fire." Gus stated.

"Yes, we do I have it right here in my briefcase, it's written on the fire report."

"They put that kind of information on a fire report?"

Jessica asked.

"Yep, it on there so when they call for a copy. The fire records personnel can make sure that the right company is getting a copy of the report. Most of the time they send their own investigator to the scene to verify what the fire department has down as cause and damage or loss is correct."

"I'm with you so far Dalton, do you think it is a local company?"

"More than likely, here it is "Forest and Home Insurance Company" they are located in Marquette. Jessica see if you can get any information on them as far as who owns them or a parent company."

"Why do you need that?"

"Gus not all insurance companies are independent. They have larger companies backing them just like you may be able to get several types of insurance from the same agent in the same office they have multiple carries and plans that they offer. The small hometown owned insurance offices are quickly becoming a thing of the past. The big guys figured out how to control the market and that means they control the price of the coverage and the cost of the premiums. The higher they drive them premiums the more money their shareholders make."

"Dalton do you think that they are running a scam again with the department store?"

"Yes, I do, I'm going to read some of these and you two tell me if they sound familiar."

I began to read the names out loud, Gus and Jessica were shaking heads, and I had gone halfway down the list when I noticed a name that floored me. Detroit Urban and Commercial.

"Holy shit!"

"What is the matter Dalton? You look like you just seen a ghost."

"This company name I have seen it before, Detroit Urban and Commercial. They were the company that had handled the arson fires in Detroit that I was working on when I was injured."

"When you got hurt what are you talking about Dalton?" Gus asked.

"I was working a string of arson fires in Detroit. They all had a similar pattern to them; the arsonist would load up the structures using the balloon method that I told you about. The last fire I went to also had, this type of fuel loading scenario, however the creep added a twist. He had set an incendiary device in the ceiling above the tiles."

"Dalton are you sure you want to share this story with Gus and me?"

"Yes, I'm okay, I told Gus that I would tell him someday how my back became scarred.

I was working these fires and was certain that the same guy was doing the torching. His technique hadn't changed much from each fire, and the Department store fire up here and the ones involving Jessica's husband all look really familiar."

"Those all happened before you were hurt."

"Yes, they did, but the fires in Detroit all had the same insurance carrier, just like the ones up here in Baraga. You said that cliff Adams was from Detroit, right?"

"Yes, that's right, but now we know that he was dead before you were injured." Jessica answered.

"Dalton when are you going to get to the part about

when you got hurt?" Gus asked becoming impatient.

Jessica came around from behind her desk and sat down beside me. Trying to show me some support so I could retell the story to Gus.

"Okay Gus, I'm getting to it right now. I was working the fourth fire scene. It was a three-story office building, that had been remolded recently the contractor had dropped the ceiling and added some wall covering and new doors, windows, brand new office furniture equipment the whole thing. It was a rental type property the kind that offers office space for rent by the square foot. There might be several companies using the same building. It wasn't doing so well; they had only been able to rent out about sixty percent of the space so I guess somebody decided to torch it for the insurance money. It was in a different district than I usually work in, but because of the similar arson characteristics the Chief on scene had me called in knowing I was working the other fires. When I arrived, the Chief filled me in and stated that they had contained the fire to about fifty percent of the building and that the sprinklers had stopped the fire from spreading to the top floor. The fire companies had made a good stop on it and there had been a substantial amount of evidence saved. The Chief had put the firefighters into a mop up mode and were basically waited for me to show up."

"Hold on Dalton, what is mop up?" Jessica asked.

"It is a term used in the fire service, it means the fire department tries to salvage anything or preserve anything from further damage. Whether it is caused from fire spread, smoke, or from water that the fire department used for extinguishment purposes.

They go around checking for hot spots in the walls

and ceilings trying not to add to the damage and cover anything that is too heavy to be moved with salvage covers or tarps to keep the water from dripping onto it causing more expense.

The building had sprinklers in place, however they had been put on two separate circuits the third floor was separate from the first two. The arsonist evidently hadn't known this, so I thought at the time, because he had only turned off the valve for the first two floors. Now that I think about it, I have to wonder if he didn't set me up.

When the fire companies showed up on scene, they only had to knocked down the fire on the first two floors the sprinklers had done their job on the third."

"If the fire was out or under control when you arrived how did you get burned?" Gus asked.

"I had started my size up from outside the building and quickly went to the inside starting on the first floor taking photographs of the burn patterns and documenting how the fire had progressed. Then moving up the stairs and into the second-floor offices doing the same. Studying how the fire had spread and the amount of burn, I noticed that there were fire trail marks on the floor and leading up the stairway to the third floor. The sprinklers had preserved the small pieces of tissue paper the arsonist had used for a wick.

"A trailer what is that?" Jessica asked.

Gus perked up and answered her before I had a chance to.

"It's where something flammable is laid down to aid in the spread of fire from one place to another." Gus was grinning with satisfaction in his ability to answer her.

"Gus how did you know that?"

"Dalton told me the other day."

"That's correct Gus you were paying attention. So anyway, I was following the fire trail or mark on the floor winding its way up the steps to the third floor. When I arrived on the landing in front of the office doors there were four of Detroit's finest waiting there for me. They had been assigned to help me in whatever I needed. They opened the door and pointed to the ceiling explaining that they hadn't touched a thing just as instructed by the Chief. The arsonist had loaded the ceiling with balloons."

"Balloons what are you talking about I heard you say something about them earlier?" Jessica asked looking slightly confused. Gus raised his hand like a school kid wanting to get a chance to answer the question.

"Go ahead Gus tell her what the balloons are for."

"The arsonist uses them the rapidly spread the fire, by filling them with an accelerant like gasoline and hanging them from the ceiling. When the fire reaches them, they explode and a chain reaction takes place the hotter the fire the faster the balloons break and the more quickly the fire burns the place. The bigger the fire the harder it becomes to put out."

"Right again Gus. The balloons were still in place hanging from the ceiling full of gasoline. The firefighters started to help me collect evidence and when we were almost through, I gave them the go ahead to start checking for hot spots or fire spread two of them were using a step stool standing on it and lifting the drop ceiling tiles and looking for any signs of fire. They had made a pass down the one side of the room and were starting back down the other side working in a straight line as one would lift the tile the other stood ready to hand up a hose line in case, he spotted anything. The other two stood ready with another hose line for back up. I noticed something on the floor under a desk that I was leaning on as I watched them progress towards me. I bent down and had my small flashlight out trying to get a better look at the shining object. The fire fighters lifted a tile and a loud explosion went off, lifting my unbuttoned coat up and over my head and sending me head first under the desk. One of the fire fighters on the back up line was thrown over the desk and the one holding the nozzle was knocked off her feet, but managed to hold on to the hose. She was able to regain her footing and extinguish herself and then turn the water stream on the one that went over the desk and myself. The two that had been directly under the blast were killed one decapitated and the other burned his lungs as he inhaled the fireball. My back was burned and I spent several months in the hospital before I decided to move up here. The two firefighters shouldn't have been looking for fire spread. I should have had the Haz Mat team take all of the balloons out first."

"It wasn't your fault Dalton. You had no idea that there was going to be a bomb in there." Jessica said squeezing my hand for reassurance.

"She is right Dalton, there wasn't anything you could have done."

"Thanks, guys, for the support."

"Was the arsonist ever caught?" Gus asked.

"Well sort of, they found him inside another building. Evidently he was in the process and something went wrong he became trapped somehow and perished."

"Just like that bastard husband of mine." Jessica blurted out.

"Yes, I guess so, didn't get to see all of the details about what had happened to him. I was only told he had died. I could probably do some calling around or we could wait and run it by the Feds when they get here tomorrow."

"Why don't we do that, they have a lot more resources than we are going to come up with using my desk top."

"Does that sound alright to you Gus?"

"Yes Dalton, sounds good to me too. I want to ask you how does all of this fit in with the old fires here and the ones you were involved with in Detroit as it seems you are leaning that way?"

"That Gus my friend is the million-dollar question. Somehow, I'm convinced they all have a common link. The way the arson fires were setup and that conglomerates name keeps popping up no matter what we look in to."

"Do you recall the names of the building owners from the Detroit fires?"

"No, I don't Jess, but I'm sure the F.B.I. would be able to dig them up. I'm beat I think we should call it quits for the night."

"Good idea, its ten thirty already, come on I'll show you guys where you're sleeping."

Gus and I stood following Jessica from here study.

The thoughts of today's discussions and investigations were still rolling around in my head as I looked at the clock for the hundredth time it seemed. Last reading of the red digital numbers 3:00 AM.

I wish I was in bed with Jessica and not on this god forsaken couch. I could hear Gus snoring from his comfortable bed through his closed door. Oh well I would eventually drift off.

CHAPTER FOURTEEN

Gus was up and standing in the kitchen preparing some coffee when Jessica and I walked in from her bedroom. I had gotten up in the middle of the night to use the bathroom and Jessica invited me to stay in bed with her. Both Jessica and I were a little embarrassed, not expecting to see Gus standing in the kitchen when we walked in and him giving the both of us that sly all-knowing grin.

"Morning Gus, how did you sleep?" I asked breaking the silence.

"Like a baby, how was the couch?" he returned.

"Soft as velvet."

"Yah I'll bet it is, umm was." He answered with a chuckle.

"How about I make you two some breakfast?" Jessica suggested, cutting our exchange of words short before we got out of hand.

"Sound like a heck of a plan, I have the coffee started." Gus said stepping aside and letting Jessica pass into the kitchen.

Jessica went to work preparing eggs ham and toast. While Gus and I set the table and poured the coffee.

Jessica had set the food on the table; Gus and I were passing the serving dishes back and forth complimenting her efforts to keep the two of us feed.

The doorbell rang and Jessica got up and went to answer it, with a puzzled expression on her face.

"I wonder who that could be at this time of the morning?" she said as she walked down the hall. Looking through the sidelight by the front entrance, before opening the door. Gus and I had also stood up and started to come around the table when Jessica opened the door.

"Good morning, can I help you?" she asked the two men standing in front of her.

"Yes Ms. Whitehorse, we are with the F.B.I. may we come in?"

"Yes of course please come this way." She instructed them as they trailed her down the hall leading them back to the dining area. "Would you two gentlemen like some breakfast or maybe some coffee?"

"No thanks on the breakfast but, I would take some coffee please." The older looking one politely answered.

"How about you sir?"

"Yes please, just coffee."

Gus and I were standing and waiting for the introductions to start and finish so we could get back to eating.

"Gus and Dalton these two gentlemen are with the F.B.I. but I'm afraid I didn't get their names." Jessica offered as she went to get them some coffee.

"Oh, I'm sorry, please excuse us. I'm Agent John Wallace and this is Agent Bill Hampton." The older of the two John was offering me his hand to shake as he introduced Bill to Gus who was making Bill's hand disappear in his as he shook it. I couldn't help but notice Bill's wide-eyed expression as old Gus put the grips to him.

"Please both of you join us." Jessica offered as she handed them their coffee, and motioned them toward the two chairs on the opposite side of the table so we were able to see each other.

"I'm Dalton James and this fellow here is Gus Jorgenson, and the lovely hostess is Ms. Jessica Whitehorse." I stated the introductions after we had all sat down.

"Are you sure you wouldn't like some breakfast?" Jessica offered again as John and Bill made their way around the table. John took the corner seat near Gus and Bill took the one next to me. Leaving an empty chair between them at the eight-place table. From their position they would be able to see and hear everyone. Gus and I had quickly finished eating I picked up the conversation from Jessica you had been providing them with small talk while we ate.

Agent John Wallace was somewhere between forty and forty-five years of age. Tall maybe 6'3" to 6"4" medium frame, it looked like he visited the fitness center a couple of times a week. His hair was cropped short in the standard issue flattop dark with some salt and pepper starting to show in the sideburn area and above the ears. He was dressed in a dark solid colored suit with matching tailored trousers, a white shirt and dark tie.

Agent Bill Hampton, was African American, shorter than John, maybe 5' 10" to 6', it was hard to be sure he was thicker than his partner his upper body was strongly muscle. His coat sleeves were tight trying to stretch over his biceps when he moved his arms in conversation. The thigh and calf muscles I had noticed were also snugly bond by his tailored cut dark suit, he appeared to be built like an NFL running back as John looked more like a wide receiver. Bill was younger maybe thirty to thirty-five, quiet for the most part John had done all of the talking and Bill more or less just nodded in agreement.

Bill had the haircut of a boot camp Marine, shaved short on the sides and finished off with an oval shaped patch of hair on the top. I noticed him stealing some quick glances at Jessica while she listened to our exchange.

"John, I thought you guys weren't going to be here until ten or eleven?"

"We arrived sooner than we had thought we were going to. Neither one of us had ever been here before, so we weren't really sure on how long of a drive it was going to be. We checked in at the motel down by the water and decided we would try to find Ms. Whitehorse's home using GPS and the address. That the home office had given us. We noticed the lights were on so we thought we would stop in and see if we could get an earlier start."

The whole time Bill sat there nodding in agreement.

"We can go into the study and get started; I'll bring in a pot of coffee. Go ahead Dalton show them into the study, and please Agent Wallace call me Jessica, Ms. Whitehorse makes me feel like a school teacher"

"I led Gus, and the two Agents into the study and offered them the couch in front of Jessica's desk as Gus and I took the remaining two chairs. Jessica came in carrying a tray with a fresh pot of coffee and sat it down on the small table in front of the two FBI agents.

"There you are gentlemen; now where would you like us to start?" Jessica asked taking her place behind the desk.

"This sure is a beautiful home you have Ms. Whitehorse, I mean Jessica. What is it that you do for a living?" Bill asked.

"I'm a lawyer for the local tribe, and thank you for the compliment about my house."

"We can start with, who and how you found the

body." Agent John interrupted the exchange between them.

"Would you like to tell them Dalton?" Jessica offered.

"I can do that as long as you and Gus help fill in anything that I miss."

I began to tell the two agents how Gus and I had originally gone out to look for the Indian Princess and then went back to show Jessica, what we had found so she could perform the ceremony that her people were accustomed to doing when someone passes on.

"While we were in the cave Jessica was in the one end doing the ceremony and I moved over to the opposite side to give her some privacy when I noticed a foot sticking up from the floor of the cave. There was a crevice about two feet wide in the wall and it went down below the plane of the floor. I tried to get a better look at the body but wasn't able to see very mush with my helmet light, so I tried to reach down into the hole and see if I could feel anything in the pants pocket, there was something in the back pocket but I wasn't able to manipulate my hand, so I had Jessica reach down and she came up with a wallet. We brought it back to her place and I dissected it the next morning. It turned out that it belonged to Cliff Adams, or at least it was his driver's license in the wallet. That is when we contacted you guys."

Jessica expressed her concerns with the removal of the body and asked if the FBI would be discreet with the location and how they handled the press so the resting place of her ancestor wouldn't be disturbed any further. They agreed telling her they had a public information officer who would handle the press.

"I have a question for you two. Any ideas on who might have knocked old Cliffy off and stuffed him in a hole?" Gus asked.

"Good question, but so far we have nothing, I'm hoping that the forensic people can come up with something, after we get the body out and sent to their lab." Agent John responded.

"What time are you expecting the rest of the team?" Jessica asked.

"Sometime between 10:00 and noon today. They said they would contact me on my cell when they were about an hour away."

"It's 9:30 right now, if you are going to the recovery site, I would suggest some different clothes."

"We were going to change at the hotel after the team calls. We should have enough time. I told them we would meet there. Then go out to the site together." John informed us.

"Sounds good to me. I think it might be a good idea for the two Agents to ride out with me. Jessica and Gus can follow us in her Lexus. If that is okay with everybody."

I noticed Jessica's expression changed with my suggestion of travel companions, but she would be a suspect in this investigation and I didn't want for her to be questioned without me present and I had a feeling that the two FBI Agents wanted to ask me some more questions about my relationship with Jessica.

"Dalton aren't you going to tell these gentlemen about the conglomerate angle we have been working on?" Jessica asked.

She had been hurt a bit by my leaving her out of the travel plans and now she was putting me on the spot.

"Yes, I was going to tell them, but I was going to do it tonight after we had returned from recovery site."

"What conglomerate?" Agent John asked.

"I guess I can give you a short version right now and later we can go into more details."

"We were planning on flying back tonight with the rest of the team that are in charge of transporting the body." Agent Bill informed us.

"I don't think you will after you hear what I have to say. Myself and these two right here have been working on the investigation of a local department store fire that happen here a while back and it is showing very similar evidence of some arson fires that happened around here when Clifford Adams and Jessica's' late husband were running their scam."

"You have my attention Dalton, please continue." Agent John offered.

The cell phone began to chirp just as I was about to continue.

"Excuse me please, Hello Agent Wallace here, yes okay we'll meet you at the Best Western in about an hour." John ended the call and slipped the phone back into his best pocket.

"Well folks the team is one hour away, Agent Hampton and I have to go get ready. We can continue the conglomerate story later tonight I think we can stick around for a day or two. I'll get it cleared with the home office on the way to hotel. Why don't the three of you meet us there in let's say forty minutes?'

CHAPTER FIFTEEN

We were sitting in the parking lot of the Best Western in Baraga waiting for the two FBI Agents to come out. I was in my Yukon Gus and Jessica in her Lexus. We were parked so we could talk thru the side windows. Jessica had lit into me at the house as soon as the two FBI Agents had left.

"What the hell was that crap about riding in separate vehicles about don't you trust me? Were you planning on leaving me out of the loop? I want to make sure they understand that I don't want the princess' resting place disturbed."

"I know, but hold on a minute. The FBI are going to put you on their suspect list, that is a given because you knew Clifford Adams when he was alive and your former husbands' involvement with him. I know and Gus knows you had nothing to do with the whole scam and disappearance of Clifford, but the FBI don't. So, I thought I would let them get me alone and ask me some questions about you, as I know they will about you and our relationship."

"Dalton is right Ms. Jessica. The FBI might consider you a suspect in the Clifford Adams deal and he is going to play them a little to see if that is the case. That's why he has to see them alone." Gus was trying to convince her that I had only her best interest at heart.

"So, you two had this planned all along?"

"Well sort of, me and Dalton talked about it yesterday. If the suspect list came up and they revealed something and we were all riding together. They wouldn't share it with us, it would be better to split up. That is why I asked the question about any ideas as to who might have killed him."

"When you put me on the spot about the conglomerate, I was going to tell them during the ride out to the site. That's why I didn't go into detail about the case we were working on. I didn't want them to think we were trying to cover any involvement they think you might have had. It's better if we play stupid and see what they have then to lay all the cards on the table and they make up some harebrained conspiracy theory about you and the missing money."

"But I'm not involved in any way."

"I know that, but I'm going to pumped them for some info and I am sure they will ask the relationship question before they divulge anything."

"What are you going to tell them about our relationship?"

"I'm going to tell them that it started out professional and turned into a friendship."

"Is that all it is, is a friendship, I thought it was more than that."

"It is Jessica but they don't need to know that, if they think we are involved they won't be so liberal with the suspect list and what they plan on doing about the conglomerate that we think is involved here. They might think that you are involved with the conglomerate also."

"Okay Dalton, I'm sorry I flew off the handle, we

better get going, and Gus and I will meet you in the hotel parking lot."

The two Agents came walking out of the hotel's front door, dressed in their field fatigues, which consisted of black combat style boots, jeans, blue tee shirt with FBI in big yellow letters stenciled across the back and carrying the customary blue wind breakers that read the same. Each had a shoulder holster with the standard issue 9mm and a hand-held radio that looked like a large walkie-talkie.

Agent John was talking on his cell phone as he crossed the parking lot coming towards us, Agent Bill walked in step just behind him.

"Hi Dalton, Jessica, Gus." Agent Bill said greeting us as he came up alongside of the parked cars.

Just then a county sheriff's car pulled in and a Michigan State police cruiser right behind it.

"What the hell they doing here?" Jessica asked.

"The extraction team is about ten minutes away, Bill would you please get the briefcase from the car?"

Bill nodded and went to get it.

"You haven't answered my question Agent John." Jessica snapped.

"They have to be here it is their jurisdiction, we don't know if that is in fact Clifford Adams that you found it could be some long-lost hiker or something and they have the right to procure the case if it is, we don't want to step on anyone's toes out here. I already informed them about the use of discretion and that we would handle any press releases."

"You don't think the body is Adam's?" Gus asked.

"No, that's not what I think but we won't be sure

until the forensic team determine it one way or the other. That is why we have to inform the local law enforcement, so they are able to gather the same evidence or use what we gather in case it turns out to be someone other than Adams."

The rest of the recovery team pulled into the parking lot. Agent Wallace and Agent Hampton got in with me, Jessica and Gus followed as the rest of the team got in line behind us.

"Do they know where they are going?" I asked.

"I told them to follow Ms. Whitehorse's Lexus." Agent Hampton informed me from the back seat.

The drive out to the site was uneventful; the two agents had developed a case of lockjaw and weren't talking about anything but the weather and the drive over from Marquette. I assumed they were going to wait and see if we really had a body or just another Native American ancestor that we mistook for someone else. I had never been asked to produce the driver' license of Clifford Adams and I was wondering why they had believed us to begin with. So, I asked them that very question.

"How come you guys didn't ask me for the driver's license back at the house?"

"I guess we figured you would give it to us when we came over tonight."

"What made you believe that I wasn't just sending you on a wild goose chase?"

"Don't worry Dalton we checked you out, the file on your service record with the Detroit fire department is impeccable. We feel that you are a straight guy and besides Bill had one of your fire investigations classes at Quantico."

"No kidding, when was that?"

"About ten years ago when I first entered into the FBI."

We pulled into the driveway of my new house to be. The rest of the procession parked haphazard in and around the trees along the driveway leaving enough room for the transport van to get close to the extraction site.

The team worked inside the cave for three- and one-half hours before radioing for a litter to be lowered so the body could be hoisted up. The skeletal remains of Clifford Adams or whoever it was were quickly loaded in the transport van and moved to the airport in Marquette. The rest of the teams cleared the gear and equipment after they left.

I noticed Jessica had the lead technician cornered by his rig and I could tell they were having a one-sided conversation Jessica was talking and he was nodding his head and reassuring her that they hadn't touched anything to do with the Princess' remains. I walked over to get her and to let the man get back to his task.

"Are you sure you didn't touch anything?"

"Yes Ms. Whitehorse, we secured the ancient remains with crime tape so the rest of the techs wouldn't bother the site, nothing was touched, but I did take a look and they are very old and they are of Native American origin I could tell by the teeth and the bone structure of the face."

"Thank you, that means a lot to me and my people."

"Come on Jessica let's leave this poor guy gets back to work."

"Hi Dalton, where have you been Gus and I are going to go back pretty soon but first we want to stop by his place. I wanted to see if Agent John had a press release ready and what he was going to put in it."

"He is right over there by my Yukon, he's talking to the sheriff and the state trooper about that very thing, come on let's see what he has ready."

Jessica and I walked over; Agent John was informing the two police officers that this was what he wanted released to the press.

"Hi Jessica and Dalton we were just talking about how we wanted the press release given. I have instructed them that this is an information blackout and that only the FBI will okay any releases to the press. There is not to be any locations of the site, or that there is also Native American remains at the site, as far as the first press release is concerned. We are going with the lost hiker story and when the time comes for the identity of the body and its location, we will be sure to move the location by at least a full square mile. Does that sound okay to you?" Agent John asked Jessica.

"Yes, very good, thank you so much for your understanding."

Gus came walking over to the three of us as the two police officers left to release their bogus story to the press.

"Hey Agent where are they taking the body to?"

"Hi Gus, they are taking it to Marquette and then they will probably fly it to the lab down state."

"How long before we find out if it was Cliff Adams?"

"Well, if they can match the dental record, maybe in a day or two. I'm sure they will be expediting everything thru the system."

"Oh, you planning on informing us if they find out who it is?"

"Yes, we are, I think we are all set here why don't we conclude our conversation back at Ms. I mean Jessica's place this evening."

"That sounds good to me as long as you two Feds bring the pizza, Gus and I have to make a pit stop at his place then we will be there."

"We do, what for?" Gus asked looking puzzled.

"Yes, we do, big guy now let's go."

"Yes mam. I'm going."

Jessica and Gus walked down the drive way towards her Lexus her arm hooked in the crook of Gus'

Why that old shit looks at him I think he skipped a couple of times. My thoughts going unheard by the two FBI agents.

"What do you say Dalton we get going too, we want to change into some less noticeable clothes before we get to Jessica's, beside we have pizza to order."

"Okay, get in." I said as I opened the door.

We had no sooner turned onto the graveled county road. When John began to ask questions.

"Dalton would mind telling me. What Gus and Jessica had to get at his house?"

"I have an idea that, Jessica is going to try and get another bottle of wine out of the old guy."

"A bottle of wine?" Agent Hampton asked leaning forward from the back seat.

"Yes, a bottle of wine. Gus has a wine cellar in his basement and Jessica and he play this little game. She puts the charm to him until him hands over a bottle of vintage wine.'

"Gus has a cellar full of vintage wine? He doesn't strike me as the type you would be a fine wine coinsurer."

"He isn't, the wine was left to him by his

grandmother. She seems to have been a collector."

"What is you and Jessica's relationship, business or pleasure?" John asked.

"It started out as business, then turned into a pretty good friendship."

"Then you two aren't romantically involved?"

"NO, just friends. Why do you ask?"

"She is a very beautiful women, I can see how some-one might want to pursue her in a romantic way." He kept prying.

"Well, we're not yet anyway and I like what I have going right now. No strings attached." I answered in a less friendly tone.

"What is this land consortium you starting to tell us about this morning?"

"I didn't say land consortium, I said conglomerate. Have you guys been checking on something about me or Jessica?"

"Yes and no. The conglomerate you were starting to talk about, wouldn't happen to own a land consortium that was interested in buying your land from you, and owns multiple corporations tied back to the conglomerate?"

"Yes, we have been doing some digging on our own and the same name keeps popping up no matter where we look." I answered just before we turned back into the hotel parking lot.

"Okay Dalton we will talk some more about this when bill and I see you later at Jessica's. Oh, and we'll bring the pizza, say in about hour maybe hour and a half."

"Okay guys I'll see you then."

"Dalton thanks for the ride." Bill said as he exited

the backseat.

"Sure thing, I'll see you later.

When I arrived at Jessica's her and Gus hadn't returned yet so I sat in the drive listening to the radio. Jessica hadn't given me a key and I didn't want to be in the house until they got there. Just in case the two FBI agents got there before them. It probably wouldn't look to good if I had a key after just telling them that Jessica and I were merely friends.

Jessica and Gus arrived around fifteen minutes after I did. They pulled into the garage after Jess hit the opener button on her visor. I walked in along the driver's side opening the door for when she got out. She got laughing and giggling, holding onto a bottle of wine.

"What's so funny?"

"This old gentleman, isn't always a gentleman." She said pointing at Gus with her free hand.

"What did he do now?" I asked knowing all too well about Gus' colorful sense of humor.

Gus got out with his all-famous innocent look on his face, and pointing a large thumb at his chest. I could see the devilish grin starting to show.

"Oh, he was just telling me a few of his most colorful jokes, nothing serious."

Gus came around the front of the vehicle Jessica hooked her arm in his.

"Let's go inside shall we gentlemen?"

Gus was grinning from ear to ear.

"You better be careful old man; I'm might get jealous."

"Well, you forgot I seen you naked Dalton and you have every right to be jealous." He laughed at his own comment. Jessica let out a snort suppressing a giggle, and slapped him on the shoulder.

"You're nasty. When are the two Feds going to show up?"

"They said they would be about an hour."

"Good I have time to get cleaned up." She said entering her bedroom and closing the door behind her.

"What the hell were you two carrying on about when you got here?" After I heard the shower come on in Jessica's bathroom. I started to question Gus.

He sat there at the table grinning, with a look of remembrance on his face.

"Dalton sits down." Gus ordered as he slid a chair out from the table.

"I have to tell you that is one great lady in there, and I wouldn't do anything out of character with here, we were just having a little fun. She charmed another bottle of wine out of me. I told her if it wasn't such a boost for my old ego. The way she turns the charm on me. That I would gladly give her the whole damn cellar full."

"So, you two are going to continue this charade? She sweet tells you and you cave in and you give up another bottle of your grandmother's vintage wine."

"Yah something like that. Here have a beer and calm your shit. I am just having a bit of fun; you know and old guy like me doesn't get much of a chance to do that anymore."

Gus handed me a beer from the six-pack he had brought in. I guess he wasn't hurting anybody and he did look to be enjoying himself more. He had lost some of his grumpiness and besides what was it hurting, other than my ego.

"You all better now Dalton? What did them two

suits have to ask you, was it, what you thought it would be? You know about you and Ms. Jessica?"

"Yes, I'm better, if I couldn't trust you with her, who you could I trust, right? They asked just what I thought they were going to ask about how involved I was with Jessica, the old business or pleasure routine."

Just then the front doorbell rang, interrupting our conversation.

"Gus you want to get that I'll let Jessica know that they are here."

Gus got up and went to answer the door I stuck my head into Jessica's room and told her the FBI had arrived.

"I'll be out in a minute, get some plates down from the cabinet and see what they want to drink, but don't you offer them any of my wine." She answered with a chuckle at her last request.

I went into the kitchen and took out some plates and silverware as Gus brought the two agents into the kitchen.

"What would you to gents like to drink, beer, soda something harder?" Gus asked.

"Anything but my wine." Jessica said as she entered from her bedroom. We hadn't heard her come onto the kitchen. I noticed all of us standing there with our mouths slightly agape looking at her loveliness. She was radiant; her hair was pulled back from her face, forming a single long ponytail that hung down nearly to hear thighs. The dress she had on was cream colored with a square cut neckline stopping just shy of where her cleavage started, the light color of the dress made her skin look darker than it actually was. The bottom hemline came to just above the knee and she was barefoot. The two agents greeted her with a tip of their heads and a soft hello.

"Hello gentlemen, please have a seat." She said offering them two chairs at the table.

"You two still haven't told Gus what you would like to drink."

"Oh, sorry Jessica, beer is fine, thank you." John answered as he took a seat.

We all sat down and began to devour the pizza they had brought, the talk around the table was mostly about the weather, where everyone had grown up, retirement and what parts of the world the agents had formerly work in. no mention of the case until we had finished. Perhaps Jessica was trying to get them more comfortable with her, she requested everyone to go into the study when we had finished.

"Let's go into the study, we can fill you guy's in on the case we have been working on."

We went to the study Jessica took her seat behind the desk Gus and I took the two chairs which left the sofa for the agents.

"Okay Dalton, we are all ears what do you guys have for us?" Agent John asked.

"What I think would be the best way to explain this, is to go in reverse order of the events that have happened. If that is okay with you two?"

"Yes, that's okay." John answered, Bill took out a small note pad and John turned on a small tape recorder.

"We had a suspicious fire here a couple of weeks ago, a small department store in town. I investigated the scene at the request of the local fire Chief; he wanted me to back up his findings on point of origin and cause. Some factors came into play while I was doing the investigation that I considered questionable. The burn patterns and spread of the fire didn't look right to me, so I played it like an arson fire and collected evidence and took photos. Then between Gus and Jessica we got talking about the old fires and I was able to get some old photos from the local newspapers. When we started comparing the fires, they seemed to show a similar pattern. I have since came to the conclusion that the same person or persons have ties to the starting of all of the fires. We thought Jessica's late husband and Clifford Adams committed all the fires in the nineties, until his wallet showed up on some corpse in the cave."

"How did you come up with the theory on the fires being set by the same person or persons?" John asked.

I opened my briefcase and produced the photos, the ones from the old fires, and the new ones from the department store.

"These are the photos from the department store, and these are from the old fires. I'll show you what I have found to be more than just a coincident. Do you see the burn patterns on the ceilings? They appear very similar, the technique used for all of the fires of loading accelerant on the ceiling points to someone with the same thought process, or the same person."

"I thought these old fires were tied to Jessica's late husband as the arsonist?" Bill asked as he compared the photos.

"They were, but when we started digging into the information on who owned the department store, it came back as a large conglomerate, who owned a bunch of subsidiary companies. The conglomerate also owns the land consortium that wanted to by my property. It was just too strange how their name kept popping up no matter where we were looking. We all thought that Clifford Adams had killed the professor, stolen the money and fled the country, but now we know different."

"I still don't see the big conspiracy?" John stated.

I explained what Jessica, Gus, and I had come up with on the insurance companies in the Detroit area, and the fire that injured me and killed two firefighters.

"So, you think that this a big case of insurance fraud, put on by a large company that started up business with the money used from the nineties fires?" Bill asked.

"Yes, that's it in a nutshell."

"How many people do you think are involved?" John questioned.

"That is the part we don't know, it could be quite a few. When we pull up the information on the computer of who the actual owners of the conglomerate are. We found that they live right here in Baraga, but Gus has lived here his entire life, and he doesn't know of anybody that has that kind of money or at least they are hiding the fact very well. They seem to have billions of dollars hidden all over the world." Jessica answered.

"You are convinced they got all of this money by scamming the insurance companies?" John asked still not convinced.

"No, not all of it. We found out about the insurance company that held the policy on the office building in Detroit, was also the owner of the building that intern were both tied to the conglomerate. We think they are using the subsidiary companies to launder drug money; they own a lot of stuff I Mexico, Central and South America. They are buying the buildings with drug money, fix them up, insure them at a higher rate of coverage, and then torch them."

"Yes, we understand that part, but how do you profit by paying out of the insurance company that you already own?" John asked.

Jessica raised her hand wanting to respond.

"The company is owned by the conglomerate, but its shares are owned by legal corporations in the U. S. These shareholders expect a return on their investment, but if the pay out on a total loss coverage by the insurance company is too much, they won't get a return, it shows as a loss."

"Yes, we are with you now." Bill interjected.

"Then the group of investors can show this as a loss on their tax returns. The conglomerate pays them off under the table using drug money."

"That's some theory." John replied.

"What can we do from our end to help you?" Bill asked.

"We need the FBI to use their great wealth of resources to investigate the conglomerate. They hold so many different interests in businesses all over the world the local authorities would never be able to handle the research." I said producing the list off companies, Jessica had printed from the computer.

"Wow, they do have their fingers into everything." John exclaimed.

"What do you think Bill, do you want to hang around here for a couple of more days and run with this?"

"Yah sure why not, I could use some fresh air."

"Okay, great you two get the ball rolling. In the

mean time I'll see if I can get the information back from the fire Chief on the department store. It should be arriving back from the lab any day."

"Dalton you may want to hold off, awhile. We can get it from them without your name coming up. From this point on don't trust anyone." John suggested.

"Then what are the three of us supposed to do in the mean time?"

"Just play it as usual, if the owners are really here in Baraga. We don't want to tip our hand to them by poking around too much, especially when we don't know who they are."

"What am I supposed to do if the stuff comes back to the fire Chief?"

"If he calls go look at it, but don't act on anything without checking with all of us sitting in this room right here. Okay?" John answered.

John and Bill left, leaving Gus, Jessica, and myself wondering who was going to turn up as the owners. Gus and she tossed around some names; I didn't add any because they were the only two people I basically knew in the area. We turned in for the night after planning our next day's strategy.

CHAPTER SIXTEEN

The day started with a loud banging noise coming from the kitchen. Jessica was preparing breakfast, fresh fruit and the muffins she was trying to get loose from the pan she had forgotten to spray. I rolled off of my couch bed, having respected Jessica's wishes to sleep alone. Staggering and stretching my way towards to kitchen still half asleep just as Gus was giving her some of his unwanted advice as to how he would get them out of there.

"What the heck is all of the noise about, and why is everybody up so early?"

"Good morning Dalton, I'm just trying to make some breakfast. How did you sleep?" Jessica greeted me.

"Morning Dalton you look like hell, rough night? Myself I slept like a baby." Gus added with a smartass tone.

"Yah, I'll bet, you old buzzard." I countered.

"Okay boys why don't we try to start the day friendly? Dalton why don't you go use my shower your clothes are on the bed. Hurry up gets going I'll set breakfast out while you get ready."

She was one of those happy perky kind of people in the morning drove me nuts. How could anybody be so damn cheerful at six in the morning? I showered and dressed; Jessica yelled from the kitchen.

"Breakfast is on the table and Gus and I aren't going to wait for you so hurry up."

"Yes dear, I'm coming." I answered in a whiny tone used by over nagged husbands around the planet.

"What is everybody in such a hurry for this morning?"

"I have to go to the office this morning, I have been neglecting my duties."

"How about you Gus?" I asked as I sat down.

"I have some things to do at home, but first I have some beer to drink and some fish that need catching. I'm bored as hell with all of this investigating stuff; besides I don't want to wear out my welcome with Ms. Jessica. So, eat up. You have to drive me home."

"Well in that case I better hurry up, I wouldn't want to keep you waiting." I said sarcastically.

Gus and Jessica went back to eating their breakfast, ignoring my sour mood.

"Well, isn't one of you two the least bit interested in what I have planned today?"

"I'm sorry Dalton, what do you have planned for to-day?" Jessica condescendingly asked.

"Nothing really important, maybe wait around for the FBI to contact us about the identification of the body from the cave."

"John said they would contact me at the office, and that I could relay the results to you and Gus. So, make sure you have your cell phone handy."

"I'll be sure to have it with me. Well Gus are you ready?"

"Yep, all set, thanks again Ms. Jessica for your hos-pitality. I'll just go grab my bags and meet you outside Dalton."

Gus left the room to go get his suitcase, leaving

Jessica and I some private time for a kiss goodbye, and to wish each other a good day. I exited through the garage and found Gus waiting impatiently by the tailgate of the Yukon.

"Hurry up Dalton, I got to get home, I'm tired of being cooped up in that house. I got some meditation to attend to out in the woods. I have a good spot to go to first thing in the morning, the trout are big, but they don't bite after the sun gets up to high. You want to go with me? It didn't sound like your schedule was too busy today." He asked when he got in the passenger seat.

"Sounds good, I have to stop by my cabin and pick up my fishing gear."

We drove to my place. The landlord had cleaned up the cabin after the break-in and fixed the door locks. He had a note tape to the door requesting me to stop by for a new set of keys. We stopped at the office and I thanked him for his efforts and gave him a fifty-dollar tip.

"We better get a move on Dalton, as clear as the sky is already and all of the dew on the grass, it's going to get hotter than two rats fucking in a wool sock. Out here today."

He informed me of the latest weather forecast in terms that Gus could only come up with. I was laughing so hard I nearly drove off the road.

"Where in the world do you come up with that shit?"

"I don't know, it's a gift. My dad used to say that kind of stuff, guess he might have gotten some of it from the old days. When he spent time at the logging camps."

We arrived at Gus'; he quickly got out and went inside. Placing his suitcases on the kitchen floor, and grabbed his fishing gear from the front porch. I loaded a small cooler with some beers and tossed in a couple of cans of soda for me.

"Let's hit her Dalton." He said with enthusiasm as he jumped into the passenger seat.

"Where to old timer, right or left?" I asked when we came to the end of his driveway.

"Left, we're going to fish the upper part of the Huron River, the trout grow big there but they are skittish as hell."

We drove in a northerly direction Gus adding to the directions as we came to different woods roads. We were at the spot by 8:00 a.m. the sun was getting too high to fish both sides of the stream so Gus instructed me to concentrate on the shady side.

With some coaching and a bit of cussing, after I hung my fly in the brush that lined the stream, I started to catch some trout. I had two brookies and one brown. When I heard a whoop come out of Gus for a net.

"Dalton! Come here quick and bring a net I got a monster on."

I scrambled down the stream, as I watched Gus pulling on his rod, which was bent in a nice big arc.

"Take him easy Gus I'm going to try and get below you so you can just guide him in the net."

I set my pole down on the stream bank and maneuvered in to place about twenty feet downstream from where Gus stood.

"I can see it Gus nice and easy whenever you think you are ready; I'll slid the net under him."

"Okay Dalton, put the net to him."

I could see the fish lying on his side, three feet upstream from me I slowly moved the net under him just as Gus's hook popped out, and the fight was all over.

"OH! Gus this is a dandy."

"Let me see, that speck has to be close to eighteen inches or maybe nineteen. Gus was as excited as a little kid. I couldn't blame him that was a nice brook trout.

"What did you catch it on?"

"It wasn't no gob of feathers I'll tell you that."

"No, really what did you get it on?"

"A Panther Martin spinner and that's all I'm saying."

"Do you think we have enough for lunch? I have three, nothing like that of course."

"I think we have enough, I have four counting this big one. Besides the sun is getting too high now and I'm sweating. The damn black flies are going to carry us out of here if we don't get back to the Yukon pretty quick."

Gus and I packed up our gear and made way for the Yukon. He was right the flies started to swarm around us as we tossed our poles in the back. Gus put the fish in the cooler and pulled out a beer, before he climbed into the seat.

"You want one Dalton?"

"No thanks, I'll take one of those sodas."

"Ahhh, nectar of the gods." Gus exclaimed after he took a long pull from his beer.

"Gus it's only ten thirty in the morning. I thought you said if a man drank before noon, he was an alcoholic?"

"That isn't what I said. I said if you have to have one with breakfast. I already had breakfast and I've been up for at least five hours, so it must be noon somewhere in the world. So, do you want one now?"

"No, I'll stick to the soda."

"That stuff will make your dick bend in the middle if you drink too much of it." He shared his theory on E.D. caused by too much soda consumption. Snickering as he talked.

"Well, I don't know if that can be proved by science but I'll take your word on it. Give me a beer."

"I knew I could talk you into one, now let's go clean them fish I'm starting to get hungry."

Gus and I drove back to his house. He was right the day was turning into a scorcher. The temperature was climbing. The thermometer on Gus's porch read eighty-three and it was only eleven o'clock. We cleaned the fish and Gus went to work preparing them for lunch. I went into the dining room and fired up the computer. Placing a disc in the drive I wanted to study some of the information I had gathered from the fire investigations in Detroit. Trying to find any clues that would tie all of the fires together.

Gus came into the room carrying a plate full of cooked trout. Then went back to the kitchen for a bowl of coleslaw, and a loaf of bread.

"Come on Dalton lunch is ready; you don't want it to get cold."

I got up from the desk and joined him at the table.

"Looks great Gus."

"What you doing on the box of brains?"

"Box of brains? Oh, the computer. I'm trying to see if I can come up with a connection between the fires that might make sense and maybe find out who the arsonist is."

"I thought the FBI was handling that stuff?"

"They are, but I have to do something I can't just sit around twiddling my thumbs."

The smell of Gus' cooking was starting to make its way into the dining room. The hint of burned bacon grease and freshly grated cabbage.

"Gus did you shut the stove off? I can smell burnt

grease or something."

"Yes, I shut the stove off." He answered disgusted at my stupid question.

I got up and went to the kitchen, the stove was still on and the grease had almost reached its flash point. The smoke was billowing up from the stove. I quickly put a lid on the pan and moved it from the burner, and returned to the dining room without ever mentioning a thing.

"Well, was I right, I shut it off?"

"Yep, you were right, just must have built up some heat from the pan, or slopped over the side when you took the fish out."

I didn't want the old guy to think he was losing his memory. No harm no foul.

"You still convinced, that the fires are all related?"

"Yes, I am and I hope we figure it out before there is another one, or someone else gets killed. I wonder if Jessica found out anything from the Feds."

"You might want to give her a call the cell phone is still in your truck and that damn computer is on so nobody can call in if they wanted to."

"Oh, shit I forgot all about that. I think when we are done eating; maybe we should give her a call and then pay the Chief a visit to see if anything came back yet. You want to go with me?"

"You go ahead, I'm going to stay right here. Maybe I'll dust off the wine rack in the basement, lot cooler down there, it's going to get really humid today, probably have a thunder storm before night fall."

"Thunder storm? It's clear as can be outside, not a cloud in the sky."

"That will change, believe me you don't live here as

long as I have and not pay attention to the weather. That big lake can kick up some nasty shit." He boasted as he started to clear the table.

I went back to the computer, studying some more files and writing done some notes.

I shut the computer down and decided to give Jessica a call to see if she had tried to reach us.

Her receptionist answered on the second ring and forwarded me after a short hold.

"Hi Dalton, where are you at?"

"I'm at Gus' we went fishing and we decided to have what we caught for lunch. Gus saved you a couple for you to fix later. Did you hear anything from the FBI?"

"Yes, I did about an hour ago I tried to call you but you didn't answer and Gus' phone was busy."

"I'm sorry I left my phone in the Yukon and I was on the computer so Gus' phone would show busy. What did they have to tell you?"

"John said we were right. The body is Clifford Adams. They said it was pretty conclusive someone had killed him; he had a bullet hole in his head."

"Did they say anything else?"

"No, you know how they are, just the facts."

"How about anything on what we talked to them about last night?"

"Nothing real substantial, but John said they were still getting information coming in from the data base."

"Good, I'm glad to see they are working on it, I'll tell Gus about everything."

"Okay Dalton, don't forget to keep your cell phone handy. They will probably try and call you if something come in that is critical to the case."

"Will do Jess, see you later."

"Okay, I'll call you later on today. I have a meeting with the tribe that is going to have me tied up for most of the afternoon. Bye, Bye."

Gus had been standing in the doorway making faces, trying to get me to tell him something while I was on the phone with her.

"Well, what did she say?"

"She said we were right. The body in the cave was Cliff Adams, it appears somebody shot him in the head before they put him in the cave."

"What about the other stuff from last night?"

"The FBI has some info coming in on their data base but nothing conclusive as of yet. Jessica said they would call me when they found something out."

"What are you going to do now?"

"I'm going to my cabin and get cleaned up, then pay the Chief a visit."

"Okay, but be careful, they don't know who the killer is and I want you to call me later and tell me where you are, or plan on going to. Besides I want to know what the FBI finds out on who owns what around here. Agreed?"

"Okay Gus, I'll call when I can."

"Good, I think I'm going down in the cellar for a while so if you call let the phone ring, it takes me awhile to get up them steps."

"Will do Gus see you later and thanks for the fishing trip today."

"Yah, Yah, think nothing of it."

I left Gus' and went to my cabin, took a shower to wash away the morning's allotment of black fly bites and changed into a pair of shorts with a Detroit City Fire Dept. tee shirt, and a pair of deck shoes.

The day had turned into a humid one, it was like a

sauna outside so I decided to go out front for a while and sit on the bench by the water. The lake was starting to show the signs that something bad was on its way. The placid calmness that was on the surface this past morning was now becoming something out of a hurricane movie. The waves and built to a modest six or seven feet as I watched them break against the pier in L'Anse. I couldn't help but wonder if the old guy was right. That was one thing about Michigan if you didn't like the weather just wait a day or two it would change. I have seen it go through all four of the seasons in one day before. Summer's stifling heat, autumn's coolness, springtime's showers, and right into winter's snows. I hoped today wasn't going to be one of those.

Now as I sat there, I wondered to myself if shorts were going to be a good choice? I will risk it maybe grab a light jacket, to throw in the back just in case.

I left my quiet spot by the lake and drove over to the fire station. I was hoping the Chief had gotten back something on the department store fire by now. I parked in front as usual.

The air outside had suddenly begun to drop in temperature; it had to be fifteen degrees cooler here then when I was at the cabin just a few short minutes ago.

I went in the front door and the rookie greeted me by holding the door open as I entered.

"Hi Mr. James, looks like we are in for a dandy. That lake is kicking up something fierce, out there. The weather channel just said to expect heavy thunder showers for tonight and on into the early morning."

"Hi Rook, no kidding? I think a bird might have whispered something like that into my ear earlier today." Well actually it was and old buzzard, but I didn't share my thoughts with the rookie.

"Is the Chief around?"

"No not since eight this morning he had to go up to Houghton for some class at the college. Said he wouldn't be back until later this afternoon or early tonight."

"Oh, I see, I was just wondering if anything came back from the lab on the department store fire."

"I don't know for sure, but the Chief did mention something about it or maybe he said it was on the way back. Anyway, he did say he was expecting something and that he would get in contact with you."

"How do you know this; did he tell you he was going to contact me?"

"No, not exactly I overheard him talking to someone on the phone." He answered showing some embarrassment in his eavesdropping.

"You said you're not expecting him back until this evening?"

"Yep, that's right, sometime after nightfall."

"Will he be coming back here?"

"No, probably not, he'll more than likely go straight home."

"Tell you what rookie, have him give me a call on my cell, here's my number in case he can't find the one I gave him earlier. I want to get this thing wrapped up, so if he calls today please give him a message." I handed him a card with my number on it.

"Will do Mr. James, if he doesn't call, I'll leave him a message on his home phone."

"That will be fine, thanks Rookie I'll see you later."

"Okay, see you later." The Rookie said as I exited the station.

On the drive back to my cabin I noticed the weather

had taken a turn for the worse. It went from hot too cold in a matter of one hour; an offshore wind was gaining in strength turning the bay into a haphazard array of jumbled wave and whitecaps. The idea of shorts today was turning out to be a bad one. I had to turn the heater on in the Yukon for the drive back.

It was around five in the afternoon and no one had called me, not Jessica or Gus not even the FBI, I was beginning to crazy with anticipation wanting to know what the hell was going to turn up on the background check of the conglomerate.

The thought of going to my cabin for a pair of pants completely slipped my mind, I remembered after I passed the driveway to the place, so I decided to go out to my new house. Maybe I could find something to do out there that would keep my mind occupied. I wanted to talk to Derrick anyway, about having some changes made and to thank him for not showing up to work the day before so the FBI could conduct their investigation. I hadn't given him much of a reason to not come. Telling him a lie about the tribe wanting to conduct a special ceremony on the bluff seemed to work. I had neglected the construction site for the past few days and imagined that Derrick would have some question about what I wanted and how he wanted to precede.

Pulling into the drive I waved a Greeting to Derrick as he backed his pickup across my path and up to a small cement mixer he was going to hook onto. Parking my Yukon, I got out and went over to help give him direction for backing up to the tongue of the mixer.

"Hi Derrick, you need a hand hooking this up?"

"Hi Dalton, sure just direct me into position, you give me a hand lifting it onto the ball hitch."

I did as he requested and helped him set the tongue onto the ball.

"What are you doing out here, this time of the day?"

"Oh, I thought I would come out and see if you needed a hand or had any questions, I didn't get a chance to look inside yesterday."

"Well, it's coming along very nicely, let's go have a look. The mason finished the stone fireplace today and I want to get this mixer over to another job, he is going to start tomorrow."

"Boy you guys were busy today; I don't remember the outside being finished yesterday."

"Yah, we finished it up today the guys have a bit of cleaning up to do, but for the most part we are done with the exterior. Let's take a look inside."

We stepped into the front entrance, as Derrick began to fill me in on what phase of the construction process was still being done.

"The plumber is almost done, maybe another day than a final inspection, we aren't expecting any problems with that. The electrician is almost through with the roof in and when that happens another inspection so I'm guessing maybe another week before all of the light fixtures, switches and plugs are in."

"Oh man, this looks great." I exclaimed as we entered my new kitchen, the ceramic tile on the floors and countertops were completed some of the Maple cabinets were placed around the room, in various locations."

"Yes, it does, when the electrician gets done drilling holes, we're planning on setting some of these cabinets. The guys have them all laid out all ready to install."

"This is going to be great."

"Thanks Dalton, but wait until you see your living

room, especially the fireplace. My mason is kind of an artist when it comes to stone work."

We entered the living room, thru the kitchen and dining room. There were pieces of broken stone and small scraps of wood on the floor, but you wouldn't notice a thing once your eyes looked upon the fireplace. A great wall of split stone went all the way up twenty feet to the cove of the cathedral ceiling, the massive support logs holding up the roof, were surrounded by stone as they entered the gable wall. The hearth was made from some kind of polished granite and the brass accents on the enclosure gave the whole thing a classy look. The mason had set a huge half log into place for the mantle.

"Well Dalton, what do you think?"

"It's gorgeous, how does he get the stones to fit so good and this piece of polished granite where did you get that from?" I asked running my hand across the smooth surface.

"The mason's brother owned a burial monument company, and anything they can't make a headstone out of he has them, polish them up and he uses it for hearth stones."

"This is a pretty big slab; I would think they could use this for a head stone?"

"Look really close, the stone is in segments he has the square the corners and then he fits it all together. I don't know how he is able to get such a good fit but he does. The grain even matches so good that it ends up looking like one big piece"

"Well, I must say that I am very satisfied and impressed this is great."

I said as I backed up into the room taking in the full view of the magnificent stonework.

"I don't mean to sound rude Dalton, but is there anything else I can do for you. I've got to get that mixer down the road before dark. It doesn't have any tail lights on it."

"No, I just wanted to make sure that there weren't any questions you needed answered."

"No nothing I can think of, take a walk around and if you find something you want changed, leave me a note on the kitchen counter or give me a call. Enjoy looking around and make sure everything is how you want it; it is easier change things now then it will be later."

"Okay Derrick thank you, and make sure you tell the guys that they are doing a great job. See you later."

Derrick left and I began checking every room in the house, admiring the craftsmanship that Derrick's crew had put into the place, and talking out loud to myself as I entered each room.

"Nice, very nice, oh man look at that."

I had wondered throughout the entire house and then made my way thru the double French doors that led out onto the large covered porch overlooking the bluff. And sat down on a bench made from a half log that they had cut from one of the cathedral widow openings before installation.

"Ahh, this is all right, old Gus and I can sit out here and tell lies to each other while we drink beer and take in the view. This is what I came up here for, to relax and let the world pass me by, not to get wrapped up in some kind of murder arson case. I wonder when someone is going to call?"

The wind had gained in intensity, since I arrived. Sitting there looking out over the bluff, I noticed the leaves along the edge of the cliff were blowing straight up into the air and circling like a small tornado, before falling back to the ground. Thinking of how Jessica had tossed the flowers over the edge, and how the idea of where the Indian princess had come to rest where she had. The wind would settle for short pause and then for some reason during one of these quiet moments I thought I heard a distant scream?

I got up walking toward the canyon's rim, somewhat dumbfounded at what I thought I had heard. The force of the air coming up the canyon face pushed me back a step as I peered over the edge. What was that noise I had heard, was it my imagination playing a trick? Walking back from the canyon toward the house the wind sound at my back I heard it again. The further from the canyon the better I could hear it. What on earth was that noise? Oh, shit! it's the cell phone in the Yukon. I ran towards it hoping I would get to it before they hung up.

"Hello? Hello? Is anybody there? Expecting to hear Gus or Jessica's voice.

"Hello Mr. James?"

"Yes, this is he."

"Hi, this is the Rookie, I have been trying to call you, but I couldn't get an answer earlier."

"Yah I was out of my rig, what's up?"

"The Chief checked in a while ago, I told him that you had stopped by and were wondering about the lab work. He said he wanted know if you would meet him at the Department store, he wanted to go over something with you at the scene."

"What time does he want me there?"

"He said sometime around 7:30 tonight would work for him."

"Tell him I'll be there, maybe a few minutes late but

I'll be there. I have to stop by my place and get my gear. It's already seven but I should make it."

"Okay I'll relay the message to his radio."

"Thanks Rook, talk to you later."

I wondered what the old Chief had for me to look at, as I walked back up to the house to lock the doors. I would have to hustle to pick up my gear and meet the Chief on time. Driving back towards town, the rain started, with lightening visible in the distance followed by a low rumble of thunder. Old Gus was right on the money about the thunderstorm. When I arrived at my small cabin the waves out front on the lake were building and crashing into the stone break wall blasting water up thirty feet into the yard.

I went in and quickly changed into a pair of jeans and boots, grabbed my fire coat, helmet, and headed towards the Baraga side of the bay to meet with the Chief at the department store. When I was at the southernmost point of the bay where the highway comes nearest to the water the main force of the storm hit. The wind was up near hurricane force, blowing water from Lake Superior all the way onto the far side of the road. The Yukon bucked sideways and rocked as the wind buffeted the exposed side. Only two miles to go and I would be into Baraga. I hoped the storm would pass as quickly as it had appeared, not looking forward to the ride back to the minimal safety of my small cabin.

My cell phone chirped indicating a call coming in, flipping on the speakerphone switch so I could drive with both hands on the wheel.

"Hello Dalton here."

"Hello Dalton, this is Jessica, I have been trying to reach you. Where are you at you sound like you are talking inside of a cave?"

"I have you on speaker, I'm trying to drive around the south side of the bay. What do you have to tell me?"

"The FBI said they have some information for us and they want to meet at my place sometime around eight."

"Sounds good, did you get a hold of Gus?"

"I tried but there wasn't any answer so I assumed he was with you?"

"No, I left him at his house he was going to work in the basement cleaning his wine racks. Said it would be cooler for him." Trying to calm the anxiety that I could hear in her voice when she asked about Gus.

"I have a few things to do in town, but I'll be there so don't start without me. Try Gus again maybe he couldn't hear the phone from the basement. Don't worry I'm sure everything is okay."

"I'll try him once more, if he doesn't answer I'll call you back."

"I'll probably be out of my truck for a while, I'll call you as soon as I get done with my errands."

"Okay, Dalton I'll see you later, make sure you call me and be careful driving in this storm."

"Will do, bye Jess."

I was just entering Baraga when Jessica hung up, the department store wasn't too far and I could see the Chief's car was already parked in the front next to the curb. The rain wasn't letting up and I wasn't looking forward to getting soaked so I pulled in behind the Chief's car and tried to put my fire coat on while sitting in the front seat. I wonder what the hell is so important that the Chief couldn't wait for a little nicer weather, oh well I've been wet before. Running to the front door of the department store with my coat collar held up under the back of my helmet, and quickly stepped inside removing my coat to shake off the water, and put it back on. The lack of outside light caused by the passing thunderstorm made it almost impossible to make out objects inside. I called out for the Chief not knowing if or where he actually was at inside.

"Hey, Chief you in here, it's Dalton?"

"Yah, Dalton back here." Came a voice from the back muffled from the rain hitting the roof, and the small streams of water flowing down from the holes that had been cut in the ceiling during the suppression of the fire.

"Okay Chief where are you at?"

"In the back, didn't you bring a light?"

I fished around in my coat pocket and came up with a small Mag- Lite, the beam it cast on the floor was small; it was more for detailed work up close, rather than trying to guide someone thru a maze of scattered debris. Moving slowly toward the direction the voice had come from, still unsure of the whereabouts of the Chief.

"Chief, give me one more hint as to where you are. This light I have isn't worth a damn."

"Over here by the old checkout counter." Came a response, then a bright light shining into my eyes. The light slightly blinding me as my pupils tried to dilate, for the darkness. Looking directly at the small beam cast onto the floor, I maneuvered myself around a tipped over clothing shelf. Casting the beam out in front of me I could see the reflective stripes on the Chief coat and helmet.

"There you are, isn't it's kind of dark for this, why didn't we wait for tomorrow?"

No answer, he was just standing their bent over studying something in the beam of his light. I moved around to the side of him thinking I could get a better look at what he was scrutinizing. The Chief stood turning towards me shinning his bright light directly into my eyes.

"What the hell did you do that for? You're blinding me."

"So, you won't see it coming." Came the voice from behind the intense light. But it wasn't the Chief.

"What the hell are you talking about?" I stepped to the side of the light and shone the small beam of my light onto his face.

"Rookie? What the fuck is you doing?"

The swing was already coming, his right arm coming towards me in a long powerful arc. See the motion I stepped into him grabbing him by the left arm and smashing my helmet into his face. The object he had swung was heavy hitting me in the left side of the rib cage. I felt a sharp slicing pain across my tender back, the rookie rocked back from the blow to his face. Recovering his balance, he swung again this time coming in from over the top.

"You mother fucker, you broke my nose." He screamed as he brought the object down. "I'll kill you!!"

"Rookie, you better knock it off right now!" I responded as I dropped my right shoulder and plowed into him. The blow went long missing my head and then a sharp stab of pain shot up from the back of my left thigh. The momentum of the heavy tool sending us both to the floor, with him on his back and me right on top of him, his light went flying from his left hand. I could feel the back of my leg being torn apart from whatever it was that he had slammed into it. Pushing my thumbs into his windpipe only made him pull and twist the thing

◆ 281 ◆

all the more, switching to a one hand choke hold I tried to wrench to thing for my leg with the other. I grabbed hold of it, recognizing what it was as soon as I felt it. The thing he had been trying to kill me with was a Halligan bar. This tool is used in the fire service and it is nasty looking, used mainly for forcible entry and ripping loose locks, by pry or just plain knocking them to pieces.

The tool is approximately 30" inches in length, with a split prying type wedge in line with the 1" inch solid steel round bar shaft, kind looks like a claw hammer type device.

The end opposite of the prying claw, is a flat piece of steel setting perpendicular to the shaft, now comes the wicked looking part that was currently stuck to the full seven inches into my left thigh. Setting at a ninety-degree angle from the flat steel blades and perpendicular to the shaft was a seven-inch curved solid steel spike. The spike is used for popping loose padlocks, by inserting the point into the loop of a lock and hitting it with a heavy hammer most of them will pop open.

I could feel the blood pouring from the wound in the back of my leg, while I tried to dislodge the curved spike, as the rookie pulled upwards tearing the flesh. Something had to happen fast or he was going to rip my leg all the up to my hip. I released the grip on his throat, and started to punch him in the face going for the nose and eyes. The rookie let go of the bar when I had broken his nose. This was my chance; rolling off of him I scrambled to the side in the dark room. The injury to my leg was excruciatingly painful, grabbing the bar close to where the spike was, I slid it out. The blood began to flow more freely, if I didn't get something in the hole fast, I was going to bleed to death. Taking the handkerchief from my back pocket I quickly packed it into the wound. The rookie had regained his footing; the flashlight lying on the floor behind him outlined his legs. I took a good grip on the bar with both hands and swung it from my lying position at the outside of his knee, the leg broke from the heavy blow. He collapsed to the floor screaming in agony. I pushed myself up using the Halligan bar like a cane, stumbled over and picked up the flashlight. Shining it on his face he was a mess his nose broken and both eyes were beginning to swell shut, that's probably why he hadn't seen me swing the bar.

"Stay where you are rookie and don't say a fucking word or I'll drive this spike right thru the top of your ugly head."

I could feel the blood running down the back of my leg and began to search for something in the department store to wrap around it, some old clothing anything?

"What the hell were you planning on doing here tonight rookie, other than to kill me?"

"You broke my fucking leg you prick."

"You're lucky I didn't kill you, now give me some answers."

"Fuck you!"

"No, I don't think so." I said reaching down and grabbing him by the hair on top of his head and lifting him to his feet.

"Now listen you little shit, start talking or you get this big fucking spike slammed thru your other knee." I said shinning the light around trying to find something to tie his hands with, when I noticed a familiar looking pair of boots between two of the isle shelving.

"Stay put Rookie."

"Where would I go you dumb ass?"

Using the Halligan Bar as a cane I slowly made my way to see whom the boots were attached to.

"Holy shit, it's Gus!" I said bending down to see if my old friend was still alive. The sight of the dear old man, lying unconscious on the floor thru me into a state of panic mixed with an uncontrollable rage and it was about to be brought full force right down on the whimpering form with the broken leg.

"What did you do to Gus you little prick? You better hope he isn't dead, because you will never see the inside of a prison." I bent down checking Gus' neck for a pulse, he had one his head showed signs of trauma the blood trickling down his forehead glistened in the light beam of the flashlight. I tried not to move him too much and rolled him on his side looking for any other injuries. He needed medical help, but first the rookie was going to talk. I left Gus on his side in case there was any blood in his respiratory system. He would still be able to breath without choking.

"All right you little fucker start talking and I mean now." I had moved behind him tying his hands with a strip of cloth I found on the shelf next to where Gus was lying.

"What's the matter can't the great Dalton James figure it out?" he said in a menacing tone.

"Let's try and you fill in the details that I miss. You burned this place and now you were going to try and burn Gus and I so we wouldn't figure it out, right? But what I can't figure out is, what's in it for you. You can't be the one who burned the other buildings back in the nineties, you're not old enough, so now start filling in the details."

"You still don't know shit!"

"Yah well why you don't tell me, or would you like me to tune up that other knee of yours." I said swing the bar back and forth in front of his kneecap.

"Okay, okay, but it won't do you any good now." He said, trying not to whimper.

"Try me."

"You know that body you and your squaw found the other day?"

"Yes, Clifford Adams, what about it?"

"He was my dad."

"Your dad? I thought his children lived in Detroit?"

"We used to until my dad fucked up the professor's murder, then he had to be eliminated. My dad was an arsonist as well as my uncle in Detroit; they came up with the scam of buying, insuring then, burning the places. The professor was willing to use his legal expertise to do the paperwork until he got too greedy and wanted a bigger cut so they decided to kill him they could always find another crooked lawyer. My uncle was assigned to kill you, in Detroit, but he screwed that up and ended up blowing himself up or he would have been killed like my dad."

"So, you're telling me this is a family operation?"

"Yep, and that squaw of yours is going to be dead in about ten minutes, along with you and that old bag of shit laying over there, and nobody will be the wiser because everyone that does the investigation on this fire scene will just dispose of the bodies when they haul the rubble away. So, go fuck yourself I'm done talking."

"What did you say about Jessica, and what about your body you little prick?" I said waving the heavy bar in front of his face.

I had to get to Jessica, she was only a five-minute

drive away but what was I going to do with Gus he need-ed help? I grabbed the rookie by the hair dragging him towards the back door and sat him down next to the wall. I would call the state police after I left, to come and pick him up. I went back to get Gus; he was starting to come around trying to sit up shaking his head.

"Hold on Gus don't move too much I'm here can you stand?"

"Dalton, what the hell happened?"

"I'll tell you later right now Jessica needs us, lean on me if you have to and I'll get you out of here."

Gus and I staggered to the back do that led into the alley. When we reached the door, the rookie was just sit-ting there grinning from ear to ear.

"What are you smiling about?" I asked as I reached for the push bar on the door.

"Bye, bye, Dalton and bye, bye to that bitch of yours. Ha Ha Ha!"

I gave the bar a push and heard a mechanical sound click come from the top of the doorjamb.

"Oh shit, Gus move!" I gave Gus a hard push thru the door just as an expulsion erupted from inside of the old department store. The blast throwing Gus and I into the alley, stunned but not any worse for wear, I tried to re-gain my footing, the blast made my ears ring and I began to holler at Gus, thinking he couldn't hear me.

"Come on Gus we have to get to Jessica!"

"So, you said but quit yelling!"

We made our way around the corner and to my Yukon, Gus was still staggering and holding onto his head with one hand and holding his other out in front of him for balance.

Gus and I both climbed in at the same time, I reached

across and fastened his seatbelt as he flopped his head back onto the seat.

"What did he say about Ms. Jessica being dead?"

"He said she was going to die too, but he can't do it now he's toast."

"He is, but his dad isn't, so step on this thing we have to get to her fast." Gus ordered.

My right leg wasn't hurt so I could drive and the left one was bleeding but I couldn't feel it the adrenaline in my system had blocked out any pain I might be feeling. Racing thru the streets, sliding around the turns on the wet pavement. The whole time Gus was yelling to go faster, and cussing between breaths.

"Faster Dalton, if he harms one hair on that lovely little gal, I'll kill him. I knew that sonofabitch wasn't any good."

"Who are you talking about?" I asked as I slid around the next turn.

"The Chief, he's the crispy little bastard we left back there's step dad."

I took the next corner to fast and slid up on the curb, the Yukon rocked up on two wheels and came down hard slamming Gus' head into the doorpost, shattering the passenger side window. His body went limp and he was out again, his body flopping over to my side as I straightened out the Yukon.

"Gus! Gus hang on Old buddy we're almost there." I said, as I pushed him off of my shoulder.

One more turn and I was speeding up the street that led to Jessica's, cranked the wheel hard and hit the gas driving right up to the garage door slamming the transmission onto park while it still was rolling making the parking pin chatter, and jerk hard, to a stop. I was out the door before it quit rolling. The force of a shoulder being put into my diaphragm took me off my unstable feet and slammed me hard into the ground, my fist swinging at my attacker.

"What the hell!"

"It's okay Dalton, she's okay she's safe."

It was Agent John; he was helping me, back on my feet, and propped me up next to my Yukon.

"She's okay, but you look like hell your leg is bleeding, where is Gus?"

"He's in the front seat." I answered, as Bill ran up and around to tend to Gus.

"Jessica is right over there." He said pointing across the drive.

My last recognizable image was of the most beautiful women running towards me in the pouring rain as my legs buckled and I hit face first into the muddy gravel.

CHAPTER SEVENTEEN

The princess' face was smiling, looking happily into my eyes; her hair was pulled back from her face into a long braid. Small arrowhead earrings adorned with feathers hung from her ears, she was talking but I wasn't able to understand what she was saying. All I could her in the distance was a steady monotonous beep, beep, beep, it sounded electronic. What the hell was this place, my leg hurt, my back and face were sore. The light coming from the ceiling was blinding.

The princess' face moved closer to mine and kissed me on the cheek.

"Dalton, Dalton, it's me Jessica can you hear me?"

"Yes, Jessica I can hear you, but I'm confused where I am?"

"You're in the hospital, you lost a lot of blood and passed out last night, don't you remember?"

"A little, but where is Gus?" The memories from the night before starting to come back into my fog filled brain.

"He is in the next bed over here behind this curtain."

"Is he all right?"

"He will be, he has a concussion, but the doctors say he will recover. He hasn't really woken up since he came in last night."

"I want to see him, help me up." I tried to sit up but

my leg hurt, so I pressed the button to adjust the bed into a sitting position.

"Now just be still, he isn't awake and you are going to tear those stitches loose in your leg. The doctors were wondering what had happened to your leg how did you get that big tear in the back of your thigh?"

"I'll tell you later, now I want to see Gus."

"All right, but stay where you are, I'll slide the curtain back." Jessica pulled the curtain to the side so I could see my old friend.

He was asleep, his white hair sticking up from where his head rested on the pillows, the big hands motionless at his side with an I V tube stuck in it. He looked peaceful enough.

"Are you sure he is all right?"

"Yes, he's all right." came a voice from behind the half-opened door.

It was the two FBI agents, John patted me on the shoulder as he moved to the opposite side of the bed from Jessica, and Bill stood behind him.

"We have some info we want to share with you if you feel up to it?" Bill asked.

I put my head back on the pillow, but my eyes went shut and I dozed off.

"They must have me on sleeping pills or painkillers."

"John and Bill, I think we better come back later." Jessica ordered.

"Hello sleepy head, are you awake?" Jessica asked.

"Yes, I'm awake, sorry I must have dozed off for a second."

"More like two hours."

"Get me out of this bed, my ass is getting sore and I have to piss." I said in a grouchy tone.

"My, crabby when you wake up?" Jessica said helping my sit up on the side of the bed.

"Sorry I hate spending time in a hospital bed, I've spent enough hours in one to last a lifetime. Thank you very much."

Jessica handed me a pair of crutches, so I could make my way to the restroom. My leg was bandaged from crotch to ankle and it hurt horribly, but I was going to get up no matter what.

"Ouch!" I grumbled as I stood for the first time. Jessica helping me get my balance.

"You sure are stubborn, now take it slow and easy."

"Yes dear."

When I came out of the restroom, John and Bill were standing by the door.

"What are you doing up?" John asked.

"I tried to tell him but he's too damn stubborn to listen, he's going to tear those stitches out." Jessica stated as she came to help me back into bed.

"I don't want back in that damn thing yet, take me over to see Gus."

Bill helped Jessica get me over to Gus' side of the room.

"Here Dalton take a seat." John slid a chair over for me to use.

I slowly lowered myself into the chair my leg hurt like hell but I wasn't going to let Nurse Jessica know it, or I would be back in bed for the rest of the day.

"Has he come around yet?"

"No nothing so far, but the nurse said his vitals were good and sometimes it takes a while for the brain to sort things out. He took a hard hit. The doctors were concerned about bleeding so they have him sedated, to keep him from moving too much." She answered as she took one of his big hands in hers and kissed the back of it, holding it with one and brushing his hair back with the other.

"I just don't know what I would do if." She softly kissed his forehead.

Just then a small grin began to move across his lips and in a low voice he started to whisper.

"I do Ms. Jessica; you would raid my wine cellar."

Jessica let out a giggle. "Oh, Gus your back, thank you." And kissed him on the cheek.

"Yes, I am, it would take more than a bump on the head to keep me from enjoying the company of such a beautiful woman."

"Hey Gus, welcome back." I said peering around Jessica from my seated position. "I thought I might have lost you, how are you feeling?"

"I don't think I'll be going dancing in the near future, got one hell of a headache, but I'll be okay."

"Hi Gus, good to see you are feeling okay." John and Bill greeted him from the foot of his bed.

"Hi guys, are you going to tell us what the hell happened?"

"Well, if everyone is feeling up to it, we can?"

We all agreed we could handle the story as long as it didn't take too long, Gus couldn't stay awake for too long. John agreed to keep it as short as possible.

John and Bill began to fill us in on the details that had led up to Gus and me landing in the hospital and the information. With the case we had all been working on. John went first retrieving a folder from his briefcase and settling down on the corner of Gus' bed.

"The theory you guys were working on turned out

to be pretty close to what actually transpired? We ran some stuff through the FBI's main database and came back with some info that we thought might interest you. That is what the meeting was supposed to have been about last night."

Bill took the folder and began to give us the details. "The big conglomerate was laundering money like you thought, but your questions about who owned it, is what had John and I interested the most, we had the data guys do some digging and their information that came back, showed the owners were here in Baraga."

"Yes, we kind of knew that, so who did it turn out to be?"

"It was the Fire Chief, his wife and stepson, it seems the Chief met Clifford Adams' wife when the investigation of the old fires was taking place. This led up to Cliff's disappearance. What better way to cover each other's story, a husband and wife don't have to testify against each other? Our theory is that they had a love affair and decided to knock old Cliff off and frame him for the murder of Jessica's ex-husband. The Chief married her and raised the son, he is the one, you and Gus, met last night in the department store."

"So, what happened to the Chief? How did, you two ends up at Jessica's? It's still all a bit fuzzy." Gus asked.

"We had a meeting scheduled at Jessica's last night, but she couldn't reach you so she called Dalton and he said he would try and find you before he came over. He had to take care of something first. Which was meet the Chief at the department store, he thought, he had information about the fire scene. Luckily, he was able to overpower the kid and get you out of there before the kid torched the place. When John and I showed up at

Jessica's we noticed an unfamiliar car in the driveway, knowing Dalton had a Yukon and you had a truck we preceded with caution. John and I took positions outside the house, we could hear the Chief telling Jessica that she was going to disappear because, she shouldn't have been poking around in old business, and that you two were going to end up the same way. John stayed in the front watching the door and I snuck into the garage where the Chief had entered. The Chief came out dragging Jessica, John told him he was under arrest and he pulled a gun threatening to kill her, if he didn't back off, but Jessica wouldn't have any of that she drooped to her knees giving John a clear shot. That's about the time you two showed up beaten and bleeding. We called the EMS to haul your butts to the hospital and that's it end of story."

"Not quite Bill." I spoke.

"Why is that?"

"The kid's said his uncle tried to kill me in Detroit, but he missed. What do you make of that?"

"The kid's uncle was his mother's brother; he is the one who trained Clifford on the finer points of arson. Cliff in turn trained the professor and then his kid; the rookie picked it up from the Chief. They all worked for his mother, who has strong family ties with Detroit's organized crime families. Who in turn are involved with the drug trade coming out of South America that is why they have holding down there?"

"Well done guys, we can expect some more arrest before we are done with this. The FBI owes you a big thank you." John said.

Gus had fallen asleep before John could finish thanking us.

"The credit doesn't just go to the three of us, if it wasn't for the Indian princess, we would have never found Cliff's body and none of this would have happened."

"That's right Dalton, maybe now she can finally be at rest. Now back to bed." Jessica said.

"Yes, my dear nurse." and I climbed back into bed to dream about my future with my own princess.

THE END

CPSIA information can be obtained
at www.ICGtesting.com
Printed in the USA
LVHW111046210421
684330LV00022B/107/J